BLACK STREET

Sidney Cooper Jr.

SCJ Publishing

To Flora and Shane my constant inspirations, and to the memory of Howard Ransom Jr. and Marvin Jackson.

Treonte _____

my

Hope enjoy

first novel.

Thanks

Prologue

We were waiting. My mother and I, both dressed in our best business attire, sitting at the desk of a loan officer at a local bank branch in Los Angeles. This was one of the larger branches in L.A. Twenty-five foot ceilings, marble floors, oak wood chairs and desks. All the tellers and loan officers were wearing navy blue or charcoal gray suits. I was a little overwhelmed by the whole environment. At age fifteen, this was my first time being involved in a potential financial transaction of this size with my mother's business.

My mother was an interior designer, applying for a small business loan to expand her growing business. Her business had flourished since its inception five years ago. She'd operated a successful business to this point, but her goal was to take it to the next level. I, her only child, had been involved with the business from the beginning. My mother thought it would be a good experience for me to get involved, and that it would keep me off the streets and out of trouble. She worried about my development due to the absence of my father. What happened to him, I couldn't begin to tell you. I never knew him. I remember when she sat me down at the age of eight and told me my father had left her before I was born. It wasn't a reflection on me. It was more of a reflection on him. She said it was just something we would have to deal with together, but it wasn't going to stunt my growth, or hers.

Our loan officer returned to her desk. She was dark skinned, African American, and a little overweight, middle aged, medium height; she wore black framed glasses, which made her look more like a college professor than a banker. She sat down at her desk and told my mother and me she had some good news.

"Your loan has been approved!"

Big smiles came over our faces, but the smile disappeared on my mother's face when we heard the loan officer say, "But, they only approved it for fifty thousand."

I could see my mother's smile transform into a frown. She was obviously upset with the amount approved. I didn't know what to think. Fifty thousand dollars sounded like a lot of money to me, but the look on my mother's face said, fifty thousand wasn't enough.

"My application was for two hundred and fifty thousand dollars. How in the hell can you come and sit down here and say you have good news?" my mother replied.

"Ms. Jackson, I know you are a little disappointed with the amount, but we can build on it."

"Build on it? You've been singing that song for over three years, and I'm down right tired of that song and dance." At this time my mother let her frustration be known. "I've been banking with this bank since I opened my business, and each time I applied for a loan, this bank has always approved me for less than I requested. Now, your approval committee sends you out as usual to break the news, and your mantra is, as it has always been, 'we can build on it', and each time I accepted it, but no longer will I go along with this farce. My company is growing. I need that money to support its growth. Moving my office from my home into a commercial space, adding some administrative and sales personnel will go a long way in increasing my client base, to say nothing about giving my company a more professional image. My company needs a face lift to go after more lucrative accounts. So, what I need you to do is to go back in there and get me approval for two hundred and fifty thousand dollars."

My mother stared at the loan officer and didn't blink. The loan officer stared back at my mother with a look of discomfort and dismay on her face.

"I can't do that, Ms. Jackson," the loan officer said hesitantly.

"Why not?" my mother responded in a stern voice.

"The final decision has been made, and they have approved fifty thousand. It's out of my hands. There's nothing more I can do, but like I said before, let's build from here."

"Are you telling me you will not even go back to your manager and argue on my behalf to approve the two hundred and fifty?"

"No, I'm trying to tell you, it's final, and there's nothing anyone can do."

My mother leaned back in her chair and just looked at the loan officer in silence. Then her facial expression changed, as if a revelation had come over her. She sat up, moved her seat closer to the desk, and leaned across the desk until she was face to face with the loan officer. I moved my seat closer and leaned in just a little to hear what my mother was saying in a clear low voice.

"For over five years I've been banking here with you, and I just now realized that I'm talking to the wrong person."

"What do you mean you've been talking to the wrong person?" the loan officer replied.

"You know what I mean. The white man ain't doing nothing but frontin' your black ass off," she said in a slow, intense voice.

"I'm offended by that statement coming from another African American woman."

"You should be offended because that's how I intended it to affect you, so you can wake up and see that you are just a pawn in this game and not a real player."

"I am a player. I'm VP of Small Business Loans."

"That's just a title to appease you and to help you ignore, the fact, you don't sit at the table where decisions are made."

The loan officer told my mother she would forget about the statements she made because they were made out of anger. She added; she knew my mother really didn't mean what she'd said. But my mother confirmed to the loan officer that she meant every word she had uttered.

Furthermore, my mother informed the banker she intended to sever all ties with the bank today. The loan officer looked surprised.

"Let's not make a hasty decision out of anger that we will regret later," the loan officer exclaimed.

My mother fell back in her seat at the statement made by the loan officer, and calmly replied, "This is not a 'we' decision. It's my decision, and the quicker you carry out my wishes the sooner my son and I can get out of here."

The loan officer got up from the desk and walked to the back of the bank, while my mother and I, again, waited quietly and patiently. The loan officer re-emerged from the back accompanied by a Caucasian man in a navy blue suit with a red tie. He was very well groomed, slightly overweight, with graying hair. They approached the desk and his 6'5" frame towered over the three of us as he extended his hand to introduce himself.

"Hello, Ms. Jackson. I'm the President of the bank, Mr. McFadden."

My mother extended her hand to shake his but never got up from her seat, making him bend down to grasp her hand. "Nice to meet you, Mr. McFadden, and this is my son Shane." She then gestured toward me. Mr. McFadden walked around my mother, and I stood up, shook his hand and exchanged greetings. He walked back to stand in front of my mother.

"It has come to my attention that you are disappointed with the amount approved for your small business loan, and would like to cut all ties with this bank. I thought it prudent to have a conversation before we took those steps."

My mother sat up straighter in her seat. Her body and hand movements became more animated while talking to Mr. McFadden. "What is all this 'we' stuff? It's not 'we' it's 'me'. And, I would like you to carry out my wishes immediately."

The bank president turned to the loan officer and nodded in the affirmative. The loan officer walked toward the back of the bank once again. Mr. McFadden walked behind her desk and took her seat.

"Ms. Jackson, although your company has reached profitability in the past couple of years, there are still questions about the company's ability service long term debt beyond the fifty thousand dollar level. Your financial ratios indicate you have good working capital, but your asset base hasn't increased significantly. The equity in your company remains stagnant. We developed a cash flow statement from your balance sheet and income statement and it revealed that you have had a negative cash flow in the second and third quarters in each year of operation."

I couldn't make heads or tails of what this bank president was talking about. This discussion was completely over my head. I just knew we ate, paid a mortgage, lived better than some, and not as well as others. Given the look on my mother's face, I wasn't sure how much she understood either. My mother was completely silent. She just looked at the bank president and began to shake her head.

"This is what you came out here to tell me? After five years of banking with this bank, one would think a relationship was being built. This conversation should have taken place a few years ago so we could have worked together to grow my business. But, since this conversation is a day late and a dollar short there's no need to continue it."

"As you wish, Ms. Jackson. Sorry I couldn't have been more helpful." Mr. McFadden got up from the desk and walked to the back of the bank. My mother looked disappointed and defeated.

"What was he talking about, Mom?"

"He was explaining why we didn't get the loan amount requested, but the reasons are cloudy to me."

My mother and I waited there at the desk for another half hour before the loan officer came out. She handed my mother a check. The loan officer wished my mother the best with her business and apologized for not being able to do more. We all shook hands. My mother and I left the premises.

When we arrived home, my mother went straight to her room. I went in the den, loosened my tie, sat on the couch and turned on ESPN. About twenty minutes later my mother emerged from her bedroom wearing some warm-ups, and carrying some folders in hand. She told me to meet her in the kitchen a few minutes later. I walked into the kitchen, where she was busy making sandwiches. She told me to sit down because she wanted to talk to me.

"Shane, I'm glad you were at the bank with me today to witness what took place. I'm not sorry for what I said to that sista, but I am sorry for the way I said it. I will send her a letter of apology because everyone should be treated with respect."

"I'm sorry you didn't get the money," I responded.

"I didn't get the loan because I don't understand the game that's being played."

"What game is that, mom?"

"The finance game. My expertise is in interior design, and numbers have always been my enemy. That's where you come in. You are good with numbers, but I've kept you on the sales side because you are a natural salesman. You could sell ice to an Eskimo."

We both smiled. She reached for the folders she had brought into the room and placed them on the kitchen table between us.

"These are my tax returns and other financial information about my company. In about three months I want to go to another bank and submit an application for a small business loan for two hundred and fifty thousand dollars so I can move my company out of our home."

"You can't do that with fifty thousand dollars? Sounds like a lot of money to me."

"It does sound like a lot of money, but in reality, for what I'm trying to accomplish it's just a drop in the bucket. It will take at least two hundred and fifty thousand to secure rental space downtown, add sales and administrative staff, implement an advertising and marketing plan, and give my company enough cash reserve to sustain itself in the down months. "

I just shook my head in agreement.

She continued. "I want you to find out how to play this finance game. Talk to whomever you need to, go to the library and do research, utilize the web, and use whatever means necessary – and you know I mean legal. If I ever catch you doing anything......." Her tone changed to a stern one.

I interrupted her. "Come on, mom. When have I ever taken that route to accomplish anything?"

"Never. And I want to keep it that way. I just don't want you to misconstrue my words or get the wrong idea. I want you to study up on financing a business. I really need your help."

"I know what you mean, mom," I said with a smile. "I can do it."

My mother smiled back at me, took her hand and stroked my face gently, then held my chin up and looked directly into my eyes.

"You're the best son a woman could ask for, I love you."

We finished our conversation over the sandwiches she'd made: Her specialty, pepper turkey stacked with tomato, lettuce, mayo, and jack cheese on wheat bread. I've loved that sandwich since I was a little boy. She knew the way to my heart was through my stomach.

So, I had my marching orders. In three months I needed to prepare a financial package representing my mom's company that would be good enough for her to secure a two hundred and fifty thousand dollar loan. The first stop was the public library. The librarians helped me tremendously in finding the books, articles, and journals on business and finance, but some of the language I encountered was difficult to understand. Math was my favorite subject in school, but I was used to concepts such as factorials, geometric squares, and improper fractions, and knew nothing about assets, balance sheets, income statements, or cash flow statements. As I left the library, on my way back home, I ran into my friend, Johnny.

"Hey, Johnny what's up? What are you doing downtown?"

"I got a summer job at Silvio's Shoes."

"Man, I didn't know you worked at Silvio's."

"Yea, my dad said he didn't want me running the streets this summer, so he hooked me up with this summer gig. What about you? What are you doing down here?"

"I was at the library, trying to learn about banking and finance."

"Why would you want to learn about that?" Johnny gave me a puzzled look.

"It's a project I'm working on for my mother. She needs to get a loan from a bank for her business."

"Your mother's no joke. Come hell or high water she gonna be the next Madame CJ Walker."

"I guess," I replied.

"Well, if you are trying to learn about banking you need to talk to Mr. Roberts. He's a banker."

"Mr. Roberts? That cranky bourgeoisie, Uncle Tom, Step and Fetch It, too good to talk to anyone on the block, Negro?"

"Yea, the one and only."

"How do you know he's a banker?"

"Well, one day I was helping my mother take in the groceries from the car, and Mr. Roberts pulled up on the block in his new 500SL. I asked my mom where he worked to afford a nice whip like that. She told me he was a banker."

"Well, he does have the biggest house on the block, and he's always wearing monkey suits. I figured he was an engineer or something."

"Yea, I thought he was a politician – you know how they steal."

Both of us started laughing at the thought of how crooked politicians were.

"I'm headed home. You headed that way, Johnny?"

"No, I'm just on a break. I need to get back to Silvio's."

"Alright, I'll check you later."

We gave each other dap (shook hands), and then headed in opposite directions. On my way home, while sitting on the bus, I began thinking of how I could approach Mr. Roberts. He wasn't friendly, and he seemed to have a genuine disdain for young black men. Once, while playing a game of football on the block, Mr. Roberts got angry with us for playing in the middle of the street. And as he passed by in his car he shouted at us. "You little niggas need to stay out the street." Then he sped off toward his house, nearly hitting a couple of us who were lingering in the end zone. The story of what happened circulated around the neighborhood and all the parents on the block got upset with Mr. Roberts. Some parents confronted him in front of his gate. From that day on, he had been almost like an outsider in the neighborhood. No one spoke or socialized with him, including my mother. Since Mr. Roberts was a banker, his ostracism was about to end. He could be a huge help in my project.

I pondered ways to approach him. First, the direct approach: I could tell him about my project and what I was trying to accomplish, but with his personality, he probably would said he didn't give a shit and to get off his porch. Or, I could lie. Tell him I was a republican, and wanted all black people to pull themselves up by their bootstraps and get off their lazy asses, but he would see right through that lie. Then, I realized I didn't really know much about Mr. Roberts and in order to devise a successful plan, I needed to learn more about the man.

I approached some of the neighbors on the block to see if I could find out any information that would help me persuade Mr. Roberts to assist me in learning about banking and finance. Everyone had the same thing to say, including my mother, about Mr. Roberts; that he was definitely a banker, uptight, antisocial, with no wife or kids to share all that apparent success. I needed more personal information -- like what his hobbies were, if he had a favorite charity, if he was sentimental about anything, where he vacationed, or what he was passionate about. I was about to give up until Old Man Roc called my name one day while I was sitting on my front porch. Mr. Darden, or Old Man Roc as we called him, was the oldest person on the block. He had lived on the block the longest. He was a retired veteran who had pulled me to the side from time to time and given me words of encouragement. He was the block philosopher, sometimes talking in riddles, leaving me to think about the words he just shared with me, like – "If you look for excellence in every aspect of a person's life, you will surely be disappointed."

"Hey, Shane, how's it going?"

"Good. Mr. Darden."

"Glad to hear you're doing well. I hear you've been asking around about Mr. Roberts."

"Yea, I was going to get around to asking you. I got you on my list."

"Mind if I ask you why?"

"No, not at all." I stood up and offered him a seat next to me on the porch steps. We both sat down. "I'm working on this project that involves banking and finance, and since he's a banker I thought he could help me out. But, I don't know how to approach him."

"So, you are doing some reconnaissance work on Mr. Roberts – that's very smart, Shane."

"Thanks."

"Well, Shane, I think you are in luck. I may be able to give you some insight about the man that others don't know and don't care to know." Old Man Roc shifted his sitting position on the steps to face me more directly. He patted me on my knee. "Mr. Roberts, or Vince as I call him, is not as much of a puzzle as one might think. He's seen a lot and been through a lot in his fifty years. He was a banker for about fifteen years, but before banking he was a janitor for about eight years. He was married and had a child by the time he was eighteen. He used to live in one of the worse parts of Los Angeles, where black on black crime was an everyday occurrence. Wanting to improve his family's situation, Vince went back to school when he was thirty and got his degree at night and still held down his job as a janitor. "

"He went back to get his undergrad degree?" I asked

"Yes, his undergrad, and all while his wife was pulling long hours as a caretaker. His son was around fourteen or fifteen at the time and with his mother and father rarely around because they were striving to make a better life for themselves, the son got caught up in some gang activity and was shot to death in front of a corner liquor store."

"Really?" I interjected.

"The story goes he was a very smart kid, but he was getting jumped in school, and bullies would steal his money. Desperate to protect himself, he joined up with another gang inside the school. The word from one of his friends inside the gang was that he never fit in, Gangbanging wasn't his thing. The rival gang had a new member and to prove himself, he had to shoot Vince's son. When the police caught the shooter, he confessed that he never had any problem with Vince's son and that he was just carrying out an order to join the gang because he needed the protection. Vince's wife never recovered from her son's death, and about five years later she and Mr. Roberts divorced."

"That's sad he lost his family," I said to Roc.

"Yes, and that's why his demeanor can be harsh at times. When a man loses everything he holds dear to his heart, his heart hardens to protect itself."

I was stunned after Old Man Roc told me the story about Mr. Roberts and his family. Now, I could understand why my mother was so worried about me staying on the straight and narrow.

"I hope that gives you a greater understanding of the man," Roc added. "He's not that bad a person, and if you need my help further, I would be willing to talk to him on your behalf. I can't promise you he will help because even though I probably get along with him better than anyone on the block, we are not buddies."

"Understood, and I appreciate you sharing what you know."

"One other thing, Shane. When a man loses something close to his heart, it leaves a void and sometimes that man tries to fill that void through financial success, but to his dismay, the void remains. Fill the void and you'll have no problem getting him to help you with banking and finance. You understand what I'm telling you?"

"I'm not sure."

"Think about it." Old Man Roc stood up and patted me on the back. "Well, I have to be moving on. Tell your mother I said hello."

"I will."

Old Man Roc walked off, and left me to contemplate his last words. I thought about his words the rest of the day. Fill the void. What did he mean by that? My mother always taught me that the first rule of sales was getting to know your potential client, and catering to their needs. What did Mr. Roberts need? From my conversation with Old Man Rock, I gathered he needed a wife and a son, since he had lost both. But my mother couldn't take the place of his wife, and I couldn't replace his son. Or could I? My mind shifted into high speed, putting together a strategy. By day's end the plan was in place.

My mother and I dressed casual during working hours, unless we were on a sales call. I hadn't shared my plan to persuade Mr. Roberts to help me with the duties she'd delegated to me with my mother. So, this morning when she saw me with a monkey suit on, her curiosity got the best of her. I only had four words for her. "Working on the project". Once I said that, she asked no more questions. I grabbed my little leather bag my mother got for me to use when we were on sales calls, threw it over my back and hit the door. I arrived at the Bank of America (BofA) building around 9:30 am. To my dismay, there was no sign of Mr. Roberts at the bank. I asked one of the loan officers if Mr. Roberts was off today. She said she had never heard of Mr. Roberts. I found that very peculiar because from all conversations with neighbors, everyone said he worked for Bank of America. The Bank of America building was a large high rise with a multitude of companies located inside its walls. So, I started to wonder if he work for BofA or if he just worked in the building. I headed for the front desk in the lobby of the building to see if I could locate Mr. Roberts that way. The building attendant looked up his name and told me he worked for Lewis, Wright, and Leland Inc. on the 51st floor. I asked what kind of company Lewis, Wright, and Leland was, and the attendant told me they were an Investment Advisor company.

I took the elevator up to the 51st floor and once I was standing in the elevator lobby, to my right I could see a receptionist. Above her head was a sign that read Lewis, Wright, and Leland, Inc. Investment Advisors in big gold letters. The reception area was really nice – plush carpet, leather chairs, nice artwork, fine wood area tables with financial magazines and newspapers lying organized on top of them. This reception area was much different than the bank my mother and I had been in earlier that week; it was smaller, but more intimate in its setting, no tellers, not a whole lot of people walking around; the space was closed, meaning there wasn't much visibility beyond the receptionist wall. Mr. Roberts not working for BofA threw me a little, but I still thought my plan had a good chance of success. I would just need to talk my way through a few layers of resistance before I would land in front of the prize. I was dressed appropriately and that is half the battle in selling anything; image. With that in mind, I approached the receptionist. She was a white woman with graying blondish hair, very stylish, wearing a pink blouse and suit that brought out her skin tone and complimented her make up well.

"Hello," I said with a smile.

"Hello, how are you, young man?"

"I'm doing well this morning, Ma'am. How's your morning going?"

"It's been a good morning, so far. The muffins and coffee delivered this morning are fresh, and I haven't had too many obnoxious clients call or come in this morning, so far, so good!"

I could tell she was in a good mood, and might be of more help than I'd anticipated, and she was a bit of a chatterbox. "A good morning is always the best start anyone could have to a day. At least that's what my mother says."

"Your mother is a smart woman. So, who are you here to see?"

"Well, I hoped you could help me with that. I go to Garfield High School and was told by my guidance counselor that there might be some opportunities for young men like myself to find a summer internship with your company. She didn't give me anyone specific to talk to, but I came down here with the hope of talking to someone."

"I think I can give you a little help and point you to someone who would be willing to speak with you. Mr. Roberts would be your best bet. He's an African-American gentleman and loves to see youths with vision and drive. I think he's on the board for the Boys and Girls Club of L.A County. I will give him a call and see if he can accommodate you in his schedule this morning. What is your name?"

"Shane Jackson." I couldn't believe my luck. This couldn't have worked out any better. "Can I ask you one more favor?"

"Of course."

"Do you have an annual report for the company from last year?" I remembered from my research at the library that you could get a good synopsis of a company from its annual report –which contains its mission, purpose, products, and principals."Yes, I think we have one around here somewhere." She looked around behind her desk and pulled out the annual report for last year. "Here you go. You can have a seat, and I will call Mr. Roberts to see if he can see you today."

"Thank you." I took a seat in one of the leather chairs. After about five minutes of reading the report, the receptionist called me up to her desk. She told me Mr. Roberts could fit me in around 10:30 am, which by my watch was about forty-five minutes away. I went back to my seat and continued to study the annual report. Mr. Roberts' potential reaction worried me a little, given his history of outbursts in the neighborhood. But, I knew if I could get past his initial suspicion and show him my intentions and objectives were noble, the chances of his helping me would be highly likely.

Forty-five minutes passed by quickly. I wasn't bored. I was reading comfortably when the receptionist directed me to go through the door on her right, down the hall to Mr. Roberts' office, the last office on the left. As soon as I walked in Mr. Roberts' office, he looked bewildered.

"I know you, don't I? You live on my block. Aren't you Irene's boy?"

"Yes, I'm Shane Jackson."

Mr. Roberts stood up behind his desk. He didn't offer me a seat or welcome me into his office. "What kind of shit are you trying to pull here, boy? I don't have time for your bullshit –this is a place of business, and I'm a very busy man."

"No, sir. This is no B.S. I am looking for a summer internship and was told by my guidance counselor that your company may have some opportunities."

"Guidance counselor my ass, any guidance counselor would know that we do not offer internships for high school students. You may have been able to bullshit your way in here, but the bull stops in this office. So, once again I'll ask you. What are you trying to pull?"

"No sir, I'm not trying to pull anything. Like I said."

He interrupted me abruptly and loudly. "Stop bullshitting with me boy." His voice drew attention to his office.

I knew his tolerance was wearing low and the odds of him just throwing me out of his office were high. My plan was crumbling under his abusive tone, so in my humblest and most articulate voice I gave him my real pitch. "Sir, I'm here to ask for your help. I didn't know the best way to approach you because I was fearful of getting the reaction, I just received." I paused, he said nothing. We just stared at each other. Then, he gestured for me to have a seat and he sat behind his desk, and nodded for me to continue. "My mother's company is in need of money, and we are at a crossroads in determining the best way to get the money. We have applied for small business loans, but each time we have been approved for less than the amount we asked for. My mother has given me the responsibility to overcome that hurdle."

"So, what do you want from me? I'm not a banker."

"Yes, I know this now. I was reading the annual report of Lewis, Wright, and Leland and to the best of my understanding, your company helps raise money for companies. I know what you do is for more money and larger companies than my mother's, but I'm thinking what you do can be applied to smaller companies as well."

"To a certain extent that is true. What type of business does your mother have?"

"An interior design company."

"How much capital does she need?" He reacted to my blank stare. "How much money does she need?"

"Two hundred and fifty thousand dollars."

"What are her plans for the money?"

"Move the business out of our home and into downtown office space and hire a few people."

"So, how far along are you?"

"Not that far, I've basically been researching banking and finance by going to the library and reading various financial publications every day. I'm learning more about the topic, but am still in the dark about what I need to do."

"And, just what are you trying to do?"

"Put a financial package together of my mother's company that will help her get the two hundred and fifty thousand dollars she needs for her business."

"Shane, you articulated that well. It was clear and concise, and you have a goal- two hundred and fifty thousand dollars. This will guide all your energy and efforts to attain that goal. I believe I can help you."

I jumped out of my seat, raising my right hand into a fist and shouted, "Thank you, Mr. Roberts," as if I'd scored a touchdown.

"Okay, calm down, Mr. Jackson. This is how it's going to work. My schedule in the morning is very hectic, so you will arrive for work late afternoon around 3 p.m. Your work hours will be Mon-Fri 3 p.m. to 6 p.m. Now, how long did your mother give you to complete her financial package?"

"The summer."

"That's perfect. By the end of summer I promise you, if you listen and work hard, you will be able to put a financial package together for your mother with your eyes closed."

"When do I start?"

"You can start tomorrow, but keep two things in mind. One, if you miss a day or if you are late without a valid excuse you will be terminated immediately. Two, you will not be compensated monetarily. Your compensation will be the help I give you in putting together your mom's financials."

I think he was telling me I could have a job, but without pay, and I was okay with that because my objective was not to get paid, but to learn. "Yes sir, I understand," I replied.

"So, tomorrow when you come in I'll introduce you around and let people know you are in my employ as a summer intern. The way you are dressed today, I expect you to be dressed that way each and every time you report for work."

"Yes sir." Mr. Roberts stood up and extended his hand, and I stood up and shook his hand.

"I'll see you tomorrow, Mr. Jackson."

"Thank you sir, you won't regret your decision to help me."

"I better not. You think my greeting was harsh, you don't want to see my reaction to you if you don't perform to my expectations."

"I can only imagine sir, and you are right. I don't want to see or experience that."

"Alright, I have work to do. See you tomorrow."

I thanked him once again and made my way out of his office and back down the hall. I thanked the receptionist for all her help and told her I would see her tomorrow.

1

250K

My mother was a little hesitant about me working for Mr. Roberts for the summer, but when I told her my purpose, she approved. She warned me about Mr. Roberts' bad disposition and his narrow view of the African American community. She told me he was a very successful man, but very bitter because of the losses in his life. She also started to go into intimate details, most of which I had gotten from Old Man Roc. I wondered how my mother knew so much about Mr. Roberts's life, so I asked her. She said she'd dated Mr. Roberts for a short period of time when I was younger. To say I was surprised was an understatement. I didn't question her about it because it wasn't my place, but I had never seen any men my mother dated until I was a junior in college. She'd made it a point not to bring men around me when I was growing up. She just thought it prudent not to present any male figures in my life that weren't looking like they were going to be around for any extended amount of time.

She opted to get me involved with athletic programs and mentorship programs like Pop Warner football and the Big Brother program. These programs had strong African American role models who taught young men the meaning of commitment, dedication, discipline, and respect. At times, the coaches were hard on us young boys, but it was all in an effort to make us young men. There was one coach in particular who really took a liking to me, and with my mother's permission, I hung out with him outside of the Pop Warner football program.

His name was coach Takufu. He drove a tricked out 1957 pearl black Chevy truck with a horn that mimicked his name every time it was blown –"Taakuufuuu". He was the coolest person I'd ever met. He kept the most beautiful women around him all the time. Sometimes one of his girlfriends would show up at practice and cause so much commotion, not only among us young boys, but also among the other coaches. Takufu would tell his girls to meet up with him later after practice. I admired this trait, and wanted to be like him.

One thing I learned from coach Takufu that stayed with me was how to conquer my fears. Fearlessness was his thing. He drilled in us that we should overcome our fears on and off the field, and those who were successful at overcoming their fears would be successful in life.

I needed this fearless quality to deal with Mr. Roberts. When I arrived at his office the next day, he was in a bad mood. He ignored me and reacted to my presence as if I was nuisance. He just threw several books on the table --each had to be thick as three short stacks of pancakes on top of each other, and said, "Read them." He never said another word to me. I looked at one of the titles. It read - *Prospectus Supplement*. I was at a complete loss, but I knew this wasn't the time to ask why I had to read these books. So, for the next three hours I read the prospectuses. When the clock struck 6 p.m., I left the office and took the books with me. I read more that night, hoping there was some information in those pages that would be of benefit to me and my goal of raising 250k for my mother. His treatment of me went on the same way for the entire week. I would just come into the office, sit at the side table in his office and read those prospectuses. Then I'd take them home and continue to plow through the pages -- taking notes – mainly jotting down questions about what I had read.

I finished reading the prospectuses over the weekend. When I reported to work on Monday, Mr. Roberts still seemed to be in a funky mood, but he had made a commitment to me and he was going to live up to it no matter what he was going through. My mother needed my help and I wasn't about to let her down or let him hinder my progress. I placed the prospectus on his desk and sat across from him in the chair facing his.

"I've finished reading the books you put in front me, but I don't know how this will help my mother build her company."

"Watch your tone with me boy!"

"Well, you said you would help me, and I just don't see how these books help."

"What did you say?"

"I said -."

"I heard what the fuck you said."

He'd dropped the F bomb. It took me by surprise and even put a little fear in me, but I tried my best not to show it.

"You asked me for help then you want to question the methods I choose to use to help you. You have a lot of nerve, boy."

"With all due respect, sir. I just want to help my mother."

"Yes, I know that, but listen to me. What you learn here will benefit you the rest of your life. Do you understand what I'm telling you?"

I must have looked confused.

"You want to help your mother, that's great, and I applaud you for wanting to do that, but what I'm going to teach you goes way beyond the loan your mother needs for her business. If you listen, learn, and apply what I'm going to teach you, not only will your mother benefit from your knowledge, but you will also benefit from it the rest of your life. Now, do you understand what I'm saying to you?"

"I think so," I responded, unsure of myself.

"Either you understand or you don't understand. Which one is it?"

"I understand," I responded firmly. That was my first lesson. When you speak, speak with confidence.

"Now, as for the books I gave you to read, they're actually called prospectuses. From your reading, what would you say is the purpose of that prospectus?"

I took my time before I responded to his question. I didn't want him to blow up and go crazy on me.

"From my reading I learned about the different companies."

"What did you learn about these different companies? Keep it simple."

"Well, the prospectuses describe the products and services provided by the company, the industry in which the company operates, how long the company's been in business, officers in the company, some legal jargon, and a whole lot of numbers from years past of which I couldn't make heads or tails."

"Shane, that's it! It's not much more complicated than what you just said. Keep that in mind." His tone changed to one of a caring teacher. "A prospectus simply tells you about a specific company, the amount of money it is trying to raise and by which means it is trying to raise capital. There are essential numbers you need to understand and manipulate, which include an Income Statement, a Balance Sheet Statement, and a Cash Flow Statement. If you are able to master those numbers and understand how the three interrelate, then you will be able to assess the financial condition of any company, as long as you understand the nature of the business."

Mr. Roberts went on about hiding or detecting the weaknesses of a company through manipulation of the numbers in its financial statements. He said the average analyst on Wall Street still had a hard time dissecting the financial performance of a company to derive its true value. He said he would teach me the basics, and if I could take the complicated financial statements of a company and understand the basics, then I would have mastered the art of financial analysis. He then took me over to the small white board inside his office.

I pulled my notebook from my backpack and started taking notes vigorously. He wrote and explained the following:

Balance Sheet: Consists of Assets, Liabilities, & Equity
Assets – Liabilities = Equity
Assets are tangible and intangible things that hold value.
Liabilities are what you owe.
Equity represents ownership
Income Statement: Profit and Loss
Revenue – Expenses = Net Income
Cash Flow Statement: Sources and Uses of Cash.
Sources: All the different ways a company makes money.
Uses: All the different ways a company spends money.

For the next few weeks all I did was read prospectuses and dissect the financial numbers of various companies. At first, it was a real struggle, but Mr. Roberts was patient with me and didn't get too irritated when I asked, what he called, a bone headed question. I began to recognize common themes, similarities, and common threads in the financial reporting of the companies. Mr. Roberts taught me how to restate the numbers reported by a company to get around some of the accounting and reporting tricks companies used to disguise their performance. I found the work intriguing. My time spent looking through 10ks and annual reports extended into the late hours of the night. To me it was like uncovering secrets of a company, or trying to find a buried treasure that a company was trying to hide from the public.

By halfway through the summer, Mr. Roberts had warmed up to me significantly. He introduced me to other executives within the company and to all of the partners as his summer intern. I was welcomed and even invited to sit in on some of the underwriting meetings and conference calls with the companies that Lewis, Evertt, and Jones represented. That was when I realized how much I'd learned about financial statements of companies, and I felt ready to secure the capital my mother needed.

I asked my mother for all her financial ledgers. I put together a balance sheet, income statement, and cash flow statement for my mother's company, then asked Mr. Roberts if he wouldn't mind taking a look at them with me. He agreed. As we reviewed them, the cash flow problems were just as the banker had said. My mother's third quarter cash flow was low and at times even negative. But, Mr. Roberts said short-term financing in the form of a credit line could take care of that.

"The most important thing you must concentrate on now, Shane, is building a future picture of your mother's company three to five years out."

"How do I do that?"

"Projections."

I must have given him a deer in the headlights look because he looked like he was going to explode, but calm prevailed.

"Okay, Shane. Sometimes I forget you are only fifteen. Maybe that's to your credit. You know the pro forma statements I had you go through on several companies?"

"Yes."

"Those are projections. All projections are estimates of how much your business will grow because of the new influx of capital."

Deer in the headlights look from me.

He continued. "In your mother's case, a two hundred and fifty thousand dollar loan. How will this money help your mother's business grow and affect her bottom line?" He paused. "You do know what I mean by bottom line?"

"Oh, of course sir."

"If you didn't, I was going to throw your ass out of here."

To work on the projections, I met with mother and had her give me in detail exactly what she was going to do with 250k and what her expectations in terms of revenue growth and net income were. I took all her information, and with the help of Mr. Roberts we were able to put together a pro forma financial statement for my mother's business with projections that extended out three years. Once the total financial package was completed I presented it to my mother and she went directly to the bank. By summer's end she had her 250k to move her business out of our home and into a downtown office space.

With a full financial picture of my mother's company and a detailed plan on how the two hundred and fifty thousand dollars would be used to improve the profitability of my mothers business, it wasn't surprising that her loan was approved in just a short time. Her company clearly had the ability to generate revenues that would support the added debt and her creditworthiness was impeccable. Most importantly, with the increased overhead from new office space and increased personnel, my mother business was projected to be in the black (profitable) in year one.

My mother and Mr. Roberts became friendly again, but nothing serious. I think she was too wrapped up in growing her business, while he was preoccupied with his career. We all got together for celebratory dinner. My mother thanked Mr. Roberts for his help and his mentorship of me this summer. He had some good things to say about me, which wasn't too surprising – I think, I kind of grew on him over the summer. She did give out some tokens of her appreciation – she gave Mr. Roberts silver cuff links that he seemed more than appreciative to receive, and gave me a game boy, which was the highlight of the dinner for me. I couldn't wait to get back home to play it.

Once I finished the summer internship with Mr. Roberts, we kept in contact every now and then. When I saw him, he would always ask me about school. He would stress education almost more than my mother, but he would put a special emphasis on quality education from a good learning institution – he emphasized Ivy League education.

2

Undergrad

My studies intensified under the pressure and encouragement of my mother and Mr. Roberts. I put less attention on basketball and more on my academics. My mother had been on me about buckling down during my junior and senior years to push my GPA to 4.0. She had a heavy influence on me, but my last interaction with Mr. Roberts was what really gave me the extra push I needed.. He said, my education would be the foundation to my success, and if I wanted to pursue a career in economics and finance, where I went to college would be important. He was adamant about two things: First, to be a true player in this financial world, one had to work on Wall Street. Second, to work on Wall Street you needed a superior education. Superior to him was Ivy League. He regretted attending an HBC (Historically Black College) for his undergrad work. In his day, he had felt his attending an HBC had hindered him.

He admitted that the experience at the HBC was a good one, but it didn't matter what he thought of his education. What mattered was the perception of others, and no matter how wrong it was, the perception of an HBC, was inferior. Mr. Roberts stressed that in order to have success one had to know the rules and play by them. And, if you didn't like the rules then be ready for a life of mediocrity. His words had a lasting impression on me and changed my life. My mother was happy with my newfound motivation and dedication toward my education.

Upon my graduation from high school I was accepted at an Ivy League school back east that had an economic undergrad program ranked third in the nation. It made my mother proud, but financing my education was an uphill battle. I received some federal assistance in the form of a Pell Grant, along with my mother's financial contributions, but it still didn't cover the $20,000 per quarter tuition fee, so student loans had to supplement the financing of my college education.

My mother and I arrived on campus two weeks before my freshman year started at Darden University. The university was located in a small city, in upstate, New York, with a total population of twenty thousand, which included the student population for the university. The downtown was about three city blocks in radius, and the one night spot in the city was an Irish Pub. This little town was more like an extension of the University. It seemed as if the sole purpose of the city was to cater to the university. The people and the town reminded me of Mayberry with Opie and Barnie Fife.

The campus was stunning, compared to the town. It was vast, gorgeous, and tranquil, with massive stately buildings. The campus took up over three quarters of the land mass of the town. Sorority and Fraternity row was larger than downtown and the houses were these large old Victorians that were built in the early 1900's. The campus buildings were made of decorative rich red brick surrounded by green lawns and autumn leaved trees. I hadn't seen anything more beautiful in my life. The campus had three state of the art libraries. The business building was the most impressive building on campus. It was made of this sort of white marble brick that made this building a beacon among the other buildings on campus, twice the size of any other building, and the interior was lined with old refined oak. The classrooms weren't huge; they were small and intimate. After we toured the campus, my mother simply fell in love with the school. She said it was worth every penny to send me there! I thought she might have been suffering from heat stroke, but she seemed to be of sound mind.

Darden wasn't a popular place with the brothers. In each of my freshman classes I only counted three blacks per class; me, myself, and I. This made for somewhat of a lonely experience. Not that the other students didn't welcome my input and participation, it was just that I wanted and needed someone with my same background and experience to enjoy this educational experience with me, and to draw from their energy to keep me focused and on track. I didn't find that inside the classroom, but I did find it in the campus dorms.

I met Walt, Earl, and Timothy in Vernon Hall. Walt and Earl were roommates on the second floor, and Timothy and I roomed together on the third floor of this five floor brick building. Walt and Earl knew Timothy. They all were from the Bay Area and had attended Jason Wright Prep School – one of the most highly rated prep schools in the nation. They hailed from families of wealth and prestige in the black community. Walt's father was a prominent criminal attorney and president of the NAACP San Francisco chapter. Earl's mother was a television news anchor on the nightly news in the Bay Area; Timothy's parents were real estate moguls. They owned residential and commercial property, in the Bay Area, Southern California, New York, Florida, and Mississippi. Evidently these properties had been passed down from generation to generation and each succeeding generation added to the extensive portfolio of real estate holdings. I looked up his family history in the library. One book estimated his family's net work in excess of $50 million.

Timothy and I had become good friends. Timothy was one of the nicest, politest, courteous, and humble people that I had ever met. I didn't know people like Timothy existed, so when I first met him, I thought something was wrong with him-- like maybe he was a couple of cans short of a six pack, but to the contrary he was perfectly normal, just the product of a good upbringing. It wasn't until I saw his goodness and courtesy up close and personal that I knew Tim was genuine in his behavior.

Walt, Earl, Tim, and I were playing basketball with some other brothas in the old basketball gym, which was open to the public and was popular for pickup games. We played regulation full court games, which took up the whole gym. In the middle of our game some other students entered the gym wanting to play basketball, but they didn't want to play the winners of our game. They wanted to split the court in two and play full court pick-up games horizontally instead of vertically, which as I said took up the whole gym. Well, needless to say, everyone just ignored them and continued to play. Our feeling was you can have it next, but we were not about to stop our game and play a shortened full court game. Timothy was the only voice of reason.

"Hey fellas, hold on a minute. It's not fair for us to monopolize this entire gym when we all can share the gym."

"What? They can wait for the next game," exclaimed one person playing basketball with us.

"But, why make them wait, when they can play now? They have around ten guys to play their own full court game. If the shoe was on the other foot, we wouldn't want to wait, either. We would want them to accommodate our request."

Tim held his ground in the face of much animosity for suggesting that we accommodate their request, but eventually his argument weighed on our minds. We acquiesced to accommodate the request of the other players.

Tim's moral fiber was intact. He was a young man of high standards and integrity. He continued to shine in that manner through the four years of our undergrad work together.

Like me, Tim was an economics major, but we only had one class together our senior year: Financial Analysis –The fundamentalist approach with Professor Falcon. This class was one of my favorites. We would analyze companies' financials, take them apart, restate them, and try to conclude the true value of the company, to indicate if it was undervalued or overvalued based on its market price (stock price). Then, we were to track the company's stock price throughout the remainder of the quarter.

The class divided into groups of four, and there was fierce competition among the groups to pick the best possible company. A trip to Wall Street was the prize, along with a tour of the New York Stock Exchange. Everyone was excited and anxious to win the trip. As students, we all had read about Wall Street and had seen pictures of the stock exchange, but most had never been there. I, for one, wanted to see the money capital of the world. Ever since my internship with Mr. Roberts, my goal had been to work on Wall Street, and a trip to see my future place of employment was more than appealing.

Professor Falon, who was in his mid-sixties, short, pudgy, balding, and a WASP, put the groups of four together himself. He partnered me and Timothy with two girls – Susan and Karen. Both were very smart and driven, both were very attractive. Susan was about five seven with an athletic build and curly brunette hair, and Karen was five-five, blond, with a slender girlish figure. Tim and I had never said two words to them in class or when our paths crossed on campus before we were assigned to the study group. They seemed to us to be very above it all; their attitudes-- I likened to musicians at the top of their game, convinced that they've never played a bad or wrong note in their entire lives. If they ever did play something off tune, it was on purpose, a ploy to take the song down a different path. Susan and Karen were not that keen on the idea of teaming up with me and Tim, but they didn't have a choice.

We decided to meet over the weekend in the old library on the south end of campus at 10:00 am Saturday morning. Tim and I arrived at the library exactly at 10:00 am on the dot, and Susan and Karen were already there waiting, giving us the evil eye, like we were a half hour late. Our first group meeting started off a little rocky. Susan took the lead, giving her choices of companies she thought would outperform, given the criteria outlined by Professor Falon. She had all her arguments and supporting documents and analysis to support her position. Obviously, she and Karen had already met and decided that they were going to captain this ship. But, much to their dismay, Tim and I had our own plan that was contrary to their strategy.

"I think that is a fine plan, and I would have to agree that the chances of success with any one of your choices is likely, but Tim and I were thinking outside the box on this one," I said.

"What do you mean outside the box? The assignment is straight forward and clear. We need to choose one company that we think has the greatest growth potential over the next two quarters," Susan responded.

Her tone was almost offensive, but I didn't want to have a confrontation with her at this time, but I also wanted to let her know her tone wasn't appreciated.

"Susan, I can understand your passion about this assignment, but if you want us to proceed as a group, please watch the tone you use. We all deserve respect, and when we lose respect for each other then the group dynamic breaks down. Now, if you and Karen want to separate from Tim and me, then do so. We can go to Professor Falon…….."

"No, we don't want to break the group up," Karen interrupted. "What is the idea that you and Tim have?"

There was a pause of silence; Tim and I looked in Susan's direction, and she gestured for us to continue with our idea.

I took the lead once again. "We were in the city last weekend and came across a clothing store located in the inner city. The store was owned by a young African American male who designed all the shoes sold in the store. The style of clothing and footwear were hip hop and the store was packed."

"So, you guys want to use this ….hip hop clothing store as our company of choice?" Susan asked.

"Yes!" Tim responded

"It's not a publicly traded company. Is it?" Karen asked.

"No, but we could put the financials together for the company and derive its intrinsic value, then devise a plan and pro forma financials for expansion to prompt the growth."

"Are you fucking kidding? That is a shit load of work!" Susan shouted.

The profanity caught me off guard and instead of her words being offensive to me I found them to be funny. I let out a tremendous laugh, which she didn't really appreciate.

"What's so fucking funny?" Susan asked.

My laugh became uncontrollable. Tears were falling down my face and I was hunched over in my seat trying my best to control my laughter. Then, to make things worse Tim joined in and his laughter was loud and rambunctious. Together we made spectacles of ourselves in the library, but the laughter became contagious because Karen joined in.

"What is so funny?" Susan asked once again.

We all kept laughing and Susan finally joined in on the laughter.

Calmer heads prevailed after our laugh fest. Tim and I explained that yes, it would mean more work for us, but the experience would be tremendous. To actually be on the ground floor of a business and be the mental engine that prompts growth and profits would be worth the price of admission to Darden. We convinced them to go along with our plan. We filled them in on our initial meeting with the owner, Calvin, who was on board with our helping him expand his business. Susan commented, who wouldn't be on board with free business and financial planning for their business?

****

Monday morning Karen, Tim, Susan, and I made it down into the city to meet with Calvin. We wanted to waste no time in looking at his books and getting a sense of his business and its potential for growth. We met in the back of the store in Calvin's office. We told him our plan of attack would be to do an initial assessment of his business and its value, then put together a proposal and business plan to expand his business through a small business loan. Calvin was excited. He told us he would give us access to anything that we needed from him. Our first request was to look at his books.

To everyone's dismay, except me, Calvin didn't keep any books. All he had was paper bags filled with receipts. When Susan saw Calvin walk back into the room with brown paper bags, claiming these were his books, she turned beet red. She turned to me calmly and asked to have a word with me outside the office.

"Let's cut our losses and go with one of the companies Karen and I have chosen," she said.

"No!" I responded.

"Why the hell not?"

"Because I'm committed to this endeavor, and I gave my word to Calvin that we would help him."

Susan was mad. If she were a bull I could have seen the steam coming from her snout! I turned to go back into the office when Susan pushed me in the back of my head, and then walked right past me. I was in disbelief. I thought to myself, she must be crazy. When I walked into the room behind her, she took a seat, a smirk on her face. That push to the back of my head must have relieved so much anxiety and anger for her. I knew I had taken her and Karen out of their comfort zones by bringing them to the inner city. On top of that I had committed us to a very challenging task which would take ten times as much work than if we were just to follow the class assignment by picking an established company that traded on the New York Stock Exchange. For putting them in this position, maybe I deserved the push to the back of the head, so I let it slide.

The next five to six hours we went through Calvin's entire collection of brown bags, piecing together a set of financials – income statement, balance sheet, and a cash flow statement – and entered the data on Tim's laptop. Together with our queries of Calvin, we were able to put together a fairly complete set of financials, but there were some gaping holes and questions that needed to be filled and answered before we could get an accurate picture of Calvin's business. First, there were questions about Calvin's actual manufacturing costs to produce his shoe line. After much prodding and pushing by us, especially Susan, Calvin admitted he piggy backed off a larger operation without their knowledge. He had a friend who worked for a company that supplied him with generic shoes before they went through design and branding, and then he would put his own brand on the shoes with some hand stitching done in the back of his store. Second, the business was a cash cow, but Calvin didn't have a bank account and hadn't filed income tax returns in two years of operation. Not that the first problem of using some other company's product wasn't bad enough, but messing with Uncle Sam was a big red flag.

Susan, Karen, and Tim wanted out at that point. And, I really couldn't blame them, but I was committed to pulling this off – giving

Calvin the help he needed to take his business to the next level while overcoming the challenges ahead of us. It was around 2 a.m. and all of us had class that morning at 8 a.m., but I had to convince them this project was worth seeing through.

"I know this doesn't look good, and the challenges are mounting against us, but we can do this."

"I don't want to offend you, Calvin, but you have indulged in some shady and illegal activities that we cannot help you with. And, you haven't paid your taxes for the last two years. No financial institution will come within miles of you if you don't have tax returns," Karen said.

Calvin said he understood if we didn't want to move forward from this point. Calvin was twenty-seven years-old, and even though he might have broken a few laws here and there, I admired the hustle in him to get his business and dreams this far. In my mind, some of us do what we have to do, to get started and hope the pieces fall in place down the line. The time and opportunity for Calvin was now with us.

"Listen, there are obvious big problems facing us in helping Calvin get his business on the right track, but each is fixable."

"Fixable? This is an illegal operation and if we are caught, we all could go to jail right along with your friend Calvin," Susan argued.

"I'm not asking anyone to take part in a criminal enterprise, as Susan puts it. What I am asking of you, is to help Calvin legitimize his business." I turned my attention toward Calvin. "Now Calvin, we need to do a formal proposal to the company you are piggy backing off of illegally, and negotiate a price for supplying you with their product. Then, we have to file your tax returns for the past two years and pay all taxes related to your income." I paused to see his reaction. "Are you on board with such a plan?"

"Absolutely!" Calvin responded.

I knew Calvin had vision for his brand beyond selling product out of one store. So, his buy in on my plan wasn't surprising. I just had to convince the others not to abandon me because I couldn't have pulled it off by myself.

"There's an opportunity here for us to be a part of something that is real." I looked around the room at Susan, Karen, and Tim. – "The American Dream! Yea, Calvin bent some of the rules to get his dream started, but let's not condemn the man, let's show him the correct path to see his dream come to fruition. We are getting an education from one of the finest universities in the country. Let's put what we've learned to the test in the real world." There was silence – Tim, Susan, and Karen looked at each other.

"I'm with you," Tim responded first.

"Count me in," Karen responded

"We must be out of our freakin minds, but count me in too," Susan joined in.

Tim and Karen were assigned the task of contacting the IRS, incorporating Calvin's business and putting together tax returns for the last two years. Susan and I were responsible for finding a company Calvin could piggyback off of, and creating a proposal to present to these potential companies. We all worked well together. It took less than two weeks for Tim and Karen to incorporate and prepare tax returns for Calvin's company. Susan and I found five potential companies that would be a good fit for Calvin's shoe business, and that had a history of helping smaller companies by letting them piggyback on their large operations for a reasonable cost. Most companies wanted a combination of unit cost and equity sharing, which Calvin didn't like, but it didn't look like there was any way around the equity sharing. At least there was no way initially.

Upon review of Calvin's financials and final tax returns, his net worth was around one hundred and fifty thousand, which was mostly cash. His net income for the last two years was two hundred and fifty thousand, so his tax liability was seventy five thousand, given his thirty percent tax bracket. We all thought the tax bill would be the hurdle that broke the camel's back. The next day Calvin came to the store with seventy five thousand dollars cash. To see that amount of cash all at once made Karen, Susan, Tim, and me nervous, but Calvin assured us the money was from his business profits. Then, I remembered Calvin didn't have a bank account. It made sense he held all his assets in cash.

We ended up partnering with an off brand tennis shoe manufacturer in Tennessee. Calvin, Susan, and myself made the pitch to the Tennessee based company. On the plane, on the way back to New York, Calvin and Susan were looking at me with a new appreciation.

"That was a hell of a pitch you did in there!" Calvin said.

"Have you done this before?" Susan asked.

"I've had a little sales experience in my mother's interior design company."

"You are a natural sales man," Calvin rejoined. "How about partnering up with me?"

"I'm a full time student. I don't have the time to commit to your business full time, but I appreciate the offer."

"Man you don't need school, you are a natural hustler, and I mean that in a good way," Calvin responded.

"My mother would kill me if I were to drop out. All the money she's paying to keep me in school. Ah man, just the thought of her reaction scares me."

"Oh, the poor baby is scared. Stand up and be a man, stop being a little boy," Susan said sarcastically.

"What?" I responded. I couldn't believe what was coming out her mouth. I know she was in the same position as me, so she had to be kidding. When I stared at her she couldn't hold back her laughter. "Yea, that's what I thought."

"All jokes aside, you go to school to get a degree to get a job and make good money. What I'm offering you now is a good job making good money, and you, of all people know, like I know, my business is about to blow up. Get in on the ground floor, Shane!"

"Everything you just said is true, but I can't. I started pursuing my degree at Darden, and I will not stop until I have that degree in hand. There's not many of us brothas at Darden and for me to set an example of stellar performance throughout my stay, would open the door for other brothas and sistas."

"I hear ya! Well, once you have that piece of paper, look me up. There's always a job here for you."

"Thanks!"

****

We submitted a small business loan application for two hundred thousand dollars to ten different financial institutions. Our plan was simply to use the funds to open four new stores in the four other boroughs in New York, lease out space and improve the space to specifications that mimicked Calvin's store in Brooklyn. We were denied by nine of the ten institutions, all stating that we needed to show three to five years of operation before they would give further consideration of a small business loan. The one institution that approved us, by a strange coincidence, approved for only fifty thousand. Calvin got frustrated with the whole process and began to think he was better off with only one store. From his perspective, he had paid the last bit of cash he had to the government for back taxes, which now left his existing business cash poor. He no longer had his supply hookup because he had severed ties at our request, which resulted in low inventory. He started to have the look and attitude that he just wanted us to go away, so he could go back to his old way of operation.

Six months had passed and we were still struggling with securing the financing for Calvin's business. We had already lost the competition in Professor Falon's Intrinsic Value Class, for which Susan did not hesitate to put the blame squarely on my head. The ending net worth of Calvin's business had dropped to ten thousand dollars. Two factors contributed to his decline: one, the failure to get the needed funds to finance his expansion, and two, the unit cost he was now paying for his inventory. Once the class ended, our group partners- Susan, Karen, and Tim – didn't want to put any more time into Calvin's business. In their minds Calvin no longer wanted our help, so we were wasting our time keeping this project going. We all met at Calvin's store after hours to discuss if we should continue to move forward with Calvin's expansion or just call it quits.

Calvin started the meeting off. "First, I want to thank all you for all your hard work, but the gig is up. I need to get back to the way I know how to do business."

"Fine by us, because we need to get back to the business of real school work," Susan said.

Karen and Tim were silent, but I couldn't let this go down the drain without a fight.

"I know we are all a little frustrated with the process, but through struggle comes victory. I can't explain it, but my intuition tells me there's light at the end of this tunnel."

"This tunnel is so dark the light you see at the end is nothing more than a match flickering in the wind, bound to blown out by the next institution you approach for money," Susan responded.

"You are such a smart ass!" I said in frustration. "Before we throw in the towel, give me two weeks. If I can't get the other hundred and fifty thousand we need then I'll join all ya'll in calling it quits."

"What is it that you think you can accomplish in two weeks that we couldn't accomplish in six months?" Susan asked negatively.

"Let me worry about that." I looked away from Susan to Calvin, Karen, and Tim. They all shook their heads hesitantly to give me the okay.

My idea was to bring individual investors into the fold, sell them on the vision of Calvin's shoe business, and win them over to his plan for expansion. I had three in mind for a fifty thousand dollar investment each. First, was his new supplier, but I knew they would want a bigger equity position in Calvin's business in exchange for participating. I would have to sell the loss of equity in his company to Calvin. Second, was my mother. Her business had really taken off after her two hundred fifty thousand dollar loan. After explaining the plight of Calvin and the obstacles he'd encountered in the pursuit of his dream, I knew she wouldn't be a hard sell. My last hope would be Mr. Roberts. I hadn't spoken to him since I graduated from high school, but if the numbers made sense, he was as likely as anyone to invest fifty thousand in a solid business with potential for future growth. The bottom line for him was the expected return and how much risk was involved.

Just as I had anticipated, Calvin's new supplier wanted a greater equity stake in Calvin's company. He wanted his five percent interest to increase to ten percent, and when I presented the plan and investment opportunity to my mother, as I thought, she was a willing participant, but she wanted a ten percent interest. My mother had not only become a successful business owner, but a savvy investor. She understood the money game now from all ends. Our experience with trying to secure the two hundred and fifty thousand to move her business out of our home had moved us both to formidable foes when it came down to financial acumen. Mr. Roberts was a lot tougher sell. He liked the business plan and the financials that supported it, but he wanted to know more about Calvin - his character, upbringing, background and education etc..... Calvin had a high school diploma, but he had no college credits. He was raised in a single parent household, like me. I thought Calvin was of good character. If I didn't, I wouldn't have tried to help him fulfill his dream. I told Mr. Roberts everything I knew about Calvin, but that wasn't enough. He wanted to meet Calvin face to face. So, I arranged a meeting and filled Calvin in on the particulars. Calvin was desperate by this time and just wanted to move forward. He knew going back to his old way of doing business wasn't what he really wanted, so he agreed to give up thirty percent of his business to get the hundred and fifty thousand we needed to get this expansion moving.

Calvin and I flew out to Los Angeles the weekend after I had talked to my mother and Mr. Roberts. I included my mother in the meeting because I thought she might bring balance to the conversation and benefit from meeting with Calvin, her new business partner. We met at Mr. Roberts' office in downtown Los Angeles, Saturday afternoon. His office hadn't changed one bit since my summer internship with him. He offered all of us a seat at the round table in his office, but he was looking at Calvin with slight displeasure. Calvin was dressed in baggy jeans, an oversized button down thick white casual shirt with a Phat Farm emblem on the right pocket, and a New York Yankees hat with the beak of the hat turned twenty degrees to the right. Calvin was the epitome of hip hop culture, and was very proud of it. In all our business meetings and presentations, he would dress in the same youthful fashion with different variations. His style was always hip hop. And Mr. Roberts didn't approve.

"I thought we were having a business meeting with a young business man, not a rap star," Mr. Roberts announced.

Calvin, by now, was used to the initial reaction to his clothing from our other dealings with suppliers, bankers, and other potential investors, but no one had been as blunt as Mr. Roberts. I actually anticipated Mr. Roberts' reaction to Calvin, but it never crossed my mind that his dress might be a roadblock to our getting the financing we needed. Even though Susan and I were always professionally dressed when we met with bankers and others, Calvin was always dressed hip hop. Susan had expressed some concern, but I dismissed her concern, using Russell Simmons as an example of a successful businessman always dressed in hip hop attire.

"I'm not a rap star sir, just a young business man with vision and a dream."

"Well, you wouldn't know it from the looks of you. If you didn't walk in here with Shane and Ms. Jackson, you would have never gotten through my front door."

For the next half hour Calvin and I convinced Mr. Roberts that Calvin was a serious and responsible business man that wouldn't take his fifty thousand dollar investment and spend it on a rap video with ten strippers half naked shaking their rumps towards the cameras. Once we got past that, the meeting was more productive. Both Mr. Roberts and my mother had pertinent questions about cost controls, management style, growth rates, cash flow, and expected rate of return. I handled all the financial questions and Calvin handled the management and staffing questions. Using my laptop, we gave them a virtual tour of the four new stores.– Loft style, eighteen foot ceilings, rich colors, cement floors, graffiti art hanging on the all white walls, and a series of unique racks and shelves displaying the latest designs by Calvin. When we finished our presentation, Mr. Roberts didn't say anything, nor did my mother. They each handed us checks for fifty thousand. As we headed for the door, Mr. Roberts stopped me.

"Shane, you made me proud today. Your presentation was excellent. You touched on all the points you knew were of concern to me and your mother, and you put us at ease with the investment we were about to make. You're a good salesman, and you are going to make a lot of money on Wall Street."

I thanked him, then we left and headed for the elevators. Calvin, my mother and I stepped onto the elevators and the doors closed with just the three of us standing there. When I looked at my mother she was wiping her eyes with a tissue. Before I knew it she, was giving me a big bear hug.

"The sky is the limit for you and Calvin" she reached for him. "For you, young man, from one entrepreneur to another, never give up on your dream. Early to bed and early to rise, work real hard and advertise."

"Thank you, Ms. Jackson, for the words of encouragement," Calvin responded.

We all embraced in the elevator.

Once we got back to New York, Calvin made a call to all his staff -- which was all of four people, and then to Susan, Karen and Tim. He told all of them he had made up his mind about some important issues that would affect the future of his business. He wanted everyone to report to the store at 9:00 p.m. tomorrow night after the store closed. He asked me not to tell anyone what had transpired in Los Angeles. I complied with his wishes when questioned by my three fellow students.

I didn't know at the time Calvin was one for theatrics and a little show boating, but when we arrived at the store there were over

100 people standing on the outside of his store front. I recognized several as family members and friends. Exactly at 9 p.m., Calvin opened the doors to his store, which had been decorated with congratulation signs, balloons, confetti, and a small stage to the right where he was standing with a microphone in hand. A DJ was set up behind him. Once everyone had entered the store, he called Susan, Karen, Tim, and me to the stage. He then made his announcement.

"Tonight I stand before you with great news. As most of ya'll know I've been working on an expansion plan for my business, and these four people standing to my right have worked long hours in helping me try to make it happen. Susan, Karen, Tim and Shane are students at Darden. For those of you who don't know, that is an Ivy League school in upstate New York. I have not paid them one dime and they have put in a lot of hard work, and just when we thought the whole project was lost... Shane, Shane, come here, man."

I moved to my left, around Karen and Tim, and stood next to Calvin. He put his arm around my neck.

"This young brotha took it upon his shoulders to carry us to the finish line, and finish we did. Yesterday we got the rest of the money we needed to start and complete the expansion. Now, not only did this young brotha find the money we needed, he was the one from the start to help me fine tune my business and financial plans to get my project off the ground. He brought the others in to help with the project. I owe this brotha a lot, and in front of everyone here, I promise you that when you graduate from school there's a job waiting here for you if you want it. I can't thank all of you enough." He turned toward the others and mouthed the words, thank you. "Thanks to my family for all your support and encouragement. A special thanks to my girl Tasha for putting up with my mood swings and never killing a brotha's dream by telling me to go get a nine to five. I'm not a nine to five brotha." He paused, looked around the room. "So, this is a celebration. I have food, drink, family, friends, and music that will be provided by DJ Kay – Let's party ya'll!"

After Calvin's announcement, Karen, Susan, and Tim huddled around me and Calvin, wanting to be filled in on our trip to Los Angeles. Calvin filled them in while Tim looked at me, saying with astonishment, "You did it, man!" He gave me a pound, handshake and hug.

Karen then gave me a hug. "You are an especially tenacious guy. You are going to go a long way in this life, and I would work with you again any day on any project."

Last but not least, Susan gave me a hug, whispering in my ear, "You're not all that!" She then turned and walked away. I wasn't surprised anymore by Susan's remarks or comments; I actually had gotten to the point where I anticipated something smart coming out her mouth. I think it gave her comfort to take me down a peg or two.

We all –Karen, Susan, Tim and I – found a little corner of the room to enjoy the food and drink Calvin provided while he worked the room, greeting all his guests. Calvin's mother came over to thank us for helping her son and extended an open invitation for a home cooked meal. She seemed like a lovely lady, too young looking to have a twenty-seven year-old son. Person after person began coming up congratulating us and thanking us for the work we did with Calvin. Everyone made us feel good and appreciated. We talked among ourselves about the time and sacrifices we'd made to make this happen. The trials and tribulations we went through from beginning to end to get Calvin's business to this point. We all promised that once Calvin had his grand opening of the stores we would come back to see the fruits of our labor.

The DJ was playing hip hop music and people were in the partying mood. Practically everyone in the store was dancing, so Karen and Tim joined in. I looked over at Susan, and she said, "Don't even think about it." Then she quickly laughed, grabbed my hand and led me to where everyone was dancing. All of us danced and laughed the night away. It was the best time I had in a long time. Between school and Calvin's project, I had no time for fun and games. It was good to let loose.

Tim and I remained friends with Karen and Susan; we hung out from time to time. Before we graduated, we did go back to the grand opening of Calvin's Harlem store. The storefront had so many people inside at the opening we almost didn't get in. We waited in a line that extended down the block until Calvin spotted us and came out to escort us in. The opening was in grand style, same old Calvin doing big things in a big way.

3

Back in L.A.

After graduation, I didn't want to go straight to grad school as Tim chose to do. He got accepted to an MBA program that was one of the top five in the country, an Ivy League school located at Columbia. I chose to return to Los Angeles. My return was welcomed by my mother. She had missed me while I was at Darden. The east coast location hadn't allowed for frequent visits by either of us. Being an only child, it was hard on my mother when I was away, but she began to realize I was becoming a man, ready to make my own way.

Upon my return to Los Angeles I didn't really hit the ground running in terms of looking for a job. I worked part time for my mother on different projects, mostly dealing with financial analysis of projects, but most of my time was spent enjoying the Los Angeles nightlife. I was partying like crazy; I hooked up with old high school buddies and hit the club scene. We all were legal and I don't think we left one L.A. club untouched. I lived at home with my mother, so she witnessed my weekly escapades of chasing women and staying out all night in the L.A nightlife. This went on for about six months and my mother never said a word to me. However, she knew I needed to put my mind to something with more substance, and the small projects she had me involved in with her company just weren't peaking my interest.

My mother still had a ten percent interest in Calvin's Designs of New York, and from what she told me it had been a solid investment. Calvin's Designs had an upcoming annual meeting for all partners in the business, and according to my mother, Calvin had sold more interest in his business to raise additional money to expand his designs to include clothing, instead of just shoes. He still owned the biggest share of Calvin's Designs, but it was no longer a majority percentage. My mother wanted me to attend the annual meeting in her place to represent her interest. She thought getting me out of L.A. would cut off or at least cut down my partying behavior.

I arrived in New York a day before Calvin's Designs annual meeting. I took the day just to do some sightseeing around the city, then I went to Calvin's store in Harlem. This wasn't my first time in Harlem, but each time I would go it was like a brand new love affair. The energy in the air was unlike nothing I'd ever experienced. I had experienced black culture in bits and pieces growing up in L.A.'s vast sprawling black community, but never to the magnitude or level I experienced in Harlem. There were black owned restaurants, clubs, theaters, galleries, bookstores, coffee shops, and other small businesses. I ended up spending the whole day in Harlem.

Calvin's store was crowded, as usual, and his new clothing line was on display. The style was strictly hip hop, featuring baggy jeans, oversized shirts, and t-shirts with faces of hip hop icons. The store theme hadn't changed -- it was like one big hip hop party – graffiti on the walls and floors, flat screens streaming hip hop videos, and a stereo system banging amps that would make the top hip hop clubs envious. I thought, I might recognize some of the Calvin's employees in the store, but I didn't. I asked for him, but he was at his other store in the Bronx. I bought two pair of jeans, and a button down shirt, along with some of Calvin's version of Chuck Taylors.

Later that night I stayed in my hotel room reviewing the agenda and financial data that was sent to my mother via email. The next morning I rose early, ate a good breakfast and arrived a half hour early for the 9:00 am annual meeting. Calvin had rented some office space in Brooklyn where he made his headquarters. I was sitting in the lobby when Calvin happened to pass by.

"What up, Baby Boy!" he shouted, which drew the attention of everyone in the lobby. He gave me a big hug and asked what I was doing there. He was genuinely happy to see me.

"I'm here for the annual meeting on behalf of my mother."

"Your mother never makes it to the annual meetings, but I make sure her money is always sent on time. How are your friends – the brotha and the two grey girls?"

"Since graduation I don't talk to them much."

"Not even yo partna, Tim."

"Tim headed to grad school and I headed back to L.A. and I haven't heard from him since."

"Ay Man, I know how that is, fallin out of touch with friends. Since adding this new clothing line, hanging out with and talkin with the homies is a thang of the past. I had to bulk up on staffing to handle the business part of running my business, so I could focus on my designs for the clothing line. I hired my nephew as my second in command. He has an accounting degree from Morehouse."

"You always did keep family close."

Calvin and I chatted some more in the lobby before he was pulled away to attend to some business prior to the annual meeting. I waited another fifteen minutes in the lobby before I made my way to the conference room. I didn't recognize anyone in the room. There were a total of five other people and all of the faces were brand new to me. I was halfway expecting to see Mr. Roberts, but he was a no show.

Once the meeting commenced, Calvin introduced everyone. I quickly found out the only original investor still around was my mother, the other five new faces in the room were Calvin's new equity partners. Calvin had taken on new partners, giving up a bigger equity share of his company while paying out old partners that didn't want to take on the newest venture of his clothing line. The meeting was a simple update of the business and the progress on rolling out the new clothing line. Calvin's nephew, who was about three years my senior, heavy set, dark skinned, full beard, five ten in height, conservatively dressed with a raspy voice, gave the financial report.

When the meeting wrapped up, Calvin wanted to get together later that night for dinner. He had a car pick me up from my hotel and take me to Julian's a restaurant in Harlem. Julian's was a soul food restaurant that catered to the young influential hip hop culture. The atmosphere inside was similar to a hip hop club, dim lights, loud thunderous base music, standing room only at the bar, and everyone dressed as if they were shooting a hip hop video. Calvin had us set up in the back at a private table with his nephew and two beautiful sistas.

Calvin's nephew, Fred, and I hit it off immediately. We both talked about our undergrad experiences – he wanted to know about my experience at an Ivy League school, and I wanted to know about his experience at an elite all black college. My stories really just covered the beautiful campus and the academic challenges. His stories not only detailed the campus and the academics, but included stories of great parties and beautiful sistas like the two who were sitting at our table. Calvin had to break up our conversation because we were so busy talking to each other about our college experience we were excluding him and the two young ladies.

Once Calvin put a halt to our conversation, my attention was drawn back to the entire table and especially the two young ladies. One was Janice. The other was Sharon. Both sistas were wrapped in dresses that looked like they were painted on their bodies. Janice was brown skin with big brown eyes. She stood about five five and had the body, cuts and curves, of a track star. Sharon was a lighter complexion and stood five seven. She had the body, legs and stature, of a classical dancer. But, if I had my choice of the two I'd pass up twenty Sharons to get to one Janice. Janice was pure brown sugar! The girls got up and excused themselves to go to the ladies room.

"Okay, what's up with the sistas? Are they spoken for?" I asked

"Janice is my girl, and I'm tryin to hook my nephew up with Sharon, but if y'all want to compete, I could throw yo name in the hat."

"No thanks, I'm cool," I responded. I should have known the finest one at the table was Calvin's lady.

Sharon and Janice returned, and later, after we all finished our dinners, I excused myself and went to check out the bar. Calvin told me after 10:00 pm the restaurant turns into one of the coolest hip hop night club spots in New York. At 10:00 pm on the dot the tables were cleared and the dance floor appeared. Before I could blink an eye the dance floor was crowded, and the restaurant/club was packed with young vibrant hipsters. At that moment, I couldn't think of a better place to be. I danced a little, walked around the club just people watching. I tried to find Calvin and Fred, but they were nowhere to be found. I didn't know anyone, so I was solo. I ended up back at the bar just people watching until Janice appeared in front of me.

"What's up? You having a good time?"

"Yea... yes I am." I nodded my head in the affirmative. "Where are Calvin and Fred?"

"They had to leave early, some kind of early morning meeting."

"Okay, so where's your girl Sharon?"

"Oh, you interested in her?"

"No," I said.

"Then, why you askin' about her?"

"I don't know. She was with you earlier, and I guess, I was just wondering where she was at."

"Okay, well... she left with Fred. So, if you were feeling her, you lost out to Fred."

"Lost out? You got it all wrong."

"I'm just playing with you," she said with a slight laugh and smile on her face. "But, my girl was feeling you, but since you didn't show an interest, she chose to see what Fred was all about."

"Well, I did inquire, but was told she was there for Fred."

"Is she the only one you inquired about?"

"No."

"I didn't think so." She then looked at me with those big brown eyes, took my hand turned and led me to the dance floor. I couldn't help staring at her backside and the dress that was fitting her body like a latex glove.

We danced non-stop for the next hour. Her body movements on the dance floor kept me mesmerized. She moved so sensually, she kept my attention the entire time. Her hands moved up and down my body and I returned the favor. Her body was so close to mine most would have thought we were one. Our faces were close enough several times for mouth-to-mouth resuscitation, but I never made a move to kiss her. I was caught up in the moment and didn't know how to withdraw myself. I was hers for the taking and she knew it. From the dance floor she led me outside the club.

"Where are you staying?" she asked.

"The Zen Hotel in uptown Manhattan."

She hailed a cab, and we got in.

"Uptown Manhattan, the Zen Hotel," she told the cab driver.

My thoughts went to Calvin. What was I about to do? I had already crossed the line by flirting with his girl in the club on the dance floor, and I was headed to the ultimate betrayal. A part of me was telling myself get out of the cab. Do something to put a stop to this, but the other part of me was still stuck on her beauty and sensuality. Her assertiveness and directness was an aphrodisiac. My loins won over.

We arrived at my room. We did things in that room that I know were illegal in several states. Janice was experienced much more than I, but I didn't take long to climb the learning curve, and she showed her appreciation over and over. When we finally wore each other out, we both fell asleep in bed. When I woke around 6:00 am in the morning, Janice was gone. No goodbye or bedside note. As quickly as she'd appeared at the bar, she disappeared into the big apple.

****

Back in L.A, I started where I'd left off before my trip to New York. I was drawn to the nightlife like a moth to a flame. I was now a regular; I knew most of the owners and security personnel at the most popular L.A. spots. I was meeting up and coming actors, actresses, producers, and directors. My life had become one big party. It almost seemed that the trip my mother sent me on to New York had backfired. She wasn't very happy with my life choices, and began to give me fewer projects, which severely affected my income.

My lack of money didn't stop my lifestyle. My mother still allowed me to stay at home and most of the nightspots I attended usually didn't charge me a cover. This pattern went on for another six months. When my mother finally got fed up with what she called my lack of productivity and indecision, she sat me down in the den and gave me two options.

"Shane, what do you want out of this life?"

"I want to live forever!"

"Stop with your foolishness. Do you still want to work on Wall Street?'

"Yes."

"What's your plan to accomplish your goal?"

"I don't know, maybe grad school in another year or so."

"A year or so? No, son, you need to get started now. You can no longer run the streets as you've done the past year without a job and live under my roof. You have two options: One, you can apply for grad school and enter this fall. Two, get a job and work for the next two years or so then enter grad school. But, the status quo is over!"

"I have a job working with you."

"You call what you do for me work? First, the little projects I have you working on, you can do in your sleep. Second, I know you are not interested in the interior design business. Your passion is high finance. When I give you a project about finding my business more financing, you come alive. If it doesn't involve finance, you're almost reluctant to take it on."

"That's not true, Mom."

"Oh, yes it is. So, Mr. Shane Jackson what's it going to be?"

I paused to weigh my options. I didn't want to go to work for some company other than my mother's in L.A, and she was right-- interior design didn't really get my juices flowing. I did want to go to grad school, however I wanted to wait two more years until I turned twenty five. Nevertheless, if I had to choose between a job and school, school would be my choice. I told my mother my preference. I surprised her when I said I wanted to attend an HBC (historically black college).

"Shane, I don't want you to take what I'm about to say wrong. But, why would you want to go from one of the top colleges in the country to an HBC?"

"I want a different college experience. I've had the Ivy League experience, and you went to an HBC, and you had nothing but good things to say about it."

"Yes, that is true, but......."

"Didn't you tell me it's not the education that makes the person, it's the person that makes the education."

"Yes but......"

"A college gets its reputation from what the graduates accomplish, and that has more to do with the people than the education they received."

"True."

"I plan to put that theory to the test by receiving my MBA from an HBC and being a finance mogul on Wall Street."

This was the first time my mother genuinely smiled at me since my graduation from Darden.

"Sounds like a good plan to me," she said with happiness in her voice.

4

Grad School

I checked out the black colleges and their graduate programs in economics and business finance. I didn't have a lot of time to research because I had to have my application for the fall in by this spring, which gave me only a few months. The HBC that stood out for me was Jordan University in Washington DC – Chocolate City. The school had a solid business school, excellent faculty members, and was located in a city that was essentially black. Only thing white in the city was the White House- I'm exaggerating a little but the city sure seemed that way, except for the tourist areas. So, I thought, if you want the black college experience what better college than one located in a city they nick named Chocolate City.

My mother was concerned about me carrying my partying ways from L.A. to D.C and possibly skipping classes. I assured her that wasn't going to happen. My primary focus was my education and preparing myself for a career on Wall Street. My Mother couldn't emphasize enough the importance of striking a balance between socializing and studying. She was very adamant about not taking my studies lightly. Coming from one of the top undergrad schools in the nation, I might have been going in a little cocky about the academic challenges that lay ahead at Jordan University. One thing my mother said that stayed with me through my two years at Jordan was, "How much you put into something is how much you will get out. If you put a little in, you will get a little out. If you put a lot in, then expect a lot back."

I was determined to make this grad school experience an all around success. I had set goals for myself. My first goal: I would maintain an A average through my two years of grad school, as I did in my undergraduate work. Second; I would join a fraternity, Alpha Delta Sigma, in my second year of grad school. This was something I wanted to do in my undergrad work, but the rushes I went to just didn't feel right for me at the time. Being on a black campus with a prominent, historically black fraternity had more of an appeal. Third, I would land an internship on Wall Street. I was always intrigued by the markets, since my internship with Mr. Roberts. The Wall Street Journal was required reading when I worked with Mr. Roberts, and I've never stopped reading the journal. By reaching my three objectives, my grad experience would be an academic, social, and training success.

My first day on campus was electric! To see all these black students in one place in the pursuit of higher learning was one of the greatest feelings of pride I've ever felt. The campus was very nice, the grounds and the buildings were well kept. Students carried books with pens and pencils in their ears, held conversations about the challenges that lay ahead for them this year. I don't know if I was expecting something different, but black academia felt good. The aspirations and desires of the students here were the same as the aspirations and desires of the student body at Darden. I think I was caught up in the partying stories about black colleges and forgot that students were also here to achieve academic excellence.

The student union was a special experience in itself. Inside the historic brick building there were pictures of alumni that adorned the walls. These graduates had made significant contributions to society in many different areas- science, engineering, civil rights, art, business, and politics. The building was filled with pictures of African American women and men with their names and a brief description of their accomplishments. I would spend a whole day in this student union hall, reading about all the distinguished alumni from Jordan. The tribute to these alumni was very inspiring. I don't think any African American could walk through that building and not get pumped to go out and conquer the world. There was one guy on the wall who really caught my eye. He was the first black man to work on Wall Street in a professional capacity. He was the first African American Wall Street Stockbroker. When I read his name below, it sounded familiar – Mr. James T. White.

I knew the name James T. White was familiar; he was my professor in my class on economic theory. His appearance was befitting his name; he wore a low cut hairstyle and beard that was completely gray. He was of a darker complexion so his gray was that much more exaggerated and gave him a very academic look. He was short but he appeared to be in good shape. When Mr. White spoke, he spoke with conviction, good diction, and the charisma of a civil rights leader. He dressed impeccably, always in a tie, sports jacket, and slacks. I never saw him once with his tie loose or his shirt wrinkled.

I was so hyped when I realized that he was one of my professors. The first day of class I waited until class was over to go up to him and personally introduce myself. I told him how intrigued I was with Wall Street, the financial center of the world. I mentioned that I had seen his picture in the student union, stating that he was the first African American broker on Wall Street. I think I might have laid it on a little thick, but I didn't care – I wanted him to know I was impressed with his accomplishments. Mr. White took to me quickly- I demonstrated, I was sharp, hungry for knowledge, and wanted to hear all his stories about his experience on Wall Street. Mr. White turned out to be quite the talker and if a student was willing to listen, he would share his knowledge and experience with you. Since I was all ears, sometimes we would end up talking for hours in his office and after class. Mostly we talked about his experience as a Wall Street broker.

Mr. White told me at the time he started on Wall Street most blacks didn't know what a stock broker was. He said only a few blacks with significant net worth invested in the markets, and a lot of times they passed over him because they thought his knowledge might be inferior to his white counterparts. He tried prospecting in the black community, but wasn't successful. Most blacks would buy insurance because they viewed that as something reasonable and practical, but to put their money in something called a stock, they just couldn't fathom. They equated investing with gambling, and they didn't have money to waste on gambling. So he had to market himself to white clientele in order to make a living. Mr. White said he did three things: First, he dressed impeccably – on Wall Street, appearance is very important. He knew he must look like he was making good money in order for anyone to invest with him. He knew he couldn't look like he was just getting by. Nevertheless, he didn't want to be flashy. A broker wanted to appear conservative. Appearing too flashy sent a signal of risky, rogue, and flying by the seat of your pants behavior. Second, he learned the jargon and studied the markets to become astute; He learned things about the stock market they never teach you in school. He learned how underwriters can manipulate prices on new issuances of stocks, and how much money was being made by people in the first couple of days of an initial public offering-IPO simply on price manipulation, not any fundamentals of the company. Third, He became convinced he was the best broker on all of Wall Street. He started to be labeled as cocky and arrogant by his peers, but that was the edge he needed to survive on Wall Street.

Mr. White became a very valued friend and mentor. Outside of my mother, I don't think I'd ever met a person with more drive and knowledge. After my first year at Jordan, Mr. White set me up with a summer internship with one of the top Investment Houses, J L Morgan. He still had a lot of contacts on the street and set me up as a sales assistant in their retail stock brokerage operation.

When I hit Wall Street for my first day at work, the day was unreal. All the herds of people on the streets, moving with purpose and definiteness back and forth; everyone suited in their Brooks Brothers suits looking like they were ready to conquer the world. The buildings of all the financial institutions that made up Wall Street were large and beautiful, and overwhelming. I'd never seen a busier city.

My intern position at J.L. Morgan was as a sales assistant to two retail brokers -- one was a brotha and the other was Italian. Both were successful brokers but their styles were very different. Jake, the brotha, was about thirty years of age, very polished; real conservative down to his Brooks Brothers suits and shoes. He had excellent credentials: Stanford undergrad and a Harvard MBA. He was in the top ten in sales the last five years. Most people would say Jake came from good stock. His family had a history in finance; his father was president of Chase Nation one of the largest commercial banks on the street. In order to be successful on Wall Street a person had to have resources and Jake was not short on resources, given his family name and history. Most brokers would kill for his client list. No cold calling for Jake, referrals were coming in constantly.

Now, you would have thought, Jake being a brotha, we would have hit it off! We got along, and he appreciated my talent and I learned a lot from him, but our political views differed drastically and that killed any chance for us to build a long lasting friendship. One day after work we went for drinks and Jake asked, "Why would you choose Jordan University for your graduate work? You are clearly a very smart young man and …with a degree from a prestigious college like Darden on your resume, you could have attended grad school anywhere in the country!"

"I wanted a black college experience. The way I see it, all colleges are institutions of higher learning. What you put into your studies is what you get out, no matter where you go."

"Black college experience - that's Bull Shit! You must play the game to be successful in this world. There's no way around it! Look around, there are rules and regulations that govern the behavior of all of us. If you step out of line there are consequences. You basically cut your earnings potential by 50-60 grand a year by choosing Jordan to do your grad work."

"You are probably correct about the earnings potential, but I'm confident in my ability to be a top earner. Initially, I may be penalized but in due time my compensation will be on par with my talent. And, just maybe I will be able to dispel the myths that black colleges churn out inferior professionals."

"Why put an obstacle in your way on purpose? Why make the mountain you have to climb steeper?"

"Sometimes it's about changing misconceptions. If getting my MBA from Jordan and excelling … as I will in my professional career …breaks down some barriers for future grads, then I'm willing to take an economic hit for the greater good."

"So now it's about civil rights?"

"No, it's about economics. Once I shine as a professional and open the door for other Jordan grads and they shine, the door will be open for other black college grads. And, corporate America will have to recognize the talent that is being produced at black colleges."

"Alright Jessie Jackson! I'll drink to that, but I don't believe it."

That was the last personal conversation we had, but what I did take away from Jake was to always have a plan to take the next step. Never settle! Keep your eyes on the prize, and the prize was what you defined. Bottom line, Jake was smart and had vision. I never thought he was passionate about sales. It was just a means to an end for him.

Tony was very different; he didn't come from money or have a family name that was recognized on Wall Street. He had an undergrad from Berkeley and an MBA from Cornel, but he had to fight for everything he got. He had a very charismatic personality and he could hold his liquor. Social settings were his strong point; even after five or six drinks he remembered names, where he'd met you, spouse's names, and children names if necessary. All the important or pertinent dates, such as anniversaries and birthdays were committed to memory. He never forgot to send cards and gifts to clients and colleagues on special occasions. Clients were taken out and wined and dined regularly. The dinners were very productive and personable. Tony only took clients to the top restaurants in the city. He felt first class service in a first class atmosphere was very important because it represented the type of service his clients could expect from him. He could get into restaurants where you needed to reserve a year in advance to get a seat. It also seemed that he got VIP service in all the popular nightspots.

One day I sat down with Tony and asked how he got into restaurants and popular nightspots that the ordinary Joe cannot get into. I wanted to know how he had cultivated such first class treatment and how he garnered such attention.

"Since you are a hard worker, and I dump a lot of shit on you … which you do without complaining, I will share my secret with you. It's not hard, matter of fact, it's easy. It just takes a little time in your down hours to make some visits and connections. First, all businesses are in business to make money, including restaurants. I go to new restaurants, check out the atmosphere, service, and food. If I like what I see and taste, I come back to the restaurant during their slow time and introduce myself to the manager or owner. I tell him I'm a Wall Street broker and I have clients that I would like to bring in to wine and dine. I make my case that all my clients are influential and high net worth individuals who have unique and special tastes. The dining experience I share with them on a business basis usually translates into a personal dining experience for them on other occasions and sometimes creates more business with other associates. The manager usually gets the point and in return, he or she gets repeat business from very influential, powerful, and rich people. What businessperson in their right mind would turn down that proposal? The key is taking the time to do your homework, build the relationships in the beginning, and not to wait until you need a spot to entertain before searching for a person who might have a connection to get you in." Tony was a good dude, and we actually built up a friendship outside of the office.

My summer internship on Wall Street was successful; I met some good people and learned some valuable lessons.

I only had a few weeks in L.A. with family and friends before I had to get back to school for the start of my fall semester of my second year. My first year was all studies and getting to know the school and the city. The last year of grad school had to be more exciting; instead of being an observer I wanted to participate and experience.

****

I pledged Alpha Delta Sigma when I returned to Jordan. Expectations from this historic and prestigious black fraternity were high. Some of the most respected political and business leaders spun from this fraternity. One thing I learned at an early age from my mother was "it's not what you know but whom you know". There's a lot of truth in that statement. I would be lying if I denied that meeting people was a strong part of the allure to pledge. One pleasant surprise was the absence of the hazing that most pledges go through when pledging as an underclassman. I've heard about and seen some of the humiliating hazing tactics perpetrated on pledges, and was not enthusiastic about being subjected to such antics, which might have played in my decision to wait until grad school. This pledging process was more subtle in its approach and had more mind games to test the strength of its candidates. The line was nine men deep. What was so coincidental was that each pledge was an MBA candidate. I think this was a first in the history of graduate pledge lines of Alpha Delta Sigma.

The pledge line quickly became "thick as thieves". We formed study groups together, carried on philosophical conversations about life, love, religion, politics, racism, and any other topic of interest. The line consisted of brothas from different walks of life, but I really had to take my hat off to three in particular. These three brothas overcame odds that truly tested their mental toughness, their self-determination, and fortitude. Big Mike, Darrell, and Charles truly possessed the will to succeed, no matter the odds.

Big Mike stood about 6'5" and weighed in around 300 pounds. He was built like an NFL defensive lineman. Big Mike spoke in a deep raspy voice that commanded attention, had a sharp mind for the law, which made his arguments and reasoning come from a legal perspective. It was as if he were emotionless. He used to be an attorney and got disbarred after being convicted of obstruction of justice in the D.A.'s pursuit of one of his top clients, who was a drug trafficker. Mike did five years in a maximum security prison. During his time in prison, Big Mike developed an interest in business and became a regular subscriber to Black Enterprise magazine along with several other business publications such as Fortune, and the Wall Street Journal. Upon his release Mike decided to pursue his business interest by first getting his MBA. Big Mike made no apologies about his transgressions. He merely described it as a risk reward decision:

"the risk was big but the reward was even bigger". He had no moral qualms about what he had done, stating he lived in the real world where the line between right and wrong wasn't black and white, but different shades of grey. The law he practiced, he said, for over eight years proved that to him on a daily basis.

Charles was a short chubby brotha with a good sense of humor. He didn't mind people ragging on him as long as they didn't have a problem with him giving them some of the same medicine. Charles was a CPA, and worked with one of the top accounting firms on Wall Street. He got dismissed because he blew the whistle on a money laundering scheme within the firm. Everyone involved, including the whistle blower was dismissed and the laundering was covered up by the firm. They gave him a good severance package, and after seeing all the money that was being made by Wall Street market makers, he understood he could make more money in the market than accounting for the money made on the market. With that notion Charles headed for Grad school. Charles knew a CPA could write his own ticket being with an MBA.

Darrell was of light complexion, a good looking brotha, who always found himself on the other end of some female's affection. He came from a good middle class background. Never knew his father, Darrell was raised by his mother, a congresswoman on Capitol Hill. Darrell was very driven and stubborn, traits he inherited from his mother. He and his mother parted ways when Darrell refused to enter the military as part of her plan to groom him for a political career. She refused to support his choice to study economics, so Darrell put himself through undergrad school at Morehouse. He bounced around a few jobs before deciding to pursue his MBA. Darrell was a natural salesman and had a deep instinctive mind concerning the stock market. He told me he had been investing in the market ever since he was twelve. His mother let him invest the family savings in the stock market. He'd always had solid returns. When he decided to pursue his dream as an investment professional that's when his mother practically disowned him. Darrell was an only child, as his mother was. He'd lost his grandmother and father, two significant memories, when he was young. He persevered with little or no contact with his mother for more than six years. "I'm doing fine!" was all he ever said to her.

The game, "Giving You the Business" was the main focus and test we had to get through to cross over the pledge line. "Giving you the Business" was based on a concept in the art of selling. In all aspects of life a person is either selling, or he or she is being sold to. If a person understands that simple concept he or she will have great success in playing "Giving You the Business" and the truth be told, the game of life.

The game had a point system which pitted pledges against each other. Pledges with the lowest points could be dropped from the line. "Giving you the Business" measured a pledge's ability to make good judgments and his ability to sell. The objective of "Giving you the Business" was for each of the pledges to sell you on an idea, concept, task, or anything else that was given to them by the Frat. If you, as the mark, bought or declined the sales offer or were persuaded to act or not act, there were points gained for the correct decision. At the end of each week, there would be a meeting between the pledges and the Frat to determine which task should have been performed and what products or services purchased.

Now, Big Mike and Charles were average salesmen at best. Their strong suits were in law and numbers respectively. But, Darrel was a different story- he was the best salesman I've ever seen. He knew his targets, their strengths, and weaknesses. He would study his targets by using casual conversations to learn more about their background, education, hobbies, pet peeves, personality and character traits. Throughout these conversations he would make intense mental notes about the person. He told us later it was a skill he'd learned from his mother at a young age. His mother, a politician, had to be a great salesperson to survive in the political arena. She sized a person up within the first ten minutes of their conversation, and she taught Darrell to do the same. I learned a lot from him, and even though he would not reveal his secrets of selling during our pledge process, he was more than willing to share with us when we all crossed. I remember the time Darrell had to sell me in the "Giving You the Business" game.

Everyone knew I was a good salesman. They also knew that it was almost an impossible task to sell to me. Darrell considered it a challenge and accepted it. Darrell's task was to sell me on stealing the Dean's first prize plaque for the best BBQ in the DC area from his office. He knew this task was ridiculous to sell me on –he would have only lost points. So, he sold the idea of getting me to clean and paint the inside of a frat brother's girlfriend's house. The frat brothers loved the idea and thought that this task was more insurmountable than the first task. But, Darrell knew if I had any weaknesses, it was for women. He thought given my weakness, he could sell me on the idea.

"Hey, Shane, what do you have going on this weekend?"

"Nothing, just going over some notes from my business calculus class."

"Well, Margret is giving a party and I hear that little fine chocolate thing, Veronica, will be there. You want to roll through there Saturday night?"

"Yeah that sounds like a plan. You think Big Mike and Charles want to roll with us?"

"I've already checked with them, they are down."

Saturday night rolled around and we all took off around 10:30 p.m. to go to Margret's for this party. I was in the mood for a little socializing and looking forward to meeting Veronica, whom I had seen around campus and inquired about through some of my close friends. The word was she was single and very focused on her education. She didn't really take too much time out for socializing, so for her to be at this party really presented the perfect opportunity for me to introduce myself and get to know her a little better.

When we arrived, the party was in full effect. There were at least 100 people already in the house having a good time. The music was pumping and there was plenty of food. I would have to say that it was one of the better parties that I had been to since I'd been at Jordan. Big Mike commented when we arrived inside.

"Fellas, I got a feeling this is going to be a night to remember."

"Man, I'm with you on that one," Charles said.

"Let the games begin," I added.

After about an hour of a little dancing, eating, and drinking, I was feeling good when Darrell approached me.

"Shane, look, there's Veronica over in the corner with a few other honeys."

She was looking good. She always dressed nice and tonight was no exception. She was a very stylish, eloquent young lady. Darrell and I walked over. As we approached, I recognized one person in the group from my calculus class, Kim.

"Hey, Kim. What's up! What are you doing here? You know you should be going over your calculus notes for the exam we're having on Monday."

"I could say the same to you. Matter of fact I had some questions about the notes he gave us last week and left a message on your voice mail. Did you get my message?"

"No, I was at the library all day," I responded.

"I should've known you were there. Anyway, enough talk about class. Who's your friend you got with you?"

I turned toward Darrell. "This is Darrell, Darrell this is Kim."

"Hello, Kim. It's a pleasure to meet you," Darrell responded.

"Likewise," she replied. I followed up quickly with, "Are you going to introduce us to your friends, or just let us stand here?"

"Oh, I'm sorry. Shane and Darrel, this is Veronica, Stacey, and Brenda."

"Hello, ladies. How nice to make your acquaintance," I said.

Darrell kept it short. "Hello, ladies."

They all responded with hellos almost simultaneously. "Hello."

Ready to make a play, I wasted no time, focused in on my target and made my move.

"So, Veronica, I've seen you around campus, are you an undergrad student or graduate student?" I asked, as I moved closer to her.

"I'm a senior, finishing my undergraduate work in Biology,"

As my conversation unfolded with Veronica, Darrell disappeared, but I didn't notice because my concentration was going well with Veronica.

Around 1:30 in the morning, Veronica and I were getting along great. We were laughing, dancing and just enjoying each other's company. I was all over her like a cheap suit. The party started to thin out around 3:00 a.m., the few people that were left started to comment on what a mess the house was. Darrell was the first to speak.

"Hey, someone turn up the lights. I see some disturbing things around this house."

When the lights came up, everyone remaining at the party gasped. There was wine and beer on the walls, along with writing. Big Mike was really disturbed at what he saw. He shouted! "Who would do such a thing? That's what's wrong with our people. We don't know how to have a good time and behave ourselves like human beings."

Veronica responded, "I can't believe what I'm seeing. How could this happen?"

Margaret played her part perfectly. "I will never give another party at this stupid university. People don't know how to treat your stuff. Look at my place. It's completely ransacked. My landlord is going to flip out!"

"Don't worry, we will help you get your place back together," said Darrell.

"Thanks, Darrell. Any help would be much appreciated."

We all pitched in to help Margret clean up her place. It took close to two hours to get her place in order, but even then the walls were beyond cleaning. They needed painting and Darrell was the first to bring that point to our attention.

"Shane, Charles, and Big Mike, let me talk to you outside for a minute."

We all walked outside to the front yard of Margaret's place.

"What's up Darrell?" I said.

He didn't waste any time. He went straight to the point.

"Look, fellas, the walls in her place need painting. We can't leave that sista like that"

And I walked right over the cliff.

"Darrell's right. We need to volunteer to help Margaret paint the walls in her home so her landlord won't flip out on her. She gave a slammin' party – the best one since I've been at Jordan."

Big Mike and Charles agreed.

The next day we arrived with paint in hand to paint the interior of Margaret's house. Little did Big Mike, Charles, and I know we had been "Givin' the Business" by Darrell. I was the target, but Charles and Mike were just innocent bi-standers. Darrell set everything up-- the party, Margret's place, and Veronica's presence at the party. We had never seen her out anywhere –that should have been a clue to me. But the setup was so smooth I never saw it coming. I didn't know what hit me until we finished painting and the frat walks in and congratulates Darrel on a job well done. Darrell then announces:

"Hey, Shane, I've just givin you the business. Charles and Big Mike, you were just collateral damage."

Big Mike was like, "What? You mean we were not even the marks and you led us to the spoiled milk to drink!"

"Yeah, that was wrong, Darrell," replied Charles.

"I was wondering why Big Mike, Charles and I were doing all the work," I responded.

Everyone started to laugh, because it was about eight of us all together who had volunteered, including Darrell, Charles, Mike, and me. However, Darrell was always running errands, supposedly picking up supplies and food, and everyone else looked busy, but really were not doing very much.

"You are going to get a tongue lashing from us when we got out of here. I think we called you every combination of lazy motha fucka we could think of, but now all I can say is congratulations!" I shook Darrel's hand.

"Thanks, man!"

The Frat pitched in and got us some pizza. We sat around with the Frat brothers, Margaret, and some of her friends, talking and eating pizza. People marveled at the way Darrell had orchestrated this whole scheme down to every detail. As we sat around I noticed Veronica never said hello and avoided eye contact with me. She was actually hugged up with one of the frat. I didn't say anything to her or bring up the fact that she had been part of the scheme to set me up. Darrell knew I wanted to get at her, and he set it up so the opportunity would present itself to benefit his mission. But, I knew my luck wouldn't hold out too long without the subject of Veronica occupying my time while Darrell did his dirty work. In this case, Veronica's boyfriend had to let me know where I really stood.

"Hey, Shane, you thought you were going to get to first base with my girl. She's fine ain't she? I know a lot of brothas want to get at her. You were very lucky I let her play a part in our game. But don't get it twisted she was just playing her part."

"No I wouldn't get it twisted. I understand the sista was playing a part and she played her part well." My eyes moved off the frat brother and on to Veronica. "I hope I wasn't disrespectful or offensive toward you in any way because that was not my intention. And, as you put it Big Brother Dame, she is a very attractive young lady and should be respected."

"If you were disrespectful, you would have heard from me. When Darrell requested that she participate I was skeptical, but as we all know he's a good salesman. He assured me that your behavior would be above board because you have great respect for women. "

His last comment upset me. Like he was gonna whip my ass or something. This mutha fucka only stood 5'8" around 150 pounds, I'm a good 6'3" weighing in around 205, but I kept it cool and humble.

"I do have great respect for women, especially sistas, because that's the way I was raised by my mother. So, Darrell was correct in his prediction of my behavior."

"Darrell had better be thankful that you did behave yourself because I would have not only got in your ass but Darrell's, too."

At this point, the frat brother was feeding off my humility and feeling a little too much at my expense.

"Well, you good people, I have an exam in the morning. It's time for me to part company. Thanks for the pizza," I said.

Darrell, Charles, and Big Mike joined me. They all said their goodbyes and we headed out.

As soon as we got inside the car Big Mike spoke first. "What is wrong with that brotha in there? He was really feeling himself too much at your expense."

"I was thinking the same thing. So, I knew it was time for me to shake that spot before I lost my temper and went upside is head. He actually talked to me like I was a punk, and if I wasn't on line, I would have shown him who the real punk is."

Darrell replied, "Yeah, Big Brother Dame is just acting like what he is – an asshole. He lied about me approaching him asking for permission. I didn't know that clown was dating Veronica. I inquired about Veronica through Margaret and she introduced me. I told Veronica about the scheme and asked her to participate. I explained that the mark had a strong enough interest in her that she could preoccupy him while I set the wheels in motion. Then she wanted to know who the mark was. When I told her it was you, she lit up, and then caught herself before her interest in you became too obvious. She and Margaret approached Big Brother Dame about Veronica's involvement. So, the real question is what really happened between you and Veronica?"

"That's a damn good question," Charles replied. "Because she looked way too nervous in that room when we were eating pizza. Big mouth was the only one talking about her part in the scheme. She was quiet as a mouse."

They all were giving me this look like something more went on than my polite little description of gentlemanly behavior. And they couldn't have been more right.

"Man, she was all over me. We had some drinks, started talking about where we were from and some of our interests and hobbies. I don't know if it was a culmination of the alcohol, atmosphere, and conversation but tides started to turn and it was more like she was pursuing me."

Big Mike chimed in. "Hey, man, I was checking you two out and she definitely was all over a brotha. I told Charles that there was a good chance you might hit that tonight."

"It surprised me and as the night progressed she got more aggressive. We got on the dance floor, man, she was running her hands all over me. She turned around and put her big booty in my crouch and started grinding."

"Get the hell out of here!" shouted Charles

"No, on the real, she was grinding me down. I got a nice little lap dance on the dance floor. I was harder than times in '29. Then, she turned her head to the right towards me and started kissing me while still grinding her butt against me. Man, I tried to put my tongue down her throat. Now, you tell me Darrell, did you sign her up for that?"

"Hell no! She went above the call of duty. Now, I really know what you meant when you said she played her part."

Big Mike said, "Ain't it funny how the finest women are the freakiest? I know you gonna hit that Shane."

"Ay an you know dat! I don't know how Dame didn't see us on the dance floor."

"He probably was busy with Darrell putting the fix in play," Charles added.

"Yeah, it was most of the frat that helped me mess Margaret's' place up."

Darrell won the "Givin You the Business" game and I was runner up. We all crossed that fall semester. We had a great big party to celebrate our new brotherhood. All four of us rented a hall with catered food, and we partied until the wee morning hours. Darrell, Charles, Big Mike and myself ended up renting a house our last semester and we had a blast. We all graduated top of our class, and people said they couldn't believe it because we partied so much. We knew how to balance our schedules and when it was time to focus on the studies that's just what we did!

5

Wall Street

Finally, I made it to my destination, Wall Street. Landing a position on Wall Street wasn't as difficult as most made it seem. Yes, there were limitations to the type of opportunities available if you didn't have what they call the right kind of education or the contacts with power and influence. Once again my ace in the hole was Professor White. He didn't have a lot of power or influence, but he still had contacts on Wall Street that could open a few doors that would otherwise be closed to the average MBA graduate. He had arranged an interview with one of the top five houses on Wall Street. One of his old associates was now a top executive at Garner, Pratt & Green. The firm had some institutional sales training programs for top candidates. My undergrad work at Darden, my internship with Goldman, along with letters of recommendation from Jake and Steve, and my friendship with Mr. White got me over the top. My MBA from Jordan didn't get weighed into the equation as heavily as my other qualifications. My graduate degree by no means hindered my chances but it didn't enhance the opportunities offered to me by Wall Street. Jake was correct in his statement about playing the game, but I've never been about playing the game. I've always strived to change the game, and that's the goal and challenge ahead of me. To change the way the game was played on Wall Street was my priority.

GPG was one of the top five financial institutions on Wall Street, not only from a profitability standpoint, but the company was also large in terms of assets and personnel. The company assets were over $500 billion and over had 50,000 personnel worldwide. The company had its hand in investment banking, research and analytics, banking, asset management, institutional trading and sales, retail brokerage, discount brokerage, mergers and acquisitions, and risk management consulting, but its specialty was fixed income underwriting and sales. It was the premier powerhouse for fixed income instruments, domestic and international, and its research, analytics, and sales of fixed income assets were second to none. The investment banking department leaned heavily on the bond expertise and sales force to secure underwritings of different corporations, hoping to raise funding in the market without giving up any equity. The mergers and acquisitions also relied heavily on bonds in structuring mergers and takeovers. I was real fortunate because I was going to be a part of the debt institutional sales force, and this presented a tremendous opportunity to get exposure to other areas of the company; e.g. mergers, acquisitions, and underwriting since all relied so heavily on sales to get a temperament of the market. In my mind, there was no better place to be starting my career!

The training program was fairly straightforward. It consisted of getting candidates ready to pass the General Securities License Exam, the Series 7. There was also training on sales techniques in how to build a book and retain customers. The training also gave candidates an overall introduction to the company and culture -- all the various departments and areas of capital markets and finance. Each of the managing directors and some of top management came by and talked about their background and experience on Wall Street. This was just a way for the company to introduce us to some of its top brass and the moneymakers. The trading floor by far was the most exciting place to be in the whole firm. The trading floor was the heartbeat of the company-- where the action took place. I never saw so much energy in one place. This by far was the largest trading floor I'd ever seen. If being on that floor didn't get a person pumped up, Wall Street was not for him.

The first part of the day was dedicated to the training program, and the latter part was spent on the desk you were assigned to, training with what they called your sponsor during your training period. Your sponsor was responsible for getting you set up on the trading desk, helping you get supplies, introducing you around, and giving you insight into the temperament, culture, quirks, and personalities of the firm and the trading desk you worked on. My sponsor was Ted, and he was the best.

Ted was an older WASP gentleman in his late 50's. Over his career Ted worked for several Wall Street Firms, from the smaller houses earlier in his career to the more established large firms as his career developed. Ted had a MBA from Princeton. A seasoned veteran, his book was solid and he wasn't looking to add to his client list, nor was he looking to climb the corporate ladder to an executive management position. He actually enjoyed mentoring and showing young sales people the ropes. He was married with two sons. His eldest son was a journalist for the Wall Street Journal and the youngest was a screenwriter in Hollywood. Ted stated, "Once sixty rolls around, I will retire and travel the world with my lovely wife." He stayed in good shape; was about 5'8, slim build with slightly receding hairline. Ted was well respected throughout the firm and actually had been recruited heavily for management positions by top executives, but he never took the leap because he said he couldn't deal with the politics of it all. Ted and I liked each other right away. My eagerness to learn and willingness to listen won him over. The one thing in my life I learned was when to shut my mouth and open my ears. My mother use to drill that into me as a youth.

"Okay Shane, you are now a part of the bond trading desk. This desk trades all fixed income products that are bonds. We do it all on this desk. There is some overlap with the smaller desk in the trading room, but the fixed income buck stops here. My point is you have to know each and every product we trade on this desk. In order to be an asset to your client base you not only need to know the products, but how those products trade, what are the analytics and research on the issuing firm. Also, how the valuation of those products fluctuate with the changing market conditions. Now I know you're saying, I was hired as a salesman and there are others that I can rely on for that information. I'm telling you no! In order to be one of the best salesmen on Wall Street and add value for your clients you need to do all the above. Do you understand what I'm trying to tell you?"

I shook my head in the affirmative, but kept silent and listened more intently than when he first spoke.

"Now I'll give you a breakdown of the trading desk. We have eight traders that trade and manage our positions in each of these securities. There are five research analysts who keep up with market data, trends, and provide commentary for the purpose of sales, underwriting, and arbitrage opportunities. There are ten institutional sales personnel on the desk who move the product- bonds from sun up to sun down. And, about 50% of our bond positions are from the companies underwriting efforts. We are the number one bond underwriter and sales on Wall Street. GPG takes pride in our bond desk and only the best get assigned to this desk. So, Mr. Shane Jackson you must be among the best in your recruiting class."

"I sure aim to prove it!" I responded.

Ted and I continued our conversation. He continued to talk and I continued to listen. He talked about the strategies to building a book, how most salespeople are lazy, and how cold calling, a necessary evil, is one true way to build your book in the beginning. He said the trick to cold calling was to make the call as personable as possible, and you did that by using the principle of three degrees of separation.

"Have you heard of the three degrees of separation?"

"Yes, it's when your acquaintance with a perfect stranger is only three people removed."

"That's it, and if you can find those three people to get the introduction to the perfect stranger, you'll build a successful and lucrative book. And, in your case the perfect strangers are pension fund managers and portfolio managers alike."

Ted kept feeding me his little secrets to success, which I greatly appreciated, probably more than he imagined. My mind was like a sponge, soaking up every word and thought coming from his brain. This conversation was one of the most beneficial conversations I'd had to date on Wall Street. I had a great respect for Ted and appreciated his mentorship and guidance.

The training went very smoothly, and after three months I took the series 7 exam. I wanted to hit the ground, the floor, Wall Street running; and I did. Passing the 7 was the first step. I passed with a score of 95%. There were others in my training class that needed to sit for the test a couple of times before they passed, which held them up in getting started building their business. Plus, there was a hundred thousand dollar bonus for the top salesperson out of the freshman class of new candidates in the first year.

****

My effort to build my book for the first couple months was futile. Cold calling all day and through the early evening wasn't bearing fruit. I had not landed one client. There were salespeople whom I knew who didn't have half my talent and they were bringing in new business every day. Ted really didn't say anything to me for a while. He just watched me closely and would shake his head in the affirmative, kind of reassuring me that I was on the right track. Ted told me not worry. But that wasn't the case with the Managing Director, Ken Marvis. He was five foot four in stature, chubby frame, red hair, and pale white skin. He looked almost like a cartoon character. Ken managed the number one trading desk on all of Wall Street and didn't have the patience for a salesman who was having a slow start in building his book.

Ken called me into a small side conference room right off the trading floor for what he called a 'pep talk', but the meeting was more like a threat.

"Ted thinks very highly of you, and believes you can develop into one of the top sales people in this firm, but the only problem is I don't have the patience or the time to wait two years to see if he is right. You have one month to bring in some new business or you can find another desk or another firm for all I care that has the patience to wait and see if you develop into a top salesman. Are we clear?"

"Yes."

Ken didn't say another word. He got up from his seat and left the room. I sat there for a moment just thinking. I knew in my heart I was much better than what I was showing, but I didn't know what I was doing wrong. About ten minutes later Ted walked in the conference room and took a seat.

"What did Ken say?"

"I have one month to bring in some new business."

"You've been on the desk for two months. That guy is amazing." Ted had a look of disbelief on his face. "Shane, I don't want you to go into panic mode and start doubting yourself."

"No, I know I can do the job, but I'm missing something, a key ingredient."

"From what I can tell you have a good work ethic, and you've been taking my advice about learning the products, analytics, and markets. You have a good phone voice and you're very personable, but you haven't tapped into your resources."

"What resources?"

"People who you know that may know some others that may know potential clients that you could call upon." Ted paused, then, reacted to my blank stare. "The three degrees of separation strategy I talked to you about during our first conversation."

"Oh yeah!" My face changed to one of recognition. "But, I don't have those types of resources. I don't know anyone who runs in those circles who would be able to give me a referral or lead to an institutional investor."

"Shane, I want you to go home early today. Make a list of all the people you know, then by each of their names jot down what they do for a living, their hobbies, any organizations they belong to, and the possible people they may have interaction with. I guarantee you, when you are finished, you will have the potential of at least five leads. Solid leads."

I left work early and did exactly what Ted told me to. When the list was complete I had about a good fifty names of people I knew and could call upon for referrals. My only problem was most of the people on my list were very young, my age or younger, just starting their careers, and they were busy looking for referrals themselves, trying to jump start their own careers. I did have four solid contacts; my mother, Mr. White, Mr. Roberts, and Calvin. The next day I brought the list back to Ted. Ted looked over the list -- a cluster of jobs, hobbies, and affiliations by each name-- and chose three names that I should call immediately: my mother, Mr. White, and Calvin. He left off Mr. Roberts because we were in direct competition with him and his firm. Even though there was a chance of him throwing me a bone, there was a certain code in the industry that frowned upon asking for help from your competition.

My first call was to my mother. I didn't want to call her and ask for her help because I wanted to make it on my own. She had always been there for me, and I knew this time wouldn't be any different. I usually talked to my mother at least once a week just to check in on her, so my phone call wasn't out of the ordinary. Our conversation started off as usual, updates on personal life, some political discussions, and then business. Instead of being vague about my job on Wall Street I was more specific this time including my difficulties with building my book, which came as a big surprise to my mother.

"Are you kidding me Shane?"

"No, I haven't brought in one new account."

"What do you think the problem is?"

"Well, my sponsor, Ted, seems to think I'm falling short on utilizing my resources."

"What resources are you using?"

"Evidently not the ones I should be using. For example, you, I haven't called you and talked about my business, to see how you might be of help in building my book."

"Building your book, what is that?"

"New business, mom, just a little street lingo."

"Well, I know why you didn't call me."

"So, why didn't I call you, mom?"

"Pride."

She knew all the time it was pride getting in the way of my asking her for help. I was her child, and she knew her child. She wasn't absolutely sure she could help me, but when and if the call came, she was ready to do her all to help in any way she could. She actually welcomed the call and was excited the call had finally come. She offered up five referrals. Three were direct clients out of L.A that were asset managers, and two were the husbands of clients who were traders for two fund families located in California.

I thanked my mother for the referrals and asked her to give the referrals a call to let them know I would be calling. We also talked about her coming out to New York for a visit, but I wanted to hold off on her visit until I got myself established. She didn't really like that but she understood. I guess as long as I kept in touch by phone it would suffice for now, and she realized I was in the midst of a battle to get my career on Wall Street jump started.

The next person I called was Calvin whom I hadn't talked to since my trip to New York for his annual meeting. I was skeptical about this call and really didn't want to make it because of what happened between me and Janice, but I did need Calvin's help. Since expanding his business, he had been on the cover of multiple magazines and he even had a write- up in the Wall Street Journal. To say I was nervous making this call would be an understatement, but the only thing that gave me the nerve was that I didn't know if Calvin actually knew about me and Janice and how we'd ended up together that night. When I really thought about it, I had a lot to gain, but nothing to lose. Calvin wasn't a part of my inner circle, and my mother actually had cashed out her investment about a year ago, so we had no tangible ties anymore. But if I could bring him into my inner circle, he would be a great asset. So, without further hesitation I made the call.

I called Calvin on his cell number, which hadn't changed since my days at Darden. He was surprised to receive my call, but he didn't sound like he was happy; more shocked that I had the nerve or the audacity to call him.

"Ah shit, I didn't think I would ever hear from you again man."

"Yea, it's been a while."

"Two years to be exact, mutha fucka!"

I thought, damn this wasn't starting off well. I didn't know how to respond to what he'd just said, and I knew there was more, so I just sat back and took what I had coming.

Calvin continued, "To be more exact since you fucked my lady." He paused, waiting for me to respond. When I didn't, he continued. "Nothing to say about that, huh, nigga? Yea nigga, she told me ya'll hooked up after we left Julian's."

Why would she tell him? I didn't understand that at all.

"After all I did for you, and you repaid me by sexin' my lady. Man, you are morally fucked up. I don't want to see you, hear from you, and don't call me ever again."

The next sound I heard was a dial tone. I had known the call was going to be rough, but I thought, I might somehow be able to talk with him and appeal to the friendship we'd developed while I was an undergrad at Darden. I wanted to apologize because I knew what I did was wrong, but he didn't give me the opportunity. I wanted to tell him I had been young, immature, and had one too many drinks that night -- truthfully, I don't know if those were the reasons. I think like a lot of people I see on Wall Street, I'm greedy. When I see something I like, I want it at any cost, regardless whom it hurts or affects, and the truth be told that's a big reason why I thought I would be successful on Wall Street.

I made my last call to Mr. White. He wasn't surprised by my call; he actually was looking to hear from me earlier just to hear updates on my training.

"Hello, can I speak to Mr. White?"

"Hey, Shane, good to hear your voice. I was wondering when you were going to get around to calling your old buddy."

"Yeah, I should have called you earlier to update you on my training, but my schedule has been very hectic with studying for the sales exam and training on the desk."

"I understand. So, how's it going so far? Did you pass the 7?"

"Yes, I took the exam and got a 95."

"Who's your managing director?"

"Ken Jacobs! Do you know him?"

"No."

"He's a very driven guy, not very talkative, at least not to the new sales people."

"Everyone is pretty cold toward the new sales people because they don't want to warm up to one who is not an earner. The Wall Street culture is all driven by money! If you make them money, everyone will kiss up and treat you like royalty, but if you don't contribute to that bottom line, then they will be looking to get you off their desk and out of the company. Make no mistakes, Wall Street is no place for the meek or weak. Now Shane, it's important for you to have a strong start."

I didn't have the heart to tell him my first couple of months had been a straight up nightmare, and Ken was looking to get me off his desk. Above all others, except my mother, I wanted to be successful in the eyes of Mr. White. He had done so much for me and believed in me. I didn't want to let him down by being a failure on Wall Street. "Yes, I understand," I responded with misgivings.

"It's great you passed the 7 on your first go round. I didn't think you would have any problem with that test. Some people get real nervous when they take the exam for the first time and end up not passing. Now, you've taken your first step, and the next step is to start building your book!" Mr. White had been anticipating this call and was excited about my potential to make my mark on Wall Street, and excited and honored that I looked to him for assistance in building my book. And to think I wasn't going to call him because I wanted to make my mark on my own. I had forgotten that there were people out there who had vested time and energy into me to prepare me for this challenge and wanted to assist me in any way they could.

Mr. White went on to tell me, "I've already made some calls to three people who manage endowments. One is from your alma mater. Her name is Nancy Whitlock. She manages a $1.5 billion endowment for New York City Arts. The second is the manager for the Jordan University endowment. His name is Mr. Jacob Johnson, and the other is a money manager for Fidelity Bond Fund. Now, he is the big fish and his name is Steve Jesowitz. You should have no problem landing New York Arts or the Jordan, but Fidelity will be a little more difficult. Mr. Jesowitz manages a 200 billion dollar portfolio, and has bond sales people making calls to his fund all the time and rarely do any of them get to even speak to his top people let alone speak to him personally. I met him at a dinner in New York for the Mayor when Dinkins was elected. He was always intrigued by my story about my days on Wall Street, since then, we've kept in contact.

So, he is expecting your call. You have an open door. It's up to you to walk through and stay in the room!"

"I won't let you down," I told him. "I greatly appreciate the referrals and your assistance in getting started. I know that you know what this means to me, sir. Thank you."

"I know you're appreciative, and I'm glad I could be of help," Mr. White said. "Make sure you stay in touch and look for my e-mail with all the pertinent information on the three money managers."

"Thanks, and I will talk to you soon!"

My mentor, Mr. White, was correct. It didn't take a lot to land the Jordan University and New York Arts endowment accounts, and to sign up my mother's referrals. Especially with Mr. White and my mother front running for me it only took a few calls, some visits to the corporate offices and some dinner dates. But, as Mr. White had predicted, the Fidelity account was going to prove more difficult. It was going to take planning and research not only on the Fidelity fund, but I was going to have to delve into the background and accomplishments of Mr. Jesowitz. I wasted no time beginning my research.

He was Jewish and had been raised in a middle class family who owned several retail hardware stores located in the different boroughs of New York. As a youth he worked in the family business, yet took his studies very seriously. He wasn't much into sports, but he did enjoy horseback riding. He completed his undergraduate studies at Harvard, majoring in economics. Upon graduating he managed the family business for five years before pursuing his MBA at Wharton. It was at Wharton where he caught the investment bug when he headed up the student investment management group, which managed approximately 1.0 billion in assets for the university endowment.

After receiving his MBA from Wharton, Mr. Jesowitz worked for a small Wall Street firm on the retail side selling equities. He strived as a stockbroker usually focusing in on small cap companies from a value oriented approach. When the mutual fund industry broke out big and opened up the market to the smaller investor, Mr. Jesowitz seized his opportunity to work for one of the more established fund companies in Fidelity. He began as a small cap analyst in the retail industry. Over several years, he worked his way through the ranks to portfolio manager. He eventually took over Fidelity's Value Fund and built it up to one of the premier funds on the market, averaging an annual return of over 18% the last fifteen years.

Mr. Jesowitz and I had similar backgrounds. He was raised in a middle class neighborhood and was part of a family business where he first developed and fostered his business acumen. Other characteristics I thought worth noting, he seemed to be a patient man, given his career path, very intelligent, and understood sales, given his experience as broker on the retail side. I felt I had adequate information about him to make my first call. I remembered what Mr. White told me: most sales people make their mistake by calling him during market hours. It is best to wait until about two hours after the market closes before making your call. He's usually in the office late, reading reports and articles and having phone conversations with business associates.

So, I heeded the advice of Mr. White and waited two and a half hours after the close before making my call.

"Fidelity Mutual. Mr. Jesowitz's office."

"Hello, is Mr. Jesowitz in?"

"Who's calling?"

"Shane Jackson from GPG."

"Hold one minute."

"Okay Mr. Jackson I will put you through."

"Hello, Mr. Jackson."

"Hello, Mr. Jesowitz. Thanks for taking my call."

"No problem. Mr. White has been a friend of mine for a long time, and he spoke very highly of you. In all the years I've known Kevin, he's never called and referred anyone to me, nor has he discussed the potential and ability of an individual like he did with you. So, I would be a moron not to talk and meet with you."

"Mr. White is great man and I'm very fortunate to have him as a friend and mentor."

"We are both fortunate to call a man like Kevin friend. All right, Shane, tell me a little about yourself."

"Well, I was born and raised in Los Angeles, California. My mother owned an interior design company where I worked, and at the age of fifteen I received my first lesson in finance. We called it project two hundred and fifty thousand. My mother was seeking a two hundred and fifty thousand dollar loan from a bank to expand her business. She delegated the task to me to get her financials together to secure the loan."

"At age fifteen?"

"Yes."

"Impressive. Did she get the loan?"

"Yes."

"Did you ever get the itch to join her in the family business?"

"After receiving my undergrad degree, I did work for a couple of years in the family business, but the finance bug had me ever since we were successful in getting the two hundred and fifty thousand."

"I had that same dilemma when I started my career on Wall Street. My family owned a small chain of hardware stores and my parents wanted me to take over the business, but my heart was just not there. They were very disappointed, to say the least, in my decision. In the beginning, my decision strained our relationship, but over time the relationship healed itself with great effort on my part."

"My mother and I had a few discussions before she really understood my passion to work on Wall Street. Her point of view was that African Americans, especially ones with education, had the responsibility to build an economic base and framework for our community by creating businesses, business opportunities, and employment. And, true financial security could not be achieved by working a job. It doesn't matter how much money you make."

"Sounds a lot like my father's objections to me working on Wall Street. I would love to meet your mom one day. She sounds like a very intriguing woman."

"We'll have to arrange something. She's due for a visit soon. Maybe we can do dinner."

"Sounds good! Look Shane I've got to hop, but let's set up a lunch in my office where I can introduce you to some of my portfolio managers and traders. You can make a short presentation. You primarily sell fixed income instruments, correct?"

"Yes, that is correct."

"Okay, I've enjoyed talking with you and wish I had more time to continue our conversation, but my wife will kill me if I'm late for dinner one more time this week."

"I understand, don't want to upset the Mrs. Does next Thursday work for a lunch and a short presentation?"

"Let me check my calendar." He paused. "Yes, that works fine. I will have my key people available for your presentation, but given your presentation will be during market hours, time will be short, but I look forward to meeting you in person, Shane."

"Thank you once again for taking time to talk with me. I'll see you Thursday of next week. Good-bye, Mr. Jesowitz."

"Good-bye."

My phone conversation with Mr. Jesowitz went smoother than I could have ever imagined thanks to Mr. White. I knew the deal could be a mammoth of a catch if I closed the deal. Opening the other accounts gave me great momentum and confidence going into my appointment with Mr. Jesowitz. Ted assured me of one thing that stuck with me. "You have the account already. Your job on Thursday is not to lose the account."

On Thursday, I made sure to order lunch from the best Hoagies sandwich shop in New York and made sure the sandwiches were delivered before I arrived at their offices. The introductions went well, and I kept the presentation short, informative, and focused. I asked them questions about their management style and other pertinent questions I couldn't get from the prospectus or company financials.

After lunch, I hung out on the desk just to get to know some of them on a personal level. That was valuable time spent. They loosened up around me and began cracking, and sharing tidbits about the financial markets. When I joined in, we all were getting along like old friends reunited. A couple of Mr. Jesowitz's PM's were Darden Alumni, so that worked a great deal to my advantage. Before I left, Mr. Jesowitz called me into his office and said the feedback was all in my favor. He said his staff was very impressed by my knowledge and my personality, and my presentation. They thought I possessed a lot of charisma. He stated that they all, including himself look forward to working with me.

"I will call Kevin and let him know how impressed we were with you. You did your mentor proud on this day."

"Thank you, sir."

Back at GPG, when the word got around that I had landed the Fidelity account, especially the Jesowitz fund, the top brass themselves came down to congratulate me. I didn't know that several sales people from different desks had tried to land the Jesowitz fund but none had succeeded. GPG did have a couple of sales people who cover Fidelity on the equity side, but their share of the pie was not substantial. So, it made me wonder, why all the buzz about me landing the Jesowitz fund? Yes, it was a good first step, but I hadn't sold one security to them yet. So I approached Ted to see why all the excitement.

"Hey Ted, how's it going?"

"Good! Congratulations on the Jesowitz fund."

"Thanks, but I don't know what all the hype is about when I haven't sold one security to them yet."

"It's seems that the Jesowitz fund recently lost a large part of their fixed income sales coverage due to a retirement. Apparently this particular salesman was a good friend of Mr. Jesowtiz and more than 50% of the fixed income business went through him. It has been made known to our managing director through top brass that it is Fidelity's intention to replace him with you."

"What? How would they know that?"

"Well, it seems that Mr. Jesowitz himself called the top brass and expressed how impressed he was with you and that he wanted to throw 50% of his fixed income business your way."

"Are you serious?"

"Yes! Like you young bucks say, 'You the Man!'..... Most people make a real good living off one account of that magnitude. There are going to be a lot of envious people around here, but don't let that affect you. You just put yourself in the running for the hundred thousand dollar bonus for top freshman salesperson."

"Really!"

"Really! Now with the big fish in your back pocket. Your book will build exponentially."

"You think so?"

"Yes! When you do an excellent job for his fund, as I know you will, he will send referrals your way, and you will build a good reputation on Wall Street, and then mark my words, institutional investors will be calling you up for your thoughts on the market."

When I talked about hitting the ground running, I never imagined it would damn near set me up for life. By my fourth month on the desk I had six major accounts with one of them being the big fish on Wall Street. This got me off Ken's watch list and gained me the respect of the entire trading desk. Nevertheless, I wasn't content with the accounts I had. I approached each day as if I had no accounts at all. This approach kept me hungry, motivated, and sprinting. Within nine months on the desk I had become one of the top three earners on the desk. This garnered me a lot of attention around the firm from my peers and the top brass, which made some colleagues uncomfortable.

Junior was uneasy with my presence. We'd met on the elevator after leaving work one day. He and his girlfriend were in the elevator when I entered. His girlfriend was striking. She was blond, tan, stood about five seven, pretty smile with a body men and women die for. I would have to say she caught my eye immediately as I entered the elevator. My eyes must have revealed how attractive I found her to be because she blushed. Junior cleared his throat. Only then did my attention get directed toward him. He clearly wasn't appreciative of my pleasurable reaction to his girlfriend. I wonder if he detected her reaction to me. If so, he wasn't enthused.

"Do you always undress your boss's girlfriend with your eyes?" He asked firmly.

He caught me off guard with his straight forwardness. I really didn't know how to answer the question because I didn't know who he was at the time, but I was really in the wrong and didn't show too much tact. So, I did what I thought was best at the time.

"Sorry, I didn't mean any harm. Truthfully, I was just caught off guard after a long day at work. Please accept my apologies to both of you."

"You don't have any idea who I am. Do you?" he said, almost shouting.

At this time more people were getting on the elevator, and I wasn't really appreciating the tone he was using. "No, I don't know who you are," I responded forcefully.

"I'm your god-damn boss, Shaun Mackey."

The elevator reached the lobby. Everyone exited the elevator. Junior, his girlfriend, and I remained in the lobby to continue our introduction. I only knew one Shaun Mackey and he was well into his sixties. I'd met him once in passing with Ted. This Shaun Mackey was in his mid thirties and was one cocky son of a bitch. I didn't know how to respond to his declaration, so I kept silent, which didn't stop him from trying to get me to bow down in front of his girlfriend. I took the rest of what he had to vent with his little short rants and raves about how if I didn't watch my step I would be out of a job and Ted wouldn't be able to save me. He didn't care how much of a star salesman I was going to be for the firm.

I didn't say anything else. I didn't try to apologize again, nor did I say goodbye when he was done ranting, but just to spite him I did give his girl another once over as they walked off -- much to his and her surprise. Junior had a little power, but the real power was with his dad. His reference to having me fired was just an idle threat that he couldn't back up. I was never nervous about the incident because in my mind anyone with real power doesn't go around saying, I have the power. The bottom line on Wall Street was money. As long as I made the company money, it would be easier to get rid of the plague than it would be to fire an earner like me.

6

Old Friend

Our trade room was huge and we didn't know or see everyone who worked there. A lot of times our desk would go to happy hour with other desks in the trading room, usually, if we were working on a deal or issuance together. We would socialize with other desks, but for the most part, given the hectic trading and sales activity, you really didn't have time to get to know everyone and you really were only concerned with those who could affect your daily grind. The only time you had the opportunity to meet others who worked at GPG were during company parties and other functions.

My tenure at GPG was coming up on one year and the annual holiday party was scheduled for the coming weekend. I had been so busy building my book I had little or no social life. All the dinners and socials I attended were strictly for business. With no woman in my sights, my attendance at my first company party was stag. The party was formal and held at the exclusive Waldorf Astoria Hotel on Park Avenue.

GPG had rented out all the ballrooms for its New York headquarters office party. Each room had a different type of music and food to go with its theme. All the rooms had live music. One room had a rock and roll theme serving an American style cuisine. Another room had a Salsa theme with a Latin cuisine. A Motown room played all the Motown oldies but goodies while serving a southern style soul cuisine. Each room was decorated immaculately with no shortage of food or drink. The rooms were over 10,000 square feet with high vaulted ceilings and plush carpet. Everyone in attendance was catered to and treated like royalty with excellent service and gourmet food. I really had to admit that I'd never attended such a lavish and decadent party.

I walked around, checking out each of the rooms and observing the service and the conversations that were taking place. I was almost overwhelmed with a feeling that I didn't belong. As strange as that sounds, that's how I felt. The feeling wasn't one of inferiority, I felt uncomfortable. I didn't see many African Americans in any of the rooms. We were sprinkled around throughout the different rooms, but I could almost count all the blacks in attendance on both hands. I think the underrepresentation was quite disturbing to me. And, the impact brought a thought to mind – what if the roles were reversed and the majority of the attendees had been African American and we owned the company and rented out this fabulous hotel to celebrate the holidays. Now, that would be a party and a sight to see, but in the meantime, I was enjoying what the party had to offer.

Ted and his wife were the first couple I ran into in the Rock and Roll room.

"Hey, Shane, where's your date?" Ted asked.

"I'm stag tonight."

"Stag," his wife commented.

"Shane, this is my wife, Lorraine."

Lorraine had red hair, wore little or no makeup that I could detect, had very smooth skin, a nice smile, and a thin frame. Father time had been good to her. For a lady in her mid fifties she was a knockout.

"Hello, Lorraine. It's a pleasure to meet you in person. We've chatted a few times over the phone when you've called for Ted."

"Yes, I remember. I've heard a lot of good things about you, but I must say I'm a little surprised you're without a date tonight ... a handsome young man like yourself. And from what Ted tells me, you have a great personality, good character and are highly successful."

"Why thank you! I appreciate those kind words. And I didn't know that I had done such a good job of fooling Ted."

We all had a light laugh.

"I didn't know I said such good things about you either," Ted replied.

And we all laughed again.

"I can see why the both of you are such good salesmen -- you both are characters. Now Shane, tell me why you decided to come stag because I know you have options."

"I really didn't have any options. I've been so preoccupied with the job and building my business that my social life has suffered. I'm hoping in the coming months to move out of corporate housing and find my own place. Then I will be in a better position to get acquainted with the city and check out some of the social night spots."

"Do you know what area of the city you are going to move to?" asked Ted.

"I've been eyeing Harlem."

"Really!" Ted responded surprisingly.

"Yeah, it's the most convenient location in the city. You can get to any part of New York from there by public transportation. The community is historic and improving, and is still majority African American, which is appealing to me."

"With the money you make you can move to any part of New York you want. I can understand wanting to be in some part of Manhattan because most of the young up and coming live in Manhattan, but my concern is safety. Do you think you'll be safe in Harlem?"

"A wise woman -- my mother once told me, never fear your own people. So, no…I'm not concerned about my safety."

"You'll have to agree it's not the best area of Manhattan."

"Best area for whom?"

"Point well taken. Hey, just be careful when you move out there."

"No reason to be careful in your own home. I'm just going home."

"Shane, I've never met a young man like you before. You are a rare breed, which explains your success."

"Thanks, Ted!"

"Shane, Lorraine and I are going to get out of here a little early. We've mingled and shaken enough hands. Don't you think, honey?"

"Yes, it's time. Shane, it's been a pleasure meeting you. When you meet a nice young lady, we'll have to have you over to the house for dinner."

"I would like that, but do I have to wait till I have a date."

"Is it going to take you a long time to find a date? Maybe we'll have to set you up," Lorraine said.

"No, No. We are not playing matchmaker. Shane can find his own date, and from the talk around the office he can have his choice of many of the women in the office," Ted expounded.

"No, I don't play that game."

"I knew you were wise beyond your years. We got to go, and whenever your schedule allows there's an open invitation for dinner at the house with or without a date," Ted said in closing.

"Thanks, I'll see you on Monday."

After my conversation with Ted and his wife, I ventured into the R&B room to hear a little soul music and try some of the dishes offered. When I arrived, the room was packed with people dancing, eating, drinking, and just having a good time. I recognized a few of them from the trade room. People I knew and didn't know were coming up saying hello, introducing their wives and dates. I would say more than fifty percent of the people I encountered were drunk or one drink away from being drunk. I guess people just let it all hang out at holiday parties. I never understood how one could drink to the point where his or her speech starts to get impaired in front of some of the most important people of the firm. Maybe it's just me, but I would reserve that behavior for my peer's eyes only. So, you can surmise my conversations weren't that lengthy or in depth for the rest of the night until my eyes spotted someone I hadn't seen or talked to in years.

I moved closer just to make sure my eyes weren't playing tricks on me. It was him. It had been about four years since I'd laid eyes on him. I had to know what brought him to this party.

"Tim, what's happening, man?"

"Shane! What's up?"

"Nothing, man. What are you doing here?"

"I work for GPG."

"Really!"

"What about you."

"I work at GPG also -- on the fixed income trading desk. And you, what area do you work in?"

"I'm on the convertible desk in sales."

"I work sales also. How long you been at GPG?"

"A little over two years now."

"I've been here just around one year. Man, it's good to see you. So, what happened to you after undergrad at Darden?"

"I went straight to graduate school at Harvard and got my MBA. Got married to a wonderful young lady I met at Harvard. Started working at this financial publication doing research in New York for a year, then got on with GPG."

"You married huh? Any kids?"

"We got a little boy, named Jordan, he's two."

"Is your wife here with you?"

"Yes, actually that's her coming towards us."

She was an attractive sista; light complexion, very regal in her appearance. I could tell she was a detailed person because I didn't see one thing out of place on her. Her hair was perfect, her dress fit appropriately for the occasion, shoes were stylish, and the jewelry complimented her attire with designer's taste.

"Jackie, I want you to meet a friend of mine from my undergraduate days at Darden. Shane. Shane, this is my wife, Jackie."

"Hello, Shane, nice to meet you."

I extended my hand to greet her. "Nice to meet you also, Jackie." Then I turned my attention back to Tim. "Tim, it looks like you've been doing very well for yourself since you left Darden."

"Thanks. Jackie, Shane works for GPG also on the fixed income desk. That desk is the biggest money maker for the firm."

"How do you like working at GPG?" Jackie asked.

"I like it. The people I work with are pretty cool and I have a great sponsor. I can't really complain."

"Yes, I bet you can't complain. While I was across the room talking to one of my old classmates, she mentioned that the guy talking to my husband was one of the top earners in the firm, and that you won the top freshman salesperson award. She didn't remember your name, but she did know your face," Jackie said.

"Ah, I do all right. Enough to keep a roof over my head."

"Oh, you are modest. That's a nice quality to possess. Are you married?" Jackie asked

"No."

"Where's your date?"

"I came stag."

"You are not gay, are you?"

I almost choked, taking a sip of my drink. Just like a sista I thought, straight forward.

"Honey, you think you could be a little more forward," Tim interjected, trying to get her to back off.

"No... not at all," I responded.

"I'm just saying, you got to watch out for brothas nowadays with that down low stuff. So, what's your story?"she asked

"Just been so busy at work haven't had time to meet a nice sista like yourself."

"Maybe I could help you out in that area. I have a lot of beautiful friends who would be happy to meet you."

"Jackie, you are not going to play matchmaker and ruin our friendship before we get it started back up," Tim chimed in.

"I think, I'll hit that dating scene on my own for now, but if I find the waters too rocky, I'll request, some assistance."

"Just let me know. All my friends are professional and independent. That is how you successful black men like them. Am I right?"

"Yes, you are right. Tim, your wife is something else."

"Yes, I know. You're not the first to tell me."

"But, you are happy to be married to this something else, aren't you?" she inquired suggestively.

"You know that's the truth, honey."

"Tim, why don't you talk to your friend about your experience at GPG. I'll leave you so you can have some privacy. Shane, nice to meet you."

"Nice to meet you also, Jackie."

Jackie walked off and started to mingle with some other couples across the room. I wondered what she was getting at with her last comment about Tim's experience. Was he in some kind of trouble at the firm, needing my assistance? Whatever it was, he knew he could count on me to help.

"Tim, what was your wife alluding to when she said your experience?"

"Ay, lets' walk out to the lobby and grab a couple of chairs so we can talk openly."

"Okay."

Tim and I walked out to the lobby, which had a scattering of people. We sat down in two big red crush velvet chairs side by side.

"My first year experience at GPG hasn't been smooth sailing. It's been a struggle to say the least. I've come to the realization that I am not a salesman and will never be one. My career aspirations when I joined GPG was to be a research analyst, but they wanted me to start off in sales because, as they put it, it would give me a good background of the company and its products. Reluctantly, I accepted the position and have been paying dearly for that decision ever since. Each day is a constant struggle to build my book, create alliances on the desk, and to gain the respect of my peers. My annual review was unfavorable and partially demeaning. My self-confidence takes daily hits because of the asshole I work for, and the daily jokes and humiliation they put me through on the desk. I tolerate the bullshit because I need the job. My mentor, who actually brought me into GPG, has put distance between himself and me. I even floated my resume out to the street to look for other opportunities, but no one has responded. A friend of mine at another firm said my name has been slandered on the street with such characterizations as lazy, a dumb ass, and personality ground zero. I'm at my wits end trying to figure out my next move. I'm afraid it may mean leaving the street."

"Do you want to leave the street?"

"No."

"Then don't be too hasty in that decision. First, we all are sales people no matter what career we're in. When you received the offer from GPG, you had to sell yourself in the interview to get the position. When you convinced your beautiful wife that you were the man for her, you were selling. And, from meeting her just now I don't think that was an easy sale."

"You got that right!"

"Tim, you've been selling all your life. So, contrary to your own belief you are a salesman. Now, I would agree that your personality is better suited for a research/analyst position, but that doesn't mean you can't be a successful salesman. You just have to learn the art of a sale, and I can help you with that. Second, don't ever let anyone shake your self-confidence. You've come too far for that to happen. You have competed with the best academically at the best schools in the nation and come out on top. And you can do the same on the street. Obviously, no one on the convertible desk knows you or they would recognize that you are a highly intelligent individual. You cannot let the characterization of you stand. You must immediately squash all notions that you are inadequate and lazy, which will not be hard because it's not true. Third, most importantly, you must demand respect from your peers and your managing director. You can no longer afford to be the butt of jokes or the petty games they play in the trade room to amuse themselves."

"How do I stop them?"

"Well, it's not going to be easy, but you must start showing resistance to staying in the hole they've dug for you. There's going to be confrontation. That's inevitable because they will attempt to keep you in the hole. Stand steadfast on the principles you've lived by all your life, and only give respect when it's received. Do not go out of your way for anyone who doesn't show you some respect."

"I might lose my job."

"Yes, you might, but that's the risk you have to take. I guarantee when you take a stand, if it means your job or not, you will feel better about yourself. If you have to find another job, you will be in a better frame of mind going to your next job."

"Yes, I guess you are right."

"There's no other way. Don't worry, I got your back. A big piece of what you're missing is a support system. Who's your sponsor on your desk?"

"He left the firm the first month I was on the desk."

"Without a mentor or sponsor how can anyone expect you to be successful? You have to start all over, and the first piece is building a support system, and you can sign me up tonight to be a part of your support team."

"Shane, thanks, man. It was truly a blessing for me to bump into you tonight."

"I'm surprised I've never bumped into you in the trade room."

"That trade room is huge, and we're way in the back corner. I'm not surprised that we never bumped into each other. We are not involved in any of the big deals. The convertible desk is a small special niche player that barely gets the attention of top management. In terms of volume, your desk sells more convertible securities than us. There has actually been talk about merging our desk with yours."

"Yes, I did hear some talk about our desk combining with another, but I hadn't paid much attention. Tim, on Monday we'll get started. I have a lunch appointment with a new client, and I want you to go with me. It's a pension account and from my research on the pension they have an appetite for converts."

"Ay Shane, I'd really appreciate that."

"It's done! Monday, you and I will go make some money."

"Thanks!"

Tim and I finished our conversation and gave each other a pound with an embrace. It was a shame what they were putting that brotha through, but I wasn't surprised. First, he was not producing and the bottom line on the street was profit and how much you were contributing to it. If he was not producing, he would get little or no respect. Second, Tim was a black man and no matter what people think, it plays a role in the way people perceive and treat you. A lot of times blacks have to break through invisible barriers by being extraordinary. When the barriers come down, they see an achiever. So, as it stands he has two strikes against him right now and more than likely he's a marked man for dismissal. The first performance review was the set-up; if the second review is the same or worse, he will get his walking papers.

I've always admired Tim's moral fortitude, and we were good friends back in undergrad. It would be a sin for me not to help him show everyone around him just how much of an asset he can be to the Convertible Desk and GPG. Tim was right that he was suited more for research and analysis, but the majority of blacks on Wall Street start off in sales to prove themselves. Then they get the breaks to move into research or underwriting. Even for the average WASP those types of positions were hard to come by unless he or she had nepotism working for him or her. So, Tim must prove himself in sales before he gets his shot in research and analysis. Even if he's successful in sales there's no guarantee he will get the opportunity in research and analysis. That's just the way things are on Wall Street.

****

Monday I arrived at the office bright and early at my usual time. Everyone was buzzing about the good time they'd had at the holiday party. I chatted with Ted a little about the party and how I enjoyed the conversation with him and his wife. I joked around with a few of the other traders and sales staffs about who had the best looking date at the party. Since I didn't have one, I really laid into some of the fellas on the desk.

"Mike's girl looked like a transvestite. Man, she was huge. Did you see her hands? When I shook hands with her, it was like shaking hands with Shaquille O'Neal."

"Larri's date looked so young I wanted to check her ID just to make sure I wasn't an accomplice to a crime just by being near them."

"And, Jerry. I thought the hotel had a sign out front that said no dogs allowed."

I had everyone cracking up on the desk. That's how it was if you were junior on the desk and hadn't earned your so called stripes. You were free game for jokes, pranks, and lunch and coffee duty. I jazzed some of the guys sometime, but I've never been mean spirited or demeaned their character or tried to tear down their confidence. Mostly, what went on at our desk was all in fun and everyone could take a joke. I was also on the receiving end of some of those jokes myself, but for the most part my early success exempted me from having to endure some of the antics.

I've seen some elaborate pranks, played with the sole purpose of demeaning a target. Some of the pranks could be on par with a fraternity line pledging, which in my view is going overboard. Once, the senior people on the equity desk left the trade room and told all the junior guys on the desk they had to work late to increase performance and the bottom line for the month. The senior people exited the trade room through the front, and about fifteen minutes later they all re-entered the trade room through the rear and came up on all the junior traders and salespeople by surprise, their hands filled with water balloons. They commenced to throwing the water balloons at everybody, not only soaking them but their reports, contact sheets, and all their personal items. I couldn't believe what I was seeing. The juniors all just laughed it off, chalked it up to the price they had to pay to make it on the desk. The equity desk was the 2nd most profitable desk behind fixed income, so most people are willing to take a little humiliation to have an opportunity to work on that desk. I'm not sure I could have taken that in stride. Some type of retaliation would have been warranted.

I believe there were similar kinds of pranks that were taking place on the convertible desk where Tim was. Ted filled me in a little about the managing director on his desk. Basically, the guy had been an underachiever since he started at the firm ten years ago. The only reason he was still around was because of his connections to top management. Evidently, he'd married one of the top dog's daughters. They actually created the convertible desk to give him an opportunity as a managing director. The desk, as Ted described it, has been a failure from day one, mainly because they never took the convertible business away from us, the fixed income desk. Ted stated we did more convertible business in one quarter than that entire desk did in one year. I was astounded when Ted made that statement. How could they allow this guy to continue? Explained in one word, nepotism!

I approached my managing director to keep him in the loop about my intention to help out Tim. Ken didn't really like the idea, but I wasn't asking for permission. I made it clear that Tim was going to join me on a sales call that day and this potential client had an appetite for converts that I was going to throw his way. Ken really heated up when he heard that, but I was steadfast in my plan to help Tim. Even though he didn't like the idea, he didn't want to press it and risk the chance of rubbing me the wrong way. I was one of his top producers, so I knew he would give me a little latitude. I wasn't surprised by his reluctance, and if I had been managing director of the desk, my reaction would have been similar. But, I had to stay true to my word.

I walked across the trade room to the back corner where Tim told me the convertible desk was. The area was kind of crazy because I'd never really walked the trade floor and all of the unrecognizable faces that recognized me were saying hello, calling me by my first name. This recognition overwhelmed me, but stroked my ego. As I approached the convertible desk I saw Tim engaged in a heated conversation with his managing director. In fact, the exchange wasn't an even one. Actually, the managing director was laying into Tim pretty heavily. As I approached the desk I heard the managing director say something to Tim that was both shocking and appalling.

"You dumb fucking nigger," said the managing director.

Tim was standing there in shock, at a loss for words. He couldn't believe what he'd just heard. He turned and saw me arrive, an angry look on my face. He turned back to his director and just stared. I was steaming and I let it be known that his behavior would not stand.

"What did you just call this man?" I asked.

"Who the hell are you?" The managing director replied.

"Don't worry about who the hell I am. Who the fuck are you to be calling this man the most racist word in the history of this country?"

"I'm his boss."

Tim interjected. "You are not my god damn boss, you are my managing director. You are supposed to assist, guide, and manage me, not ridicule, demean, or degrade me, which you do a damn good job of."

Before long, the argument drew more and more attention around the trade room. All parties had reached a shouting pitch that could be heard throughout the room.

"If you did your job, I wouldn't have to ridicule you. You are the lousiest salesman I've ever seen in my life. You cost this desk $25,000 by not processing that ticket on your desk last Friday."

"I told you, it wasn't my ticket and I didn't know that ticket was on my desk," replied Tim.

"I asked you to process it," his managing director replied.

"You did not ask me, and if you did, I didn't hear you."

I was still fuming and dying to lay into this man some more, but I didn't want to steal Tim's thunder in defending himself. But, I couldn't help myself.

"Don't you guys have sales and trading assistant's on this desk? Their only duty is to process tickets?" I asked.

"I don't want to hear another word out of you," the managing director told me.

"What! You must be out of your god damn mind telling me you don't want to hear another word out of my mouth. Man, fuck you! I know one thing ... you better apologize to this man or you're going to have some serious trouble on your hands."

"Both of you can kiss my ass."

At this time, Ted had walked over, along with some others from my desk and a few traders from the surrounding desks. They attempted to calm the situation down, but when Tim's MD replied to my request for an apology with 'kiss my ass', I lost it.

"Kiss your ass! Why don't I just whip your ass?"

I moved toward him, but Tim and Ted grabbed me. You should have seen the look on Tim's managing director's face. He was scared shitless. It was almost gratifying enough just to see the fearful expression on his face. For someone to talk that much shit, use the n-word, then show surprise and trepidation when blacks are upset, was beyond me. Like it's okay for someone to verbally abuse another, but when the person abused reaches his limit, and escalates it to a physical nature, it's frowned upon. He's seen as uncivilized or hotheaded.

Ted was there for me. He calmed me down and walked me back to our trading desk. As we walked back, Ted was talking to me.

"Shane, as I told you, this guy is a loser. And, now you've seen firsthand just how much of a loser he is. He is not worth ruining your career over."

"You're right, but the audacity of that guy got the best of me."

"Believe me, Shane, I understand."

"Is there any recourse Tim can take against him for the racial slur?"

"There's mediation, where a neutral third party outside the firm would hear both sides of the story, and negotiate or recommend a settlement between the two parities. The settlement could be in the form of penalties or punishment."

"What kind of penalties or punishment?"

"It can range from monetary fines to complete dismissal. Shane, I want you to be careful in how you get involved with the resolution of this dispute. Between you and me,, the firm would frown upon any outside involvement and there would be repercussions if any outside sources were involved in resolving this problem. You could ruin your career on Wall Street if you don't play the game the right way."

"Are you telling me not to involve any civil rights organizations?"

"By no means am I trying to tell you not to involve those organizations. We all are men. And we have to follow our conscience to do what we feel is right, but you have to know there would be consequences to such action here on Wall Street."

I understood what Ted told me and appreciated his candor. In my mind, it was up to Tim to say how he wanted to handle the situation. No matter what, I had his back all the way. I let that be known to Ted. He said he appreciated my position as a man of principle and could not argue with it. We eventually made it back to the desk and sat down, but I wasn't right for the rest of the day. Tim and I still kept our lunch appointment with a potential client. Tim lined up some convertible business.

After the lunch appointment, I asked Tim how he wanted to handle the situation with his managing director. He'd decided on company mediation. He was afraid of using any outside help because he knew the firm would find displeasure in that and with his current reputation, the end of his Wall Street career would be certain.

Three months later, a hearing took place. The outcome was disappointing. Tim's manager was found guilty of the racial slur, but the penalty was a mere apology to Tim and the entire trade room for his behavior. There was no monetary fine, demotion, or anything else that would indicate the firm was reprimanding him for his conduct. Matter of fact, with that so called penalty, they almost condoned it. After hearing about the decision, I was very sensitive to any hinting of racial jokes, stereotypes, or anything considered to be in that realm of language.

About a month after the decision, I was sitting on the trading desk reading the market news and reviewing some charts when a trader from another desk, whom I knew, but not well, got up from his desk, walked towards me and shouted. "Do you know how to moon walk?"

My head was lowered, as I was reading, but it quickly registered that he was talking to me. I tried giving him the benefit of the doubt but he continued to walk in my direction, and shouted once again. "Do you know how to moon walk?"

I looked up at him and said, "Why are you asking me?"

He knew by the tone of my voice that he had made a mistake, so he tried to clean it up.

"No, I wasn't asking you specifically. I was asking everyone on your desk."

"But, you are walking towards me."

"Ah, man you're too sensitive."

"Damn that. Look. I don't sing, I don't dance, and I don't tell any got damn jokes! So, you take that shit back where you came from because I don't play that shit."

He was embarrassed and stunned, and walked his butt back to his trading desk and sat down.

7

Harlem

I had been at GPG for over a year now and still living in corporate housing. My schedule actually got much more hectic with me assisting Tim in building his book. But, I was determined to take some time and find myself a home in Harlem. I took time after work and weekends to go into Harlem and walk around the community. Harlem to me was a paradise. The architecture of the buildings was beautiful, and some of the small art galleries and community centers paid tribute to its rich history. The African and African American vendors on the street had the spirit of entrepreneurship that America was built on. It was very inspiring just talking with them. The mix of different African cultures and African-American culture was very educational to see and experience. I went into a lot of shops and talked to a lot of people about Harlem in general. I found a local barbershop where the barbers were both down to earth and had intimate knowledge of Harlem.

When I first walked in, Chuck greeted me from behind his chair. He was about fifty years old, 5'8", slightly heavy build, and with a nice old school style of dress. There were five other barbers in the shop, but they all were young, cutting all those new school cuts with different designs in a brotha's heads. That wasn't for me. I was looking for a new school cut with an old school feel, and Chuck was the man for the job.

"Come on, brotha. Gotta chair waiting right here for ya," Chuck said.

I walked over and took a seat.

"How you want to cut um up today?"

"Just hit me with a phillie fade."

"Sounds like a winner. What's your name, brotha?"

"Shane."

"Nice to meet you, Shane. I'm Chuck."

Chuck started in cutting my hair. "Do you live around here, Shane?" Chuck asked.

"No, but I'm looking to buy a house in Harlem. What can you tell me about the area?"

Another barber interjected, "One thing I can tell you, is don't let the sun set on your ass before you get in your house or you subject to getting robbed."

"Man, don't listen to that brotha," Chuck replied. "I lived here all my life and never had any problems. I keep telling these brothas there is no place in Harlem that is bad for a brotha. Now, other parts of Manhattan outside of Harlem can be a god damn headache for brothas walking around, but if we keep moving out, we are going to find ourselves without a community to call our own. And, believe me that's part of the plan."

"Yeah, you may be right about that, Chuck," another barber said.

"I'm telling all of you right now, Harlem is a geographical gold mine. It's central to every major borough in New York. I was born and raised here and know there's another change on the horizon. It's called gentrification."

"What the hell is gentrification?" one of the patrons asked.

Chuck explained. "Gentrification is when the property values are driven down in areas occupied by African Americans. Developers come in and take advantage of the cheap prices by buying properties for half their true value and redevelop the area, at prices most African Americans cannot afford. As a result, the demographics of the area change. Meaning, they move ya'll black asses out to less desirable areas."

"Preach, brotha!" one of the other barbers yelled!

"Y'all can make all the fun you want, but don't say you weren't informed. This brotha in this chair got more sense than all of you. People used to work four and five jobs to get out of Harlem, now they work four and five jobs to move into Harlem."

"Brotha, I hope you ain't working day and night to move into Harlem?" asked one of the barbers working next to Chuck. Then he laughed loudly.

"No, I don't have four jobs."

"Where do you work, Shane?" Chuck asked.

"I work on Wall Street."

"Wall Street! That explains the Brooks Brother's suit."

"So, you must be making some cheese working on Wall Street?" the barber next to Chuck asked.

"I do all right."

"Shane, you are making a smart move buying in Harlem. Not only from an investment point of view, but because we need more of our middle class to stay and start building this community back to what it was during the Harlem Renaissance. I commend you for taking the steps to move into this community. If we had more upwardly mobile brothas and sistas thinking like you, we could change this community for the better and maintain its blackness. Most of us, once we start making some money, we move to the suburbs, trying to get as far away from our community as possible, and we only return to make appearances, like that's really going to make a difference."

One of the patrons chimed in on the conversation. "Chuck, you can't blame black folks for wanting to better themselves by moving into better communities not plagued by drugs, crime, and an inept educational system."

I didn't interject my opinion; I was taking this time listening, taking in the thoughts expressed in the conversation among these black men.

"You right, but sometimes my passion gets the better of me. I know you can't judge people for trying to make a better life for themselves and their family, but what incenses me, is that we don't see that by staying in the community, we can make the community a better place to live for all. When successful blacks leave the community there are economic consequences that impact -- property values, taxes, services, and business commerce, not to mention, the mentorship and role models within the community. All this is lost, and we wonder why there isn't a decent grocery store in the community. In my humblest opinion, the best and greatest effect comes from doing it from within the community, not from outside."

The conversation was lively and very informative. Chuck was what they called a 'Harlemite'. He had been born, raised, and started his own business in Harlem. To say Chuck had a deep love and respect for Harlem would be an understatement. He spoke with passion at the very mention of his beloved community. The conversation continued and they each took turns telling me the advantages and disadvantages of living in Harlem, but no matter what, I had made up my mind a long time ago. Harlem was the place I wanted to call home.

My Mother was a successful businesswoman and I guess you would have considered our family middle class, but we lived in a community of mostly black families. Just like Chuck, my mother didn't believe in moving away from our community. Maybe that's the thrust of what makes me want to purchase a home in Harlem. Before I left the barbershop, Chuck turned me on to a realtor who knew Harlem like the back of his hand.

I contacted the realtor about two weeks later. He was expecting my call, and told me Chuck had spoken about me in a very favorable light. We chatted a little about what I was looking for and my price range. I really didn't have a price range and just wanted good value for my money. One thing I did specify was a brownstone. My mother was raised in a brownstone and always bragged that they were the best built homes. The Realtor and I made an appointment to view some properties the following week.

The Realtor did turn out to be very familiar with Harlem. He lived in the community and was involved with several community projects. Like Chuck, he was a Harlemite. We got along well. I was impressed by his knowledge of the real estate market in Harlem and New York in general.

The first brownstone we looked at was on a very nice block, but the house was smaller than what I wanted. The Realtor thought, since I was a bachelor, square footage was not that important. The block was full of black professionals which he thought would be a good fit for me, but I didn't think it was good value for the money. I didn't like the second house because of the floor plan. As soon as you entered the house, the bathroom was the first door to your right. The ceilings seemed too low for a brownstone and although the house was a good size, the bedrooms were small with minimal closet space. The third house was very nice, but just wasn't appealing. The fourth and last house was the one. As soon as I opened the door, I knew this was home. The brownstone had these beautiful hardwood floors and high vaulted ceilings. The bedrooms were spacious and the master bedroom had its own private bathroom. The kitchen was outta site, large with granite counters, oak wood cabinets, breakfast nook, and large appliances with designs dating back to the 19th century. This place had a lot of character.

What I didn't understand was why this place had been on the market for so long. It had to be one of the nicest brownstones in Harlem. My realtor said the brownstone was owned by an African American woman who was a doctor with a private practice in Harlem for many years. She was retiring and returning back to her hometown in Virginia. He said there were two things that kept this house on the market for this length of time. One was the price. She was asking a price that most people moving into Harlem could not afford, and two she refused to sell to anyone other than another African American. I asked how that was possible. He said he was the listing broker on the house and controlled who had access to the dwelling. Isn't that called redlining? I asked. He said, he had been in realty for over 30 years and to this very day he knows of areas around New York where, if you're African American you cannot buy a house. I still didn't quite understand her reasoning, since her goal was to sell her home. The realtor explained that she didn't want to contribute to the gentrification of Harlem, but still wanted a good price for her home, so she was willing to wait for the right buyer. Well, she had found her buyer, I told the realtor.

I purchased the home and moved in about two months later. I didn't have anything to move into the house except me and my clothes. My mother visited to help me get situated into my new residence. She couldn't wait to see my brownstone; she wanted to help decorate and furnish. I hadn't seen my mother in over a year, and the excitement of seeing her made me want to throw a party at my new home. So, I invited some close friends to celebrate my mother's visit. I figured this was the best time to throw a party at my home since I didn't have anything of value in it that could be damaged by guests.

I invited Ted and his wife, Tim and his wife, and some others from work. Mr. White and his wife flew up. A few of my new neighbors joined in on the special occasion and some other special guests that I hadn't seen since my start on Wall Street: Big Mike, Charles, and Darrel. We had kept in contact since we graduated from Jordan, but we hadn't seen each other. Big Mike was living in Oakland and was having a difficult time finding a good job because of his criminal record. He was working as a consultant in San Francisco at a manufacturing company in their legal department, reviewing contracts. Charles lived in North Carolina and worked as a fixed income trader for a large commercial bank. Darrel worked in Los Angeles for a small investment banking firm that specialized in underwriting government bonds. It was good to see all of them.

I surprised my mother with the party. She was even more surprised that I had the audacity to throw a party at my home, which was virtually empty. Yet she loved my brownstone. When she first arrived, she raved about the floors, the layout, the kitchen, my closet space, and the overall size of the house. She couldn't wait to help me decorate and furnish my new home.

I rented some tables and chairs for the party, and had the party catered by a soul food restaurant in Harlem -Betty's. The party was lively, everyone was socializing, and there was plenty of food. I had told my mother about Mr. White and Ted and all that they had done for me in getting my career started on the right path. When she met them for the first time, she couldn't hold back her gratitude for the two men who had aided her son.

"I know you are proud of your son and the accomplishments he's made in just a relatively short amount of time," Ted said to my mother.

"I'm very proud of my son." My mother grabbed me and pulled me close. "But, I do expect a lot more from him in the future. The mark of a successful man is not solely measured by the money he makes, but success is also measured by the contribution he makes to society."

"I can see where Shane gets his vision and drive from," Mr. White said.

"Shane has told me you two have been great mentors to him, and his success at GPG is directly attributed to your advice and guidance."

"When you find a young man of Shane's caliber, you know right away his development and training started at a young age, and that is a direct reflection of you," Mr. White replied.

"I appreciate those kind words, Mr. White, but as we know, it takes a village to contribute to a young man's development into manhood, and you and Ted are a part of that village."

Ted interjected. "I don't know how much credit I can take in his development, but one thing I can say is that Shane has the qualities of a true leader. His vision and determination are what great men use to move mountains, and in my opinion, he will do nothing less than move mountains. He's definitely a young man who has a sense of history and his measure of success expands beyond monetary compensation."

I excused myself from the conversation and the three continued their discussion late into the night, talking about business, economics, and politics. Mr. White's wife and Ted's wife joined the conversation shortly after I left to interact with my old college buddies.

We started off our dialogue just updating each other about the job scene. Big Mike was having the most difficulty because of his felony conviction; he wasn't being shown a lot of love in the professional ranks.

"The interview process is always a breeze, and the resume is tight. Having a law degree and an MBA has most employers dripping at the mouth, but as soon as the background check comes back with a felony conviction, you can hear a rat pee on cotton. No call backs, no follow ups, they don't even return my phone calls or emails."

"That's really unfortunate. Do they even look at the fact that you went and got your MBA after you served your time?" I replied.

"Shane, they don't give a damn about that! All they see is a convict."

Charles exclaimed, "What about redemption?"

"What about it?" Darrell replied.

"Big Mike has paid his debt to society and all he's looking for is an opportunity. And you mean to tell me society will hold that one mistake against him the rest of his life?" Charles asked.

"Big Mike has two strikes against him, one is the felony and the other is that he is a black man. So, the way society views him is, he has one more mistake before game over, and they are not willing to take the risk of hiring him," Darrell answered.

"That's bullshit!" I shouted. Darrell looked surprised. "Not what you are saying, but how they are treating Big Mike."

Tim had walked over a few minutes earlier and was listening in on the conversation. He had his own opinion of Big Mike's situation.

"Darrell, I have to disagree with your assessment of Big Mike's situation and how society views him. There is equal opportunity for everyone. There are probably other factors that he probably hasn't considered as to why he didn't get the job he desires."

"Where did you meet this clown, Shane?" Big Mike replied.

"Be cool Big Mike," I said.

"I mean, did you hear what I said earlier? The whole process is a cake walk, until they notice that I'm a convicted felon." Big Mike started to breathe a little harder, and became more animated with each word. "There are no other factors to consider. They practically hire me before the word comes down."

"I didn't mean to offend you…I just…."

"Don't say another god damn word!" Big Mike said loudly.

Heads raised up around the room to see what was going on, and some people came in from adjacent rooms to make sure everything was okay. Tim's wife casually walked over and pulled him away into another room to mingle with some others.

"That brotha's living in a fantasy world," Darrell said

"He's a good brotha, but I am a little surprised by his comments, given the problems he's encountered at work."

"Is that the brotha you took under your wing?" Darrell asked.

"Yes."

"Then what the hell is his problem? They calling him nigga on the job and he thinks there's equal opportunity for everyone. Is he smoking?" Big Mike said.

I had to turn the conversation to another topic quickly because they were ready to go find Tim and give him a good tongue lashing. So I asked Charles how was North Carolina. He said that his background in accounting and math and his knowledge of the market led him to become a trader. He was really enjoying his time working in capital markets, and would like to eventually come to New York and work on Wall Street. He said when he's ready, his first call will be to me. I told him, I'll be there when he needed me.

"I expect you to own a piece of Wall Street at the pace that you're moving, so I will just work for you as a trader."

"That would be a dream come true. Hiring you, Charles, would mean I could provide an opportunity for Big Mike and Darrell. Can you see all of us working together on Wall Street?"

"Wall Street wouldn't know what hit them," Darrell responded. "Big Mike could oversee all legal issues of all financial transactions, Shane and I could lead up sales, and Charles could be head trader."

"Ah man!" Big Mike said. "Whew that's a dynamite vision." You could see the excitement on Big Mike's face just from the thought of all of us working together on Wall Street.

"Alright, let's cut out all the dreaming," Charles commented

"But, that's not a farfetched dream at all. I mean that is attainable," I responded.

We just looked at each other and knew that one day we would make that dream come true; it was just a matter of time. The very thought of our working together on Wall Street lit a fire in me. With these guys by my side, the sky would be the limit. I trusted these guys and we have always kept it real between us; that's the reason we were able to build strong friendships during grad school.

We broke it up after a while and I went to mingle with some of my other guests. It was starting to get late and I needed to say my goodbyes to my other guests. Big Mike, Charles, and Darrell stayed behind to help with the clean up. They were staying in a hotel in Manhattan since I didn't have accommodations for them yet. They tried to convince me to hit some night spots with them later. My mother was staying with me, so I declined because I wanted to spend more time with her.

Later that night, my mother and I sat down with hot cups of cocoa and talked. She wanted to talk about a wife and family. She spoke passionately on the topic. You would have thought I was a forty year-old bachelor. I was amazed at the way my mother was coming at me.

"Shane, you need to find you a nice African American young lady and settle down. It's time."

"Mom, I'm only twenty-six and just getting started in my career."

"Getting started in your career!" She was very animated. "Boy, let me tell you something, most people if they are lucky end up where you are starting off."

"You say that like it's a bad thing."

"No, no not at all. I'm very proud of your success and it's nothing to be ashamed of. I just don't want you to get caught up in the monetary success and think that's what life is all about. You must have balance, and family brings that balance. And I know you're twenty-six, I'm not saying get married right now, but start looking for that special lady now and take your time in getting to know her so you both can build a solid foundation together."

"Mom, you are getting a little too deep for me."

"Listen, you take after your father, you are not the humblest of individuals. When I first met your dad, he had the biggest ego, and I put up with it because he was a fine looking man and I was young, but ego translated into arrogance and self centeredness. And, those qualities led to a quick end to me and your dad."

"I'm nothing like him," I said in defiance.

"Shane, I know we don't talk about your father a lot, but you do have some qualities that your father possessed, and that is not necessarily a bad thing. Your father had some very good qualities, but he could never see beyond himself. I want for you what I never had, and I know you, son. You are going to need a strong black woman to handle you."

"I like how you emphasize black woman each time," I commented.

"Well, I'm not ashamed of saying I would like you to marry an African American young lady. You're a successful African American man, and you need to take a black woman along for the ride. I'm so tired of seeing black men reach a certain level of success and think they need to have the white man's version of beauty… blond hair and blue eyes, by their side."

Mom was getting a little worked up over this subject. So, I gave her reassurance that when the time came for me to choose a wife, I couldn't see myself with any woman other than a strong down to earth black woman. A lot like my mom. She had the last words as always.

"Above all I want you to be happy and if you find that happiness with a woman that's not of the same ethnicity, then who can argue with that, as long as you are true to your heart. But that being said, you find you a black woman!" She chuckled a little, got up, headed to the kitchen and asked if I would like some more cocoa.

I retired to my bedroom, and mother stayed up a little longer, then retired to her room. The only thing I had in the house for the most part were those two king size beds. My mother was staying with me for a month to help me in decorating and buying furniture for my home. She knew my taste and style, so I left everything up to her and just told her to surprise me.

As I went off to work on Wall Street each day my mother spent most of her time decorating the house. Everything she was doing, I loved. She purchased some unique furniture that had an antique look to it, but with a hint of modern style which matched the style of the brownstone perfectly. The couches were huge and comfortable, with rich earth tones. The dressers and mirrors were made out of fine oak hand crafted wood. She decorated the kitchen with kitchenware that looked like it was from the 1940's, but everything was brand new. She also bought some really nice pieces of art from some prominent African American artist. One piece I liked in particular was a huge piece by an artist out of Oakland named Kelvin Curry. This was an abstract piece of an African American woman standing strong and sensual, admiring every shapely curve of her body in a mirror. The colors were in pastel blue with a backdrop in blue and gray. My mother really outdid herself in decorating my home. I told her price was no issue, and I could tell you now she sure didn't pay attention to price. When my mother wasn't decorating the house, she was touring New York and just making her way around Harlem.

During the month my mother was staying with me I tried to make it home at an early hour so we could spend some quality time together. I would take her to the movies, which I hadn't been to in over a year. We ate the fine cuisine of New York, and we saw Broadway plays. One day I made it home a little earlier than usual, so I could accompany my mother to a shop where she was getting a dress made. It was a small shop and was only about five blocks away. The day was nice, and after changing clothes, we walked to the shop. As soon as we entered, a beautiful African American young lady greeted my mother at the door. Man, she was beautiful. She was a nice chocolate sista with dreads. Her skin looked like she had been using cocoa butter since she was a baby. She stood about 5'9" and was wearing a white sun dress, by no means was it tight fitting but when she moved you could see the contour of her body, she was all sista. Her smile was amazing with those pretty white teeth gleaming from that dark skin. My mother saw my pleasurable reaction to this sista and you could see a big smile engulf my mother's face. She did not hesitate to introduce me.

"Kendra, this is my son I've been telling you about. Shane, this is Kendra and this is her shop."

We looked at each other, shook hands, and exchanged hellos. Our eyes met and her brown eyes just made a brotha stop for a moment to take her presence all in, my mother couldn't resist the moment.

"You alright son?"

Enthralled, I said,"Yea, yea I'm okay."

I really was at a loss for words. My mother had given me no warning, no indication, at all of what she was up to. I had no idea I was going to meet someone so pleasurable to the eye. I asked her about the shop, and how long she had been in business. She responded, then asked about my job on Wall Street, and about my new home. Evidently my mother had frequented her shop more than a few times since she was having four dresses made, and had spent some time talking about me with Kendra, while getting to know her, too.

"Shane, Kendra makes suits for males also."

"What kind of suits for men do you make? Do you have any in your shop I can take a look at?"

"No, I mainly just do women's clothing, but I have made some business and formal wear for my brother."

"I told her you wear those tired Brooks Brothers suits, and that you need to add a little more style to your business attire," My mother added.

"Those Brook Brothers suits are standard."

"Standard for whom? If I know my son, you set your own standard, don't you?"

"As usual, you are correct mother."

"Let's take some measurements and you tell me what kind of style you might be looking for and we'll go from there," Kendra said.

"I can go for that."

Kendra, mother, and I walked to the back of her shop. We stopped in front of this large three panel mirror, each mirror skewed at a different angle. Kendra began asking me about my style and personality.

"To make you a suit that not only fits your body but encompasses your personality, visions, and goals I will need to get to know you just a little bit," Kendra said.

Was she hitting on me? I thought or was this all business? I wasn't going to leave any questions about my intentions.

"Well, I could pick you up around eight tonight for dinner." She'd opened the door, so I had to walk through it.

"I was thinking more along the lines of just talking with you now about interests, work, job, goals, and the plans and dreams you have for yourself."

"Oh, okay, my bad," I said in an apologetic voice.

"No, I don't mean to insinuate that I wouldn't like to have to dinner with you. After all a girls got to eat and that actually was a nice invitation, but tonight at eight doesn't work."

"What does work for you?"

"Friday at eight."

"Sounds like a date," My mother intervened.

"I think my mother just landed me a date."

"I believe so," Kendra responded.

.   "Well, we all have to do our part," my mother said in a boisterous voice.

We all laughed and exchanged glances. As we started to settle down, Kendra got on with taking my measurements. She asked me a few more questions about my position on Wall Street and where I saw myself in five years. When I responded, saying, "Owning my own investment firm," I surprised her.

"Aren't you the ambitious one?"

"Is there any other way to be?"

"When you really think about it, I guess not," she said. She wanted to make me a three button navy blue suit with an orange pinstripe. At first I was thinking that sounds kind of loud, but after talking with her, she made me more comfortable with the color selection. I could tell right away this was not going to be an ordinary suit, but once she got finished with explaining to me her conceptualization of the suit I became anxious and couldn't wait to see it. Kendra and I exchanged numbers for our date on Friday. My mother said goodbye and told the seamstress she would be back to see her before she flew back to L.A.

I only had a few more days with my mother before she left. She had been a busy woman since she landed in New York. She had decorated my house, toured New York and Harlem, and hooked her son up with a gorgeous female. All in all, the way she saw it, this was mission accomplished, I would have to agree with her.

8

Training

Work had been going especially well. My book was continuing to grow and my commute had turned from just getting back and forth to the office from home, to more of a meet and greet as I walked through my Harlem community. I was slowly becoming a Harlemite, like my barber, Chuck. The commute back home was especially nice when I would make a detour on my walk from the subway to drop in on Kendra to just chat and visit or pick up one of the many suits she made for me. The only real challenge I had at GPG was training Tim in sales. His training wasn't an easy task. Tim's personality was introverted -- more so than I remembered from our undergrad days. But, he was a hard worker and was dedicated to becoming a better salesman. Breaking down the basics was the first step in building a foundation of understanding the art of selling. After the basics, I would show him some more insightful tactics and tools of the trade.

Initially, most of our training happened after work. I would grab a conference room with a white board and lecture him on the fundamentals of sales. He thought I was crazy because most of this he had already heard through the sales training at GPG. But, I explained that most sales people know the principles but never how to implement them, or don't know how to translate them into real world achievement. That's where my knowledge would help him. My sales experience expanded beyond Wall Street. My mother is an entrepreneur, and from a young age, I was dealing with her clientele and financiers, so I was very comfortable around people. I thought that was his primary weakness, and if he couldn't increase his comfort level then he would fail as a salesman.

"Whether you know it or not, your body sends out signals, and if those signals are signs of discomfort, then a sales call will be an uphill battle for you. Also, your voice has more than a hint of nervousness when you are on the phone making a sales call. Most will interpret that as insecurity and no one wants to do business with an insecure salesman."

"I really sound insecure on the phone?" Tim asked.

"Not when you are talking with your wife, but on sales calls you definitely do. So you have your work cut out for you. The phone is the most essential tool for a salesman."

"Most guys I hear on the phone on the trade floor sound like arrogant assholes."

"You don't want to sound arrogant but you do want to come across as confident. That's the line you want to tow. Once you conquer the phone then your personal interaction should improve also."

"Man, you make it sound as though I am completely inept."

"No, I don't mean to come across like that, but we must change your mind set in order to make you a successful salesman."

Tim and I continued our sessions after hours, trying to build his confidence and work on his interpersonal and phone skills. A big part of his training included him accompanying me on sales calls, dinners, and other activities I used to entertain clients. Our first dinner was with a client of mine who ran a pension fund with over three billion dollars in assets. Each time he came to New York I would take him to an exclusive popular bar then follow up with a dinner at one of the finest restaurants in New York. These were what I called my Tony rules; treat your clients to the best and the most exclusive. The Tony rules served me very well in building and retaining my client list. With this particular client, he liked a little added entertainment, which I was able to provide to him on a very confidential basis. My client was a white male from the Midwest and he had a "jones" for black women, and for him, the darker the better. So, each time he made a business trip to New York, after drinks and dinner I would take him to a strip club that featured black women. On this occasion, Tim was with me, but I had talked to my client to make sure he was comfortable with Tim coming along for the after hour activities. My client trusted me and said any friend of mine was a friend of his.

So, the three of us hopped into a cab after dinner and went to a club called the "Black Tail". This was not an exclusive gentlemen's club, and wasn't in the upscale area of New York. It wasn't uncommon to see criminal elements inside the club, but I knew the owner and had become acquainted with some of the regulars at the club. This gave my clients a sense of comfort and security. I never knew so many white men favored the company of black women until I started entertaining my clients. I was skeptical about bringing Tim along because I wasn't sure what his reaction would be and I knew he wouldn't be comfortable, but he needed to see some of the things that a good salesman did to accommodate valuable clients.

As we entered the club, I could tell Tim was ill at ease, but my client was glowing like a light and smiling from ear to ear. The club was dimly lit, spotty dingy red velvet carpet, the main stage extended from the front of the room down the middle of the room like a runway for a fashion show, surrounded by theater style chairs that were over due for a cleaning. The bar was in the rear, and to the right was a hallway that led to private and VIP rooms. There were ten to fifteen sistas walking around in the most exotic and sexy lingerie, their bodies were curvy in all the right places, and so much flesh was hanging out from their outfits a man got exited just by casting eyes upon them. We walked over to the bar and I ordered drinks for all of us and told the bartender to start a tab. Within minutes, we had over five dancers all over us. One thing about strippers, they were very similar to Wall Street salesmen. They were all about the money. Two brotha's and a white man all dressed in corporate suits, and we smelled of money to these women. Tim was not enjoying the scene, so I told the ladies to give us a minute and we would get with them later. However, I told them to go ahead and give my man over here all the attention he desired. My client wasted no time; he walked off with two women under his arms and just gave me a nod to say he was in good hands. I nodded back to assure him I would take care of everything. Then I turned back to focus my attention on Tim.

"Man, you alright?"

Tim responded in a shaky and nervous voice, "What are we doing here?"

At that moment, the owner came over and I introduced him to Tim. Then the owner motioned to me that he wanted to talk in private. We walked a few feet in back of Tim.

"Is your boy okay?"

"Yeah, he's cool. I think this may be his first time in a strip club. There's so much ass in here, it can be overwhelming for a brotha, if it's his first time."

"Okay, but if he hadn't come in with you I might take him as an undercover coop."

"No, no, he works with me, and I'm just trying to show him the ropes on entertaining clients."

The owner nodded his head, showing understanding.

"Speaking of clients, he's back there with Diamond and China in VIP," The owner said.

"Make sure you take him a bottle of champagne and give him every accommodation available." I then reach into my inside left suit pocket and took out a white envelope and gave it to him.

"Don't worry brotha, all will be taken care of."

We gave each other a pound and a half hug and he vanished. I walked back to the bar where Tim was standing.

"Are you some kind of pimp?" Tim asked in a concerned voice.

I started laughing, thinking this brotha has definitely led a sheltered life.

"No man. What are you talking about?"

"You gave that man an envelope and I can surmise given the type of joint this is there was money in the envelope."

"You are correct. There was money in the envelope, and that was given to him to cover the cost of the VIP room, food, champagne, and the girls."

"Like I said, you are a pimp."

"Since when have you seen a pimp give money to someone to cover the cost of the company of a woman? If anything, I'm a trick?" And I started chuckling.

"You think this is funny but this is illegal," he said in a very stern voice.

"What's illegal? Lap dancing?"

"You know that man is getting more than a lap dance. How much money was in the envelope?"

I was a little hesitant to tell him the amount of money, but in order to teach I had to keep it real.

"Three thousand dollars."

"Three thousand dollars!" he said in amazement. "What the hell, I may have never had a lap dance, but I know for damn sure it don't cost three thousand dollars."

"Yeah, you're right. He may be getting a little more than a lap dance, but not the type of more, you are thinking about."

"What other type of more is there?"

"Well with this guy it's mainly about the attention. The last time we were here I didn't see him the whole night, once we got into the club, and when I went looking for him he was with one chick in the VIP room with his shirt off, and she was rubbing her bare feet on his chest. When I walked in, he didn't try to cover up what he was doing and he wasn't embarrassed. He just looked up and asked me was I ready to go."

"Are you shittin me?"

"No, I'm keeping it real. He evidently has a feet fetish, and he usually gives the girls massages and makes comments about how beautiful their skin is, but he never takes off more than his shirt."

"How do you know all this?"

"A few of the girls he has kept company with told me."

"Then, why the three thousand dollars?"

"Well, he keeps company in the VIP room most of the night. We will not see him again tonight until almost closing, and if he is in there with two or more women that runs some dough."

"What about the SEC."

"What about them?"

"You are breaking rules of ethics?"

"Maybe, maybe not. Look, we are competing in the real world with big stakes. Entertaining clients is a big part of staying competitive. Now are there times when we may cross the line -- to keep it real with you -- Yes! Is there a line that I won't cross? Yes, but the line I draw in the sand may be different from the line you draw in the sand."

"The line is drawn for us by the SEC and we all must adhere to that line or suffer the consequences."

"If you were to truly examine the SEC rules and compare them with your daily activities as a salesman on Wall Street you would be in violation of at least twenty five percent of them."

"How do you figure that?" Tim said sarcastically.

"Your desk sends a case of champagne to each of your clients for Christmas, is that right?"

"Yes."

"Now, the brand you guys send out runs about five hundred a bottle and there are about twelve bottles in a case is that right?"

"Yes."

"So, each case you send out is approximately six thousand dollars in value, and to be totally honest you probably send out more than one case to special clients, and you don't think you are breaking SEC rules."

"Well that's different."

"How is it different?"

"Uh, it's just different," Tim said, frustrated.

"Tim, we all draw our own line in the sand to determine how far we will go to accommodate our clients. You have to determine for yourself how far you are willing to go and your comfort level with the line you've drawn."

"Yeah, I guess you're right. Does Kendra know you come here?"

"Hell no! All she knows is that I'm out entertaining clients. She doesn't need to know the details"

"Why? Because you know morally it's wrong."

Now, Tim was pissing me off, acting so self righteous. I paused and caught myself before I cursed him out for calling my moral character into question. I explained to him in a very calm way that that kind of talk could end his career on Wall Street immediately, and it's no wonder that he hasn't been exposed to some of the late night activities that take place with some of the clients on his trading desk. I continued telling him, in my matter of fact, calm tone that no one brings him along because they don't trust him and without your colleagues trust you are dead on arrival.

"Your clients have to know or least believe, that you are not judging them when they come to New York for a night on the town. My client back there trusts me and that's due to the fact that I never draw any conclusions or opinions on his moral character. I make no judgments of his behavior because I understand he has a need. It's not my place to approve or disapprove; we are all grown men and none of us are perfect, including you." And, the last thing I told him, "If you get your client to trust you with his personal business then he damn sure will trust you with his corporate business. Keep that in mind when you start to draw your lines in the sand."

"Does Ted know about your late night activities?" he responded.

"What? Man, are you that naive? I'm trying to show you what it takes to sell on Wall Street, and you still don't get it. Ted would never say anything to me if he did disapprove, and the only time he would, would be if he thought I was too close to the edge and in danger of falling off. Then and only then would he pull my coat tail and pull me back."

I then finished my drink at the bar, grabbed one of the dancers who was thick as molasses, and pulled her close to me. I looked at Tim with my arms around her.

"I understand if you don't stay. I will see you back in the office tomorrow. I'll explain to my client that you had an early appointment in the morning." I walked off with the dancer.

"Where you going?" I heard Tim ask.

"To get a lap dance." I gave him the peace sign from behind.

The next morning, Tim walked over to me on the desk and apologized for leaving me the night before. I told him there was no need for an apology. All I was trying to do was show him a road - "It's up to you to travel down it or not." He said he appreciated the time that I took to train him and to help him build his book. If any of his comments last night had offended me, he hadn't intended such. It was just his first time being exposed to something like that, and he just wasn't ready. I told him not to worry about it. Then, I let him know there was an opportunity for him to pick up a client in a couple of days. On Thursday, a client from Seattle was flying in and was bringing another money manager with him. The second manager was a heavy buyer of convertibles. Tim gave me a pound with his fist and walked back to his trading desk.

Ted overheard our conversation, and once Tim was far enough away he asked, "What was his first time?'

"Strip club."

Ted started to laugh, "Are you serious?"

"Yes."

"Where has he been? He has no life experiences, at all, does he?"

"I really don't know, to tell the truth."

"I take my hat off to you for taking him on, because from where I'm sitting he doesn't have what it takes."

"He'll be alright."

"The only possible reason he will be alright is because you are feeding him business. Sooner or later he'll have to stand on his own and that's when the real test begins."

Ted received a phone call on the desk, and I was happy, because it looked like he was about to go on a roll. Ted was a veteran in the business and was very perceptive about people. And I really never knew him to be far off the money in his evaluation of anyone in the two years we'd been working together. For the first time, I started to wonder if Tim had what it took. It was becoming more apparent that the odds weren't in Tim's favor, but I was determined to help him come hell or high water. We had another appointment that week to help Tim build his book.

Thursday came, the day of our appointment with my client from Seattle. I told Tim that we were going out for drinks. This particular client wasn't big on dinner, so more than likely we would spend the entire evening in bars. There were two in particular that the client really enjoyed. Both were located uptown. The crowd was real Wall Street, mostly sales people, traders, money managers, investment bankers, and such. Tim said he'd be ready and would be more comfortable in this type of environment. I cautioned him that this gentleman could hold his liquor, and he shouldn't try to keep up with him. I wasn't sure about the other money manager who was making the trip with him, but if he hung out with Clyde, more than likely he wasn't a light weight. I went over the objectives with Tim in terms of what he should accomplish on this appointment.

First, I told him to start off with small talk just to get a feel for the guy. "Fish for some common ground that will lead you to a deeper conversation and he'll open up to you. Let your true personality and knowledge of the market shine through. You are smart, witty, honest, and possess a fundamental and technical understanding of economics that are your strengths. Play off of them. As the night unfolds get into the business, but not until you connect with him on a topic, hobby, interest, or something else."

We were supposed to meet Clyde and the other money manager around five p.m., so Tim and I grabbed a cab around 4:30 p.m.

I knew the owner of the bar so I had called earlier in the week to let him know I was coming through with some clients and just needed a table for four reserved for me. We arrived early and the table was already setup. Tim was surprised that we had a reserved table and I told him it's all in the planning. Most would not imagine trying to reserve a table at a bar, but this was an upscale bar where they prided themselves on service and were well aware of the clientele they served. One of the cocktail waitresses showed us to our table. We had two bottles of wine that I had ordered ahead of time on chill at the table; one was white, the other was red. Tim and I sat and chatted, going over some of the strategic tactics that I wanted him to implement tonight. I didn't want to harp or ride him too hard, but this was an important meet for him. We were sitting toward the back of the bar, but I spotted Clyde walking in and asked the waitress if she could show him to our table. As Clyde walked toward the table with the waitress in lead position, I noticed that the person with him didn't look at all like what I had expected.

He was a she. She was a brunette young woman in her early thirties about 5'8" and very much an eye catcher. Clyde was an older Irish man about mid fifties, overweight, but very charismatic, with a great personality. Tim and I stood as they approached the table, and from the corner of my eye I could see Tim had a big smile on his face, staring at the woman as she approached. It was too late to nudge him and make him aware that he was staring. Once they'd walked to the table we all shook hands and Clyde introduced Susan to me and I in returned introduced both of them to Tim.

"I see as usual, Shane, you have my favorite red and white wines," Clyde said.

He poured himself a glass and asked Susan which she preferred. She chose the white.

"Excellent choice, Shane knows I love wine," Clyde said as he poured a glass of white wine for Susan. "How long have we known each other, Shane?"

"Coming up on two years," I said.

"Is that all? Man, it's like we've been knowing each other for at least five years. Susan, this guy is a hell of an athlete. Some of the research analyst and traders took him mountain bike riding when he came out to visit his first time, and as you know, Susan, there are some die hard mountain bike riders at the company. Shane kept up and actually did better on the trail than some of the seasoned riders."

"How long have you been mountain bike riding?" she asked me.

"That was actually my first time mountain bike riding, but I did enjoy it."

Susan said, "I love mountain biking. The majority of my exercise comes from riding. The outdoors and fresh air, you can't beat it."

Tim entered the conversation with, "How long have you been riding?"

That was a good lead in on Tim's part.

"Practically all my life," Susan answered. "My father was a bike rider who used to take the whole family on bike rides. And once I moved to Seattle I got caught up in the rave of mountain bike riding. What about you, Tim? Do you ride?"

"No I don't, but I am interested in the sport. I've been looking for some kind of exercise program, but I don't really like the gym. I'd rather be out in the fresh air and sun. I started doing research on road bikes, but mountain bike riding sounds like a lot of fun."

"Oh, I can tell you anything you want to know," Susan said excitedly.

Tim and Susan's conversation began on a high note. He had established a common interest between the two of them; she opened up enough for him to get a good read on her. Clyde and I were just catching up. I hadn't seen him since last year. Clyde was the same, no change, full of jokes and observations of other people in the bar. Some friends of his joined us. They started in on the harder liquor. I went one round with them, then bowed out. After bowing out of the drink fest, still in its early stages, I didn't want to join in on Tim and Susan's conversation because he was doing well by himself, so I wandered off to the bar. To my surprise my frat brother Charles was standing at the bar having a beer. I made my way to him quickly, and gently tapped him on the shoulder.

"What the hell?"

Charles turned around and looked happily surprised.

"Hey, man, I've been trying to contact you since last night. Do you ever check your messages?"

"You called me?"

"Yes. I tried to hit you at the house and on your cell. You didn't get my messages."

"Well, I stayed over Kendra's last night and I forgot my cell phone over there."

"Man, you slippin'. That girl has got a nice hold on you."

"When you meet her, you'll understand why. But, I want to know what brings you to New York."

"Management signed me up for this conference in New York on Friday."

"What is the conference about?"

"Economic Outlook for the bond market."

"Really, I may have to crash that conference. How many people from your company are attending?"

"It's about eight of us all together."

"Where you staying?"

"With you!" Charles said with authority. "Why you think I've been calling you? I know it's kind of last minute but you my boy, so?"

Charles stepped back and raised his hands above his head. He always had been a bit of clown.

"You know I got your back. We should just make a weekend of it."

"Yea, that was my plan. My flight doesn't leave New York until Sunday."

"Sounds like a plan to me."

"What are you doing here?"

"A client of mine came in from Seattle and brought a colleague who could potentially throw some business Tim's way."

"Tim's here?"

"Yea."

Just then, one of Charles' colleagues walked up to us and asked Charles if I was the friend he had been trying to get in touch with.

"Yes, isn't that crazy? I've been calling all around New York to track this guy down and he's here having drinks."

"I told you there was a high probability you would run into him here. This is the spot if you are a player on Wall Street," Charles' friend said.

Charles introduced us. We chatted about business, markets, and New York. He was a knowledgeable guy. I was soon engaged in discussions for the next two hours with Charles and his colleagues.

When I looked at my watch, I was surprised how time had slipped away. I worried a bit that my absence from Tim and the others had been too long. I told Charles I needed to go check in on Tim. He walked with me to the back of the bar. From afar I could see Tim and the others laughing and getting along. Once in view of the whole table I surmised that they had been doing shots, several rounds had been consumed. I arrived at the table and couldn't believe my ears.

"I'mmm tellllingg yoouuu thaaaaat I caaaann haaaangg wit yooooou and and gooo a feu mo rounds," Tim said drunkenly.

I thought to myself, I know he is not drunk. I turned, looking at Charles. He was laughing with the rest of the people at the table. Tim was certainly intoxicated. He was beyond drunk, loaded to the gills. I couldn't believe it. I had warned him not to try and keep up with Clyde, but evidently he didn't heed my advice. Tim was making a spectacle of himself; he was slumped down in his chair, talking to anyone who would listen, making no sense, and he'd become the butt of jokes from the others at the table. I had to intervene quickly and try to do some damage control.

"Ay, Clyde. What did you do to my man?"

"I'm innocent. Susan did it. She challenged him to some shots and drank the poor man practically under the table, as you can see."

I looked over at Susan, who looked as fresh as when she'd hit the door.

"I thought mountain bike riders only drank fresh spring water, milk, or some kind of tofu soy mix drink." Everyone laughed. Susan looked up at me with a big smile.

"Clyde, you set my man up. You come here with a pretty brunette looking like Cindy Crawford. Is she a money manager or a swimsuit model?"

Everyone was inebriated, howling and cracking up. "She's a got damn runway model!" Since we'd all been drinking, the mood was light. I couldn't let up. I had to keep going and find an out. "Look at her. What man in his right mind wouldn't want to have her drink him under a table? Raise your hand if you would sign up for that duty." Every man at that table raised his hands. Clyde was laughing so hard he nearly busted his gut. "Is she related to you because we know your whole family can drink a mere mortal under the table?"

"Stop, Shane, stop you're killing me." Clyde tried to contain his laughter enough to ask me about Charles. I introduced them. Tim had fallen asleep, snoring loudly. We heard him and laughed. I couldn't help myself.

"Let me get this man home to his wife."

"Alright, Shane, thanks for the drinks and for hanging out with us. I think, besides a huge hangover tomorrow morning, Tim should be okay," Clyde said.

We said our goodbyes and shook hands. I closed out the tab. We literally had to carry Tim out of the bar. Good thing Charles was there to help me. While we were standing outside waiting for a cab, Charles said, "Looks like the gray girl was giving you a little action."

"I didn't notice," I replied. Just then she walked out of the bar, alone.

"Hey, Shane, sorry about Tim. I didn't mean for this to happen."

"He's a big boy. He'll learn not to tangle with a pretty face." She smiled.

"Look, some friends and I are going to this nightclub in the village tomorrow night. Why don't you and Charles come hang out with us? Here's the phone number to the hotel where I'm staying. Give me a call." She handed me the number and walked back into the bar. I looked over at Charles.

"We for damn sure are going to be there," he said

"I've got plans."

"To hell with your plans. You got company, and I want to be shown a good time. So cancel whatever you got going on. Call Kendra and tell her you can't make it because you have a date with Patty Duke." He started to laugh

"Man, you crazy."

Just then, the cab pulled up. We put Tim into the cab.

"Let's just send him home in the cab. Do you know his address?" Charles said.

"We can't send this man home alone in his condition."

"Why not?"

"Because I owe his wife an explanation and it's my responsibility to see that he gets home all right."

"What? He's a grown ass man dog. You are not responsible for him."

"Get in the cab and let's go," I replied.

Charles and I got in the cab. He sat up front with the driver and I sat in the back seat with Tim. We arrived at Tim's house and we told the cabbie to wait. We carried Tim to his driveway, but before we saw her, his wife was coming towards us.

"What happened?"

"He just had a little too much to drink. We were meeting with some clients and he just had one too many," I said in response to her question, hoping she did not want to hear more.

"One too many, from the looks of him he had several too many."

"Well, yea, he had several too many," I agreed.

"Can you guys bring him around back? The kids are in the front of the house and I don't want them to see their father like this."

As she directed us, Tim revived, raised his head and ranted unintelligibly for a moment. I told his wife we'd had several episodes of this in the cab. We took him around back and up to their bedroom the back way. His wife thanked us. We headed back to our cab. Charles always had smart remarks, so I expected nothing less once we got back into the cab.

"You know you should have told his wife the truth, that some white woman drunk his ass under the table."

"I knew you'd say something crazy."

Friday morning Tim called in sick. I wasn't surprised. He must have had a mammoth hangover. I tried to keep what happened at the bar under wraps, but given the venue where we had been, it was next to impossible. Rumors and gossip traveled fast on Wall Street; often moving as fast as market information. The word circulated late morning, a few people from the firm had been in the bar the night before, so the headline of the story circulating was "Tim Suckered into A Drunken Stupor". Since I wasn't at the table when it happened, I only had limited information to defend him, but evidently there were a couple of guys from the firm who had seen everything. So, they dismissed my defense of Tim. When he called in sick, an announcement was made over the speaker in the trade room.

"Tim will not be in today. He has a very important appointment all day with the toilet!" The whole room roared.

The day was slow; I was close to leaving the office and crashing the conference where Charles was, but I had some clean up and updates to do on some client files. My whole day ended up being a prep day for the coming week. I was entertaining Mr. Jesowitz and his wife next week. The planning for this outing had been three months in the making -- six tickets to one of the hottest Broadway shows that had been sold out for the next two years. No one could get their hands on these tickets to save his life. Not even reliable brokers could get these tickets. I managed to get them through a stroke of luck.

****

I was walking home one day. One of the street hustlers stopped me. He was a short slender man, in his late twenties early thirties, very smooth talking, and kind of a laid back attitude. He cultivated the look of a New York street hustler. He was standing next to his '67 gold Cadillac with a black vinyl top. I had seen him around Harlem a few times but we had never spoken to each other.

"Say brotha hold on for a sec," he said.

"What's up?"

"You know, brotha, I see ya walkin through Harlem almost everyday in your fly ass suits with a Wall Street Journal under your arm and your bag swung over your back, and I say to myself this brotha must be heavy into some financial shit. Am I right?"

"I work in finance."

"And, from what I can tell there aren't too many brothas or sistas that work in that field. That leads me to believe you work with a lot of white folks."

"I guess you could say that."

"Reason why I'm asking, brotha, is because white folks have different taste than us, and I find myself in possession of something that is appealing to white folks, but black folks in Harlem don't give a damn about it."

"What you got."

"I got six tickets to some Broadway play that I can't even pronounce. I think they box seats and the mutha fucka I got them off say they worth about four g's."

"Let me check them out."

I couldn't believe that this cat had tickets to a play that no one could get his or her hands on. I didn't know how they came into his possession. He either stole them or somebody lost them and he found them.

"I was thinking you might know somebody who'd like the tickets, since you work with white folks. If you found a buyer, I'll break you off a little cheddar for finding a buyer. You interested?"

"First, let me ask you a question, and my intention is not to pry but if I find a buyer and the tickets are stolen or lost, the buyer might have a hard time at the theatre. You see where I'm coming from?"

"Yea, yea my brotha, I hear ya. I got these tickets from a white boy uptown who was into me for about eight g's. He only had four of the eight and gave me the tickets to make up the other four. Being the good hearted person that I am, I took the tickets. Now I assure you, whoever takes these tickets will not have any problem. Straight up! You feel me?"

"Yea, I feel you."

The guy he was talking about probably worked on Wall Street, developed a drug habit because he couldn't handle the pressure and turned to drugs for an escape. Some turn to alcohol, some to drugs, and some to suicide. It amazed me how much drug and alcohol abuse was on Wall Street.

"Are you going to be around here tomorrow?" I asked

"Yea, but you can take the tickets now and when you sell them just break bread with me. I trust you brotha. A lot of people around here know and respect you. I have no reason not to trust you until you give me a reason, and another thing, you doing me a fava by getting rid of these tickets because if you don't get rid of them for me, I'm just out four grand and may be tempted to pay that white boy another visit, and I don't need that in my life right now."

"Look brotha, I'm not going to sell them for you, but I will buy them from you."

The brotha look surprised.

"All six of them?"

"Yes, all six, you said four grand?"

"Yea,"

"If you are here tomorrow, I will buy the tickets from you."

"Solid brotha and don't worry I'll be here. Your name is Shane, right?"

"Yea, what's yours?"

"I'm Ice."

Ice and I gave each other a pound and parted ways. So that's how I got tickets to the most popular play in New York, from a street hustler in Harlem.

****

I finished up at the office around four o'clock and then met Charles at my house. I ordered Chinese food and Kendra came by to eat with us; she and Charles got along great. He couldn't keep his mouth closed. Every question she asked him, he answered. Charles was so caught up in the conversation I don't think he was aware of all the information he was giving away; some of the history he revealed, good and some was bad. Kendra had a talent for drawing people in and getting out of them any information that she wanted or needed. Thus, the success of her clothing store. Her personality was suited for sales. She bonded with people quickly. In a short period of time she got information without the impression of probing. She was trustworthy and honest, and she was very pleasing to the eye, always an asset. She and Charles bantered, so we stayed up snacking and playing card games until about one in the morning, causing Charles and I both to completely forget about our date in the village.

In the morning, Kendra got up and fixed a dynamite breakfast. She made omelets, muffins, fried plantain, fresh fruit, grits, chicken sausage, and Chai tea with Agave Nectar. I know she didn't make all this from my bare cabinets.

"Aw baby, this is a nice spread you put together here. I know you didn't make this from what I had in this kitchen."

"No, I went to the grocery store to pick up a few things."

"Thanks, babe."

"I'll do almost anything for you," she replied.

"Almost anything, huh? I haven't lured you to the point of doing anything for me?"

"No, you haven't lured me that far yet, but you are a good brotha, and I'm thankful to have you as a part of my life and as my man."

"Well, I can't let all the compliments be one sided, now can I?" Kendra gave me a smile and chuckled. "You are a beautiful sista and I don't just mean that as a physical description. Your soul carries with it a quality I haven't seen in very many people. It makes you a pleasure to be around, and makes people gravitate to you. Your beauty is radiant. The mere sight of you brings me pleasure, and I'm proud and privileged to call you my lady."

She became silent and just looked at me and her eyes swelled up ever so slightly. She jumped in my arms and gave me the best kiss I ever had in my life. Then Charles walked in.

"Please, don't get any slobber on this food you two, because a brotha is hungry."

Kendra and I both broke into laughter.

"Sit down, man, we're getting ready to get our grub on! This wonderful breakfast my lady cooked for us," I said. I looked at

Kendra, still in my arms, and gave her a nice peck and we all sat down and enjoyed our breakfast.

After we finished breakfast, Kendra had to leave to open her shop. I told her I was just going to show Charles around New York today and that we would come by the shop later. Charles wanted Kendra to make him a suit. He had seen the suits she had made for me and wanted one for himself. He just had to have a suit custom made by Kendra. She agreed and told us to come by the shop just before closing around 5:00 p.m.

Charles and I walked, talked, and ate lunch. Our day shot pass, but we didn't really go too many places. I took him to this barbeque joint in Harlem for lunch, then to Chuck's for a haircut, and then we hung out at a sports bar, watching college basketball. While we were kicking back at the sports bar watching games and shooting pool, Charles brought up Kendra and couldn't stop saying good things about her.

"Kendra is a cool sista. How did you meet her?"

"You won't believe it, but moms hooked that up when she was down decorating the crib."

"Moms hooked you up with a keeper. That's just like a mother to find the perfect woman for her son."

"I don't know about perfect, but she is special."

"Man, I'm telling you she is perfect for you. She is wifie material."

"You think so?"

"I know so, and if you don't marry that sista, you're not as smart as I give you credit for."

"Hey, don't jump the gun. We've only been dating coming up on a year."

"A year? I'm surprised you haven't taken that off the market already. Man, I love you like a brother and I'm telling you don't let this one get away."

We finished up our pool game and headed back into Harlem to Kendra's shop. We arrived a little after 6 p.m., about an hour later than she told us. We knocked on the door because she had already locked up, but we saw the lights were on. She appeared from the rear with her genuine smile that would brighten up anyone's gloomiest day. As I watched her walk to the door to let us in, Charles's earlier words about taking her off the market resonated. She welcomed us in and led us to the work area of the shop. She took Charles's measurements and talked with him about the style of suit he would like. Before they were finished she had an order for three suits for Charles and another two suits for me. Kendra was an excellent seamstress and tailor, but she was a better sales person; her sales came effortlessly. In less than an hour she had closed on a five suit deal that would gross her close to ten grand.

Charles wrapped up his weekend in New York with me and Kendra. I'd forgotten how well he and I got along and as the weekend drew to a close, Kendra had completely won over Charles. We ended up at a few nightspots and hitting a couple of dinner spots. Some of Kendra's close friends joined us. A few I hadn't met. It was a different experience for me; watching Kendra interact with some of her friends. She had such a pleasurable demeanor, and people were naturally drawn to her. This weekend opened my eyes to see Kendra in a whole new way; personally I began to see her as a possible lifelong mate, and professionally I began to see her as a most astute businesswoman.

9

Opportunity Knocks

I was in my third year at GPG and my book was continuing to build, and as one of the top salesmen on the debt desk I got exposure to the underwriting side of the business as a consultant to clients about market conditions and pricing. Upper management noticed my talents beyond sales, thanks to Tim. My training and mentoring of Tim had taken on a life of its own and the relationship rekindled the friendship and trust that we had in our undergraduate days. The relationship developed into a two way street: As I continued to help Tim sharpen his sales skills, he helped me understand the intricacies of market research. His strength was indeed market research and trends, but he became a solid salesman in his own right. The criticism, jokes, and questions about his ability as a salesman ceased, but Tim didn't like sales. His personality was more introverted than the average sales person, but he enjoyed research and analysis. I saw the passion and excitement in his eyes each time we discussed market trends and economic indicators, or any aspect of the economy. He was an economist at heart. His mind was sharp and he had a good feel for the pulse of the market and how to project its direction. I wished GPG could have seen what I saw in his ability as an economist or researcher. I mentioned it to some top people in the firm, but none were willing to give him the opportunity to show his talent as a research/analyst.

One day while Tim and I were having our regular after market hour's ritual, where we discussed markets and sales tactics, we were interrupted by Ted. He knocked, and then stuck his head through the door of the conference room where Tim and I were meeting.

"Hey, Shane, sorry to interrupt but I need to talk to you in private right now." I gestured for him to come in the room. Ted walked in and looked at Tim.

"Tim, can you give Shane and me a minute?" Ted asked

"Sure, not a problem!"

"We will continue this conversation tomorrow," I said to Tim. We gave each other a dap and Tim left the room. Ted took a seat and in his usual calm demeanor he commenced to tell me some shocking news.

"Ken, our managing director, has just turned in his resignation."

"Man, that's news! Where is he going?"

"What I'm hearing is he has partnered up with a couple of people to start a small firm specializing in debt underwriting, but that is not the half of it. More than three quarters of the trading desk have turned in their resignations this afternoon also."

"What? Ken is taking them with him, huh? Did you know all this was going on?"

"No, the word is that this was kept very quiet. They didn't approach me because Ken and I never got along and the only reason he ever became managing director of the desk was because I turned the position down. They didn't approach you because you are close to me. They thought you would have leaked the mass exodus to me."

"They were right in that calculation, but I would have never accepted the offer because Ken never had a hand in my success on the desk. So, how is management handling the news?"

"They are in a state of panic. To lose close to three quarters of your top desk in the firm is no small setback. I've just come out of a meeting. They offered me the managing director position."

"Congratulations! You know you can count on me to help build the desk back up."

"Shane, you've known me close to three years now. I have never had any desire to be a managing director or to take on any other management position."

"Yeah, I know this, so what did they say when you turned the promotion down?"

"They tried to get me to step in as an interim MD until they can hire a permanent one, but I turned that down also."

"Man, I know they are pulling their hair out!"

"You know they are!" Ted laughed lightly. Then he looked at me seriously. "I suggested you for the position."

I was silent, at a loss for words, my mind worked overtime contemplating the opportunity. Ted's comment had me deep in thought, weighing the pros and cons.

"Shane, I took the liberty to contact Professor White before I came in to talk to you. He's available for a conference call if you would like."

I looked at Ted and told him, "Let's make the call."

From the conference room we called Professor White. The three of us discussed this potential opportunity that stood before me. Ted spoke first.

"Professor White, I've just finished telling Shane what has taken place on our trading desk. I informed him of my recommendation of him for the managing director position. I've also told him I briefly talked to you, but we haven't discussed my recommendation yet because we decided to bring you in on the conversation."

"Shane, I hope you don't mind that Ted shared his recommendation with me before he told you."

"No I don't mind that at all. Ted knows how much I value your, and his, advice."

"Well, one thing I want you to know is that neither Ted nor I are trying to determine your future. Your future is in your hands and if this directorship position doesn't figure into your plans, then we don't need to have this conversation."

"I know, I haven't shared my long range plans with you or Ted, but that's because I haven't thought much about the future up to this point. My relationship with Kendra, training Tim, and continuing to build my book has left little time to ponder the future. I've been too much in the moment."

"So, how do you feel about my recommendation of you for the opening?"

"I like your recommendation, and appreciate that you think enough of me to make that recommendation."

"It wasn't hard for me to make the recommendation, given your success on the desk in the three years you been at GPG. You are one of the top salesmen at GPG, and your market knowledge has improved tremendously."

"Thanks, so where do I go from here if I want to pursue the MD position?"

"Well, they have agreed to meet with you in the morning to talk about the possibility. To be totally honest, they weren't sold on the idea of you as manager," Ted disclosed.

Professor White chimed in, "What were their concerns?"

"The major concern was Shane's age and his lack of experience."

"Okay, how do I put those concerns to rest?"

"Before we go there let's make sure we are seeing the total playing field. Now Ted, were there any other reservations about Shane? And you can be candid with us."

"We are dealing with one of the oldest and top Wall Street firms in GPG. So, that good old boy's network is in place and still harbors some of the pre-civil rights era mindset. When I made the recommendation, there was silence and surprise on the faces of some of the top executives."

"Are they giving me this meeting just to appease me and for show?"

"That is a strong possibility."

"You have the sit down, Shane, and that's a good step," Professor White said. "You just have to convince them you are the best person for this position. Historically, African Americans had to be three to four times better than their competition to succeed, and you are three to four times better than any alternative candidate, and that's the attitude you have to possess when you walk into the meeting."

"Professor White is right. You are the third most productive salesman on the debt desk and top five in the firm, and the four salesman that rank above you are at least ten years your senior. What no one tells you is that your market knowledge ranks above all the top salesmen, and your work with the underwriting division has been stellar and clients have taken notice and appreciated your input and advice."

"Shane, the bottom line on Wall Street is money. If you are a producer, no matter what kind of backwards thinking any of the top executives have about African Americans, they will look at your bottom line, and they will not be able to deny that you are making money for them. This fact will make them tread cautiously around you and take all precautions not to offend you. Use this to your advantage to push for the position!"

"I understand. Should I be ready to give a laundry list of my accomplishments on the desk?"

"That shouldn't be necessary. Your accomplishments are well documented, and they even know that you are responsible for the tremendous turnaround in the production of Tim, and that speaks volumes of your ability to manage and cultivate talent. I think you should concentrate on a strategy to bring the debt desk back from this tremendous setback," Ted said.

"I agree with Ted. If you can put together a plan and sell them on that plan, there will be no denying you this opportunity."

"I think you are both right. I can put together something that will knock their socks off. Looks like I'm going to have a long night putting this plan together."

"One other thing Shane, I was going to retire in another year, but if they give you the MD position, I will stick around for an additional year to help build the desk. You can factor that in as part of your plan, and I will let that be known to them."

"Thanks Ted, I appreciate all your support." I extended my hand to give Ted a handshake and hug.

Professor White gave me his last words. "Shane, you know you can count on me if you need a sounding board on any of your ideas. You have my home number -- call me anytime, tonight if needed. Last thing, they may offer you the position on an interim basis, but do not settle for that. Tell them it's all or nothing!"

"That's a good point, Shane. If they push for anything temporary, it's imperative to stand your ground."

"Understood!"

Ted and I said goodbye to Professor White, thanking him for his time. Both Ted and I left the conference room and walked back to the trade room. By this time mostly everyone had gone home. There were a few sales and trade people left in the trade room. When they saw Ted and me, they came up to us and wanted to gossip about what they heard had taken place today. Ted and I didn't fully engage them and dismissed ourselves, saying we had to get home.

Ted and I walked to the subway station. I caught the subway to Harlem and Ted got on the subway headed to the suburbs of New York. While on the subway, my mind was working fast, thinking about the promotion to manager and how big of an opportunity that would be at this stage of my career. I could barely contain my excitement. Just the thought of becoming a managing director enthused me. Once I got off the train, I jogged to Kendra's boutique to share my news.

Kendra was busy with three women when I entered her business. She was measuring, sizing them up, and taking orders. When I walked in, she excused herself to come and greet me. She gave me a light peck on the lips and a hug. Then, she took a step back, gazed into my eyes and said, "What's up?"

I commenced to telling her an abbreviated version about the new developments at GPG. She smiled broadly. Then hugged me and said, "That is your job and all you have to do is go claim it. I'm so proud of you." I told her I don't have the job yet. She made eye contact again and stated. "That's your job, baby. Just visualize yourself in the position and the position will manifest itself." I told her that I had to get going to prepare my presentation to executive management tomorrow. She told me to call her tomorrow after the meeting, and if I needed her tonight just call, but she thought it would be better if she went home after work instead of coming by my place to give me some quiet time with my thoughts. I gave her a kiss to show my appreciation for her support and headed out.

I arrived home and went into the kitchen to make my favorite sandwich, pepper turkey on rye with tomatoes and cheese. Then I put on a Miles Davis CD in and went to my study. It's there that my plan for the debt desk crystallized in my mind. I thought to myself, *What do I need to do immediately to turn the tide of this coup that initiated on the Debt Trading Desk?*

The first step would be to replace key personnel who were part of the mass departure. Research and Analysis wasn't directly a huge part of the profitability on the desk, but the desk had one of the top economist of debt markets on Wall Street. This person brought the firm much publicity and exposure with his appearances on money and financial news television shows. His wasn't a key position of concern in terms of profitability, but a knowledgeable and articulate candidate would be of high priority, and I could think of no one better than Tim. Rising above the earlier problems, he had proven himself to be a good salesman. In my estimation his market knowledge was second to none at the firm. In that position he would prove himself to be a formidable asset.

Losing the head trader position was a huge blow to the desk. Someone with trading experience and a broad knowledge of debt instruments and how they trade in different market environments was needed. This person would have to have the personality of a salesman, but the drive of a Managing Director. One person came to mind who had the experience, knowledge, and personality needed, Charles. He would be able to fill the position immediately with little or no learning curve. Charles wouldn't be a hard sell to the executives because of his accounting background and trading experience. He only had been in this field three years, but he was a rising star in his firm and would have impeccable references from his current company, which happened to be a major player in the debt markets out of North

Carolina. Currently, his position title was VP of Trading – Assistant Head Trader.

The bloodline of any firm, let alone a trading desk, is its sales' personnel, and the debt desk had lost all its sales personnel except Ted and me. We counted for almost 40% of the sales production on the desk, but you take a 60% chunk out of any entity and that entity is on life support. Ted, being number one on the sales desk, brought in twenty five percent of the sales production, and I accounted for fifteen percent, which trailed the second top producer on the desk by five percent. My biggest challenge was to put a sales team together that could rival the old sales team. A good first step would be Darrell. He was already tops in sales at his current firm, and I don't think he would need much convincing to draw him to Wall Street. Head of Sales would be the opportunity I would present to him because I knew even though Ted agreed to stay on another year, he wasn't open to taking a formal management position. Ted would be my informal confidant and advisor in the management and direction of the desk.

That would cover the key positions immediately, but general staffing would also be critical to bringing the desk to profitability. My staying true to my commitment when I first started this journey on Wall Street was also important. Not only did I want to create opportunities for myself, I wanted to create opportunities for other African Americans. Now this crisis at GPG had provided great potential for my becoming a Managing Director. There was one other person who would need no interview, and I would bring right in, Big Mike. Mike was big and intimidating, but very personable with a sharp legal mind. Mike wasn't very well suited for a sales position, but an analyst research position his legal background and attention to detail would be of benefit. I thought maybe a hybrid position that would have him doing some sales and some analytical work would be best.

With these key people in place, Charles – Head Trader, Tim – Head of Research and Analysis, Darrell – Head of Sales, and Ted which was my main support in this endeavor, I could present and articulate a good first step to stop the bleeding on the Debt Desk and return it to some kind of solid footing. My biggest hurdle was to convince them that I could handle the responsibility of managing a whole desk with the same success I had as a salesman. I think most saw me as a very capable and competent hard worker, but most importantly, management had to believe I was smart and savvy enough to handle the desk and the transition.

My next step was to make some calls and make sure that the key pieces to my plan were all on board. My first call was to Ted. We talked about my decision to go for the MD position and the role he wanted to play on the desk going forward. Just as I thought, he wanted no formal position. He just wanted to lend his knowledge and experience to my building and developing of the desk. He wished to stay low key and be an advisor and confidant to me. My next call was to Tim. He was elated with the possibility of advancing to research and was excited for me. We briefly chatted about his accomplishments as salesman, and he took that moment to say how much he appreciated my help, support, and continued belief in his ability. My last call, which was the most gratifying, was a conference call to Big Mike, Charles, and Darrel. I made them aware of the problems on the trading desk at GPG, shared with them that I was interviewing for managing director, and outlined what I saw as their respective roles if I got the position. They all expressed an eagerness to work with me on Wall Street. Charles was the first to express his excitement.

"Man, I told ya'll we would all be on Wall Street working together. Now the opportunity is here, and there's no doubt that Shane will close the deal on this MD position."

"Let's not get ahead of ourselves. Shane doesn't have the position, yet," Darrel replied.

Agreeing with Charles, Big Mike added, "Ay, I'm down with you, and I agree with Charles, you are going to get that MD position, so just let me know when I need to be there and I'll be on the next train smokin."

"Darrell's right. Let's not put the carriage before the horse. There's still work that needs to be done before my meeting tomorrow. So, I got to get started. Knowing you guys are all onboard gives me that much more confidence going into this meeting."

I knew they would all commit to this plan, but I didn't want to make it seem like I was taking them for granted. We all had talked about the day we would work together on Wall Street, and now perhaps I could make it happen. For the opportunity to present itself so early in our careers was both exciting and a little frightening. If I landed the MD position, it would put Tim, Darrel, and Charles in power positions in the firm, and I don't think even one desk at any of the large houses on Wall Street had a Managing Director, Head of Research and Analysis, Head Trader, and Head of Sales all of African American descent. This would be a first. Even some of the African American owned firms didn't have an all African American professional team working at their firms.

I told my team I would give them a call tomorrow night, letting them know how the meeting went, but I didn't expect a final decision on my candidacy until a few days afterwards. I called Kendra next, whose voice always seemed to put me in a good mood. Her words always fed my soul the proper nutrition at the time. Our conversation wasn't that lengthy, we talked just enough to fill her in on the highlights of my plan. She was very supportive, she liked the way I was including people whom I trusted and who had my back through the years. My last call of the night was to my mother. After I told her the details of the days' events, she was happy; nevertheless, she warned me to be myself and to keep my eye on the prize.

"What is the prize, mom?"

"This journey you are on now is just the training ground, there are bigger and greater challenges ahead beyond GPG. Shane, don't get me wrong. This is a great opportunity, and if you put everything you have into this, there's no doubt in my mind that you will succeed."

My mother had a vision way beyond the scope of my immediate future, so I had to stay focused. I told her I'd give her a call tomorrow, letting her know how things went. She said she would wish me luck, but I didn't need it.

I think my mother's expectations for me were greater than the expectations I had for myself. She had to be proud and satisfied with my accomplishments at this stage of my life. And for the life of me, I didn't know why I felt she expected more. Most parents would have been ecstatic about seeing their son making the sums of money that I was making. I was already a millionaire and well on my way to becoming a multi-millionaire, if things went well tomorrow, but she was not as excited as I thought she would be. Sometimes I felt my mother was saying, so what? I expect more from you! What more, she never told me. She exclaimed that I had to find it out for myself, on my journey; it would reveal itself when the time was right.

The next morning I got up at my usual time -- 4:00 a.m., fixed a light breakfast of wheat toast, one egg over easy, and fresh squeezed orange juice. I read my Wall Street Journal and caught some of the morning market news on CNBC. The pre-market news was non-eventful, which made for a smooth opening and no special attention was paid to the debt markets. Well, not immediately, which allowed me to focus in on the meeting I had at 9:00 a.m. with executive management.

I arrived at work at my usual time of 6:30 a.m., Ted was sitting at the trading desk, almost all alone. Management had dismissed all that were part of the mass exodus, telling them to get their things and not to bother reporting in tomorrow. Man, I thought that was pretty harsh, but on second thought, it made sense. Management didn't want those who were leaving to linger around the trade room, affecting morale, undermining operations, or even trying to recruit others to join them. Out with the old and in with the new, I hoped. A few minutes later, more of the remaining sales people and traders walked in, joining us. Most had negative attitudes.

"This desk is dead. I hear Robert and James is hiring."

"I hear they are going to merge our desk with the convertible desk which is sure death for all of us."

"I hear we are getting out of the debt markets all together and we all will be switched over to equities."

"Hey, I don't want to work in equities," one the salespersons cried. "I signed on for debt markets and if they force me into equities, I'll quit."

Ted and I didn't respond to any of the comments made by the others, even when they directly solicited our input. Both of us just glanced up at them without words and continued our conversation between ourselves. Ted asked if I was ready to meet with the executives this morning, and I responded, "Ready as can be." We then reviewed the major aspects of my presentation. He asked me some quick questions covering areas he thought they would probe, and made objections and observations on plausible weaknesses in my plan. After about a half hour, he asked if I would like him to go in with me. I knew Ted was responsible for my getting the opportunity and his presence could only help my situation.

"Yes, I would appreciate your presence if you would care to join me."

Ted and I arrived in the executive conference room on the 81st floor about ten minutes early. I had never been in that conference room. It was all mahogany, glass and leather, with huge windows overlooking the city. There was a long mahogany table in the middle, surrounded by soft black leather chairs. There was a fifty by sixty inch white board on the west wall of the conference room and four plasma wide screen televisions on the south side, broadcasting business news from around the world on four different stations with the volume muted. We were the first to arrive for the meeting and we took the two middle seats on the north side of the conference room. Quietly, Ted spoke to me about some of the details in my presentation.

A few minutes later, all the top executives arrived, along with some MD's on the other trading desk. As they entered, Ted and I stood and greeted each one, while Ted did the introductions to those I did not know. There were executives from all the profit centers; Underwriting, Mergers and Acquisitions, Corporate Finance, International Markets, Portfolio Management, Economic Research, Retail Trading and Sales, and Institutional trading and Sales. Mr. Mackey was over all institutional business and I had never been introduced to him formally.

Mr. David Mackey was about sixty years of age and had been at GPG for about twenty years. He was a tall slender man with gray hair balding from the top of his head to the middle, looked in fairly good shape for his age. I'd been told he wore nothing but Brooks Brothers' suits and today he was wearing one. I had briefly run into his son, David Mackey Jr., whom Mr. Mackey was grooming to take his place once he became a partner in the firm, but I'd had no other interaction with him. Junior was about forty years old, tall, like his father, had blond hair that never seemed to be out of place, and was married to Italian suits. Ted briefed me on father and son when I first started at GPG. He said both were politically connected and were driven not by money but the family name and tradition. The Mackey family had been in finance and banking for over five generations. They were a prominent, wealthy family in the New York area. With his father moving into a partnership position, they would once again stamp the family name as major players on Wall Street.

There was a lot of envy among some of the other executive VP's because Mr. Mackey's division had been the top producer for the firm for the last ten years and he was pretty cocky about letting the others know. Some resented the nepotism. They thought others who had been with the firm longer and who had better experience should be next in line to succeed Mr. Mackey. Now, with this mass exodus on the fixed income desk, everyone was betting he would delay the move.

First, his pride wouldn't let him leave on a down note. Second, the partners of the firm were putting pressure on him to see the fixed income desk through this critical time. There were also those who enjoyed seeing him and his son sweat. If the fixed income desk fell, the Mackeys would fall, too, and open up opportunities for other employees. So, the Mackeys had a lot riding on the salvation of the fixed income desk. With all that in mind, Mr. Mackey's son opened the meeting.

He spoke directly to Ted and me. He got right to the point, saying that the fixed income desk was hemorrhaging from all areas and there was an immediate need to stop the bleeding. The only way to do that was to bring in a MD that could set a new path for the desk and return the desk to its status as the top producer. He was blunt in his overview. He continued, saying the first logical choice was Ted, but Ted had declined the job and had recommended me. He went through my accomplishments on the desk over the four years, and stated that as of this year's end numbers I'd become second in sales on the desk behind Ted; the latter was news to Ted and me. While Junior was making his initial comments, his father said nothing. In his silence I could feel his eyes looking me over and studying me. Then Junior threw the curve ball.

"Any decision made about the MD desk in the next couple of days would only be for the interim, and we fully intend on doing an inside and outside search for the best MD for the position."

At that moment, I felt it prudent to assert my feelings and my intentions. I wanted that position. An interim position would not be the end of the world and most might jump at that opportunity to show what they could do, but I wanted all or nothing and was willing at that moment to put it all on the line.

"I don't mean to interrupt you, but my intention and purpose is to present my plan for the fixed income desk for consideration as the permanent MD. If we are not gathered here for that purpose, then this meeting has no purpose for me. I am not willing to take this position as an interim assignment, and if I cannot have your full consideration for the position then I can have my letter of resignation on your desk in the next fifteen minutes."

No one said anything. They sat with stunned looks on their faces. Even Ted appeared somewhat shocked. The senior Mr. Mackey's expression didn't change, his eyes continued to study me.

Junior, I felt, had made a huge mistake by showing his hand so fast. Evidently, he hadn't thought about the response I might make to his proposition.   Judging from the look on his face, my response blindsided him. There were whispers in the room, but no one spoke, until Mr. Mackey broke the silence.

"Let's not get stopped in our tracks before we even begin. Like David has said, our intention is to find the best person for this position at this time, but who's to say you are not that person? David's words do not mean that we would exclude you from consideration as the permanent MD, but we would open it up to competition."

Mr. Mackey was making direct eye contact with me as he spoke, and I never broke eye contact while he was speaking.

"I've always been under the impression that there would be competition for the position and that's something I've never shied away from in my life. I just want the same consideration you give to others, and I do not want to be named MD of the desk unless it's permanent."

"You have my word that's the course of action we will be taking," Mr. Mackey responded. "Now, please lay out your plan for the desk for us."

I pushed my seat back from the table and stood up, then proceeded to take off my suit coat and paced the conference room as I presented. I began by giving an overview and my take on the current situation on the desk in the context of its history, goals, and strategic direction as it related to the goals of the firm overall. This was to show I had a command and appreciation of the history and tradition of GPG. Then, I showed my understanding of the current economic climate and how the fixed income desk could position itself to rebound, given these current conditions. As I started to lay out my plan and get to the nuts and bolts of my presentation Ted handed out my presentation package which laid out my plan specifically. The package was equipped with profiles and history of the key personnel I wanted to bring aboard. I proposed a revised mission statement for the desk and ten objectives that I wanted to accomplish in the first year, along with my strategies to attain those objectives. I included colored charts and graphs for percentages of sales, breakeven analysis, and other key indicators and ratios that measured the profitability of the desk. I discussed each point in the presentation package without looking at it once, as I elaborated on the key areas that would drive profitability, while glossing over small details.

I kept the presentation on a high level, except when it came down to my diagnosis of the strengths, weaknesses, and the challenges facing the desk as a result of the mass departure of personnel. I laid out my plan to replace the critical positions that were lost and talked about the talents of each of the replacements. Respectively, I shared each candidate's experience, education, current book, and market knowledge. I knew the most important factor in my getting the MD position was profit and how soon I could get the desk back to earning money. That's why my emphasis was on the personnel and their ability to contribute to the bottom line. At the end of the day, I had to sell them on my plan and have them see and share in my vision for the desk. This was the most important sales pitch of my career, so I was professional and personable, making eye contact with key individuals whom I knew would have influence in the decision, touching the shoulders of individuals, asking for affirmations on key points and resolutions. Nothing was forced. I was very calm, cool, and collected, commanding the attention and respect for my knowledge. I ended my presentation with the following:

"I am not a perfect man, but I'm the perfect man for this job."

Mr. Mackey stood up walked over to me and extended his hand. I took his hand, and as we were shaking hands he told me that my presentation was top notch and he was very impressed. His son didn't say anything. Mr. Mackey then announced that he would like feedback on my presentation from everyone in the room today. I walked back to my seat to gather up my things, while Ted whispered, "Good job." The others in attendance came by to say, "good job" or simply to give me a pat on the back, before they left the conference room.

Ted and I headed back to the trading desk where those who remained were up to little or nothing. They were still meandering around, feeding on negative remarks and rumors. It was like they never even knew that Ted and I had ever left the trading desk. It was around midday, and I had cleared my calendar for the day to concentrate on the MD position, so there wasn't much to do. The market was pretty calm. I leaned over to Ted and told him I was going to take off, but if he needed me, I could be reached on my cell phone. I gathered a few things and headed for the door. Tim spotted me heading for the door and ran over to me. Without too many words I greeted him and told him the plan was in motion. Now we just had to sit and wait, but I told him to touch base with me tonight at home and I would fill him in on the details.

I got outside the building and it was a beautiful day in The Big Apple. The sun was beaming through the spaces between the tall buildings. It was a perfect day for a walk, so I decided to walk home - - all the way to Harlem. I didn't know how long it would take but the concept of time was the farthest thing from my mind. I spent the time outside under sun, admiring the Manhattan architecture, reflecting on my presentation, thinking about the opportunity before me, and my future with GPG.

It was time well spent. Still contemplating the day's events, I arrived home. When I looked at the clock, the time was 4:00 pm. I showered and watched some of the economic and world news. Around 5:30 the calls started to come in. First, my mother, then Ted, then Mr. White, then Tim, then Charles, then Darrell, and then Big Mike, but I hadn't heard from Kendra, which struck me as a little peculiar.

Around 6:30 there was a knock at my door and I knew that could only be one person; Kendra. When I opened the door, she walked in and gave me a hug, a long one. We embraced for a good two minutes or better. Then she stepped back, gazed into my eyes and, "I'm so proud of you, baby," rolled out her mouth.

"I don't know if I got the job, yet."

"Baby, you got that job!" She gave me the nicest and sexiest smile I'd ever seen a woman give a man, then she gave me the most gentle and sensuous kiss. She backed up after the kiss. "Aren't you going to take my coat, baby?"

"Aw, I'm sorry, babe. Let me get that for you." I walked around behind her to take off her coat, a beige three quarter length wrap, which I thought was a little heavy given today's weather. As I helped her out of the coat, I saw she was wearing white lingerie that was a sensual contrast to her chocolate skin, along with thigh high white stockings with thong underwear and a skimpy bra that pushed her assets to a higher level of value. But, the topper was the white pumps she had on that threw me into overdrive. I tried to play it cool, but could barely maintain myself. She turned around to face me. I could have taken a seat and stared at her beauty for eternity. She smiled at my reaction, and for about ten to fifteen minutes, she modeled for me. I stared without a word. It was all non-verbal communication, but she kept her distance, not allowing me to get close enough to touch her. She then asked me," Do you want to go upstairs and play?"

I stuttered a little bit because I was truly mesmerized by her beauty. My lady was sexy. I finally uttered the word, "Yeah."

She couldn't help but laugh. She knew she had me.

I had to pull it together to let her know she didn't have that much control over me. So in my smoothest voice I told her, "Please lead the way." And I gestured towards the stairs. She was doing the sexiest walk going up those stairs, looking back occasionally, making sure she had my full attention. I didn't think we would make it to the bedroom, and we didn't. We started in the hallway to the bedroom, and then made our way into the bedroom, then out of the bedroom to one of the guest bedrooms, back into the hallway, to the stairs. I have to say, some of my best work was done on the stairs, then to the kitchen for the finale. Good thing we ended in the kitchen because both of us were in desperate need of food and water after that session. We ended up in the den on the couch butt naked feeding each other and drinking wine while I filled her in on what had taken place that day.

Two weeks went by without a decision from the executive management. There were rumors about different people having been brought in with their whole team intact, but they were just that, rumors. I kept to my regular routine, servicing and maintaining my book while keeping up with training Tim. The few traders that were left on the desk, after the mass exodus, either absconded to different companies or transferred to other trading desks within the firm, leaving Ted and me to man the desk. The desk was now on life support and there still was no word on the MD position. With no trading, research, or analysis, we had to rely on the convertible desk, which was sub-par at best. Since we didn't trust those guys, Ted and I were a two man show, sharing the trading and analytic duties, and still advising underwriting on sales of all fixed income instruments. I've never worked so hard in my life and have never learned so much. Ted went into overdrive, like a man on a mission. Ted was usually relaxed, on cruise control, but now he began to maneuver and make sharp turns and accelerate like a race car driver in a grand prix event. I followed his lead. I think I surprised him with my trading knowledge. Ted was aware of my market knowledge. He knew Tim had helped me in that capacity, but he didn't know that over the years with my experience on the desk and with the help of Charles, I had significantly increased my trading knowledge of fixed income securities. Ted and I were working diligently. Two months passed and still, there was no word on the MD position.

It was an early market close and Ted and I were just sitting on the desk and watching the news, questioning why a decision hadn't been made. We knew they had brought in at least five other candidates but still to this date, none had been hired. After the market closed, my phone rang. It was Mr. Mackey. He wanted to see me in his office. I hung up the phone and looked at Ted.

"That was Mr. Mackey. He wants to see me in his office."

"That's the call we've been waiting on."

"Yeah, either they decided to go with me or they are going a different way."

"Only one way to find out," Ted replied

"Yeah!"

I arrived at Mr. Mackey's office about five minutes after I hung up the phone. I knocked on the thick wooden door to his office, and entered once prompted. This was my first time in his office. The top floor office was huge; about one thousand square feet with old English style furnishing. The light in the office was dim, but he had a desk lamp that lit up his desk area like the fourth of July. He had a large antique rug in the middle of the floor that covered almost half the room. His desk was a large oak wood antique that looked like it was from the 1900's. His desk faced the entrance to his office. On each side of the entrance he had two widescreen TV's that were on the business or world news channels with the volume down low. The walls were decorated with pictures of himself posed with past presidents and dignitaries.

As soon as I walked in the office, I noticed he was alone. His son was nowhere to be seen. I didn't know if that was a good or bad sign, but I didn't dwell on it too long. He offered me one of the two seats in front of his desk. I sat down in front of him and without any hesitation or prelude, he said, "The job is yours!"

Now was the time to deliver! I wasted no time putting my plan into action. I contacted Darrell, Big Mike, and Charles and told them to give their two week notices. But a two week notice was not needed for Big Mike since he was between jobs. He caught the red eye that night. I pulled Tim over from the convertible desk and, as promised, made him head of research and analysis.

Two weeks later Charles and Darrell arrived on the scene. Big Mike was staying with me in the Brownstone because he didn't want corporate housing. I offered corporate housing to Darrell and Charles and they declined, too, and opted to stay with me in the brownstone until they could become acclimated and learn their way around the city. The brownstone was plenty big enough for all of us, and we felt that it might be best to share the same space, given the enormous challenges that lay ahead. Under the same roof, we could have middle of the night strategic meetings or early morning meetings, which we called war room meetings. The dream we had talked about in grad school, we were now living.

My team consisted of myself, Managing Director; Tim, Head of Research and Analysis; Charles, Head of Trading; Darrell, Head of Sales; Big Mike, Sales Executive and Analyst; and Ted, Sales Executive. The first day all of us were on the trading desk, I called for a closed door meeting to make sure they understood the direction I wanted to take the desk in and the challenges we must overcome to accomplish my objectives. It was imperative that everyone shared my vision and everyone's actions were in tune and harmony with the bigger picture. We met in the small conference room right outside the trading room.

"All eyes are on us and the bets are against us making it, but the executives of GPG don't know the character and drive of the people who sit in this room. They don't know the abilities of each of you and that you will work non-stop to make this desk a success, realizing our goals and dreams. I looked at Tim. "Tim, they don't know or care about what you went through on that convertible desk during your first three years at GPG, and they don't have an inkling of your ability as a researcher or economist. I know you will outperform any of the economists in the firm. I didn't bring you over because you are my friend. I brought you over because I know you are the best, and with this opportunity, you will be able to prove me right. I plan on putting together a daily newsletter on our thoughts about the fixed income market, and you will head that up." I patted him on the back, and then turned my attention to Charles.

"Charles!" He looked up at me. "You are a genius with numbers. You know how these fixed income instruments trade in different market environments, from domestic to international. We will follow your lead with any trading information you provide and include a technical analysis feature in our weekly."

I continued my pattern. "Darrell, you are Head of Sales. You are a gifted salesperson, and I've known that since our days at Jordan. I've never seen a better salesperson in my life, and I want you to share that talent by training the salespeople we bring on board. Now, when I call you the best, I mean that. There is no better salesman that I know and that includes Ted."

Everyone was surprised by my statement, even Ted had a look of dismay. "But, I would have to say there is no better man than Ted. I have never met anyone more giving, honest, and bull shit free than Ted, and I want all of you to know this opportunity for all of us would not be available without Ted. Now, on the subject of Ted, he has free will, and reports to no one on the desk, not even me. We are in partnership. He is my confidant and mentor, to whom I have great respect and admiration. He will continue in his capacity as a sales executive, but he will have influence in the direction of the desk. Last, but not least, Big Mike, I have huge plans for you. You are of good character and have a great personality that resonates with everyone. Your legal background and analytical mind will serve the desk well in the company's underwriting endeavors for existing and new companies. I want you to work with Darrell in sales and Tim in research and analysis, but I also want you to take the lead along with me in working with the underwriting group in raising capital for new and existing companies via debt issuances. In conclusion, I want to thank all of you for taking this journey with me, and I promise you, I will do everything in my ability to provide the tools, training, and information to make us successful."

After my little speech, everyone, respectively, took turns telling what the opportunity meant to him. Each thanked me for inviting him along on the journey. It was truly gratifying to hear each of them express confidence in me and my vision. The most moving words came from Big Mike.

"When I met Shane, Charles, and Darrel in grad school, the fact of me being a convicted felon had already circulated around campus. But Shane offered me his friendship, and Darrell and Charles followed his lead. That offering of camaraderie came at the right time for me because I was on the verge of throwing in the towel by not finishing up my MBA. Right then I knew you, Shane, were a person of integrity and compassion. Through you brotha, I think those qualities are shaping and refining my character. Shane, you exude leadership, and I would follow you into battle any day of the week. You've been there for me more than anyone, and this opportunity is just another example. I was feeling I'd be under employed forever, before I received your call about the potential opportunity with you on Wall Street. Thank you, my brother."

When Mike finished, I almost broke down. It took all my strength to hold back my tears to hear such kind words of appreciation about a friendship that I really cherished. Big Mike then walked over and gave me a pound and a hug. He was really pushing me to the edge of tears, but by the grace of God, I was able to hold back.

We adjourned the meeting and went back to the desk. I had a total of five people on the desk and that included me. So I knew my next big task was to staff the trading desk with smart, competent professionals, but I had made my mind up that I wouldn't take the traditional route of most trading desks.

The first step was to make contact with human resources and hand pick the HR representative that I wanted to work with. I wasted no time, and after our staff meeting I went straight to HR to talk to someone about recruitment. I was met by Diane Peters, the head of HR. We discussed some HR representatives that had traditionally worked with the Fixed Income Trading Desk. I politely rejected them, telling her the fixed income desk was blazing a new trail, and I would like someone who hadn't been involved with the desk in the past. I actually had a woman (who was African American) in mind, but I had never spoken to her. I had seen her around the office from time to time. I described her to Diane, and asked could she be available to speak with me. Diane called her on the phone immediately and asked if she had time to talk with me. The woman I was seeking was Betty Johnson. We made an appointment for the following morning. Betty sounded very mature and professional over the speakerphone. From what I could remember Betty was around 5'7", a brown skinned sista, well dressed, and appeared to be in her early thirties, but with sistas' you can never tell, so I guessed she was late 30's, early 40's. She had a very conservative look about her and a good reputation in the firm. She did the recruiting for the convertible and the equity desks. She had recruited Tim into GPG from Harvard.

I arrived in her office ten minutes before our appointment at 9:00 am. When she walked into her office around 8:55, she was surprised to see me. I think, I actually startled her, but she kept her composure.

"Mr. Jackson, you are a little early for our 9 o'clock."

"Yes, I wanted us to take our meeting outside and maybe get some lattes at the coffee shop down the way."

"Why is that? My office will not suffice?"

"For our first meeting, no. I would like to make this less formal and get to know you a little, so we can relax and chat without interruptions. I think the best place to do that is outside of these corporate walls and where we can enjoy some fresh air. Are you okay with that?" She was a little hesitant and her body language showed her discomfort. "Look, don't take this the wrong way, I'm not trying to get at you or anything like that. I'm just new to this MD position and I would like to have a good working relationship with my HR representative. I'm of the opinion that if we get to know each other a little better, our relationship can be more productive."

"I wouldn't disagree with that Mr. Jackson, but it is highly unorthodox for us to take our first meeting outside of the office, but if you think it is necessary then I will join you for a latte."

Now, considering her reluctance, I'm thinking she may not fit into my plans. Nevertheless, we both proceeded to go outside for our first meeting. As we left the office for the elevators, she told the HR receptionist she would be out the office for the next hour. If needed, she could be reached on her Blackberry. We both were silent on the elevator. We stepped outside into a crisp sunny New York morning. Betty waited to see what direction we were going. We turned left and headed toward the coffee house just a few blocks away. I asked, "So, Betty how long have you been at GPG?"

"This September will be my ten year anniversary."

The fresh air and a walk seemed to change her tone from a defensive one to one more gentle.

"Wow ten years!" I paused and smiled at her. "What do they give you after ten years, a gold watch?"

"Yes, I think it's something along those lines."

"Are you from New York?"

"No I'm from Mississippi."

"Aw, a southern woman, I should have known. Do you miss the South?"

"Sometimes, but I still have family down there, and I get back home at least once a year. What about you? Where you from?"

"From L.A."

"Are you kidding?" She had a surprised look.

"No!"

We arrived at the coffee shop. We walked in and ordered lattes, and found seats in the back of the coffee shop at a table where we couldn't be easily seen by entering patrons. When I stood at the table and pulled out a chair, she had a quizzical look on her face.

"Thank you," she said and took a seat.

"Now, why are you so surprised that I'm from L.A.?"

"Because you strike me as a New Yorker, from your dress, your demeanor, your drive, and your attitude."

"What do you mean by my attitude?" I said smiling.

"Don't take that the wrong way. It's just that most New Yorkers, especially on Wall Street, are convinced, and you carry yourself like that."

"Convinced?"

"Yes, convinced. Convinced that they are better, that they are winners, and confident they are second to none."

"I come off that way?"

"Very much so, like our appointment this morning. You decided in your mind, you wanted to hold this meeting outside the office, and you were convinced I would agree with you." She paused and smiled at me. "Am I right?"

"Maybe!" We both were silent, taking sips of our lattes. "Where did you go to school?"

"I did my undergraduate work at Spellman, and then got my graduate degree at Harvard. You went to Darden. Then did your grad work at Jordan."

"Pulled my employee file, huh?"

"You bet. I wanted to know something about the person who didn't want to work with their assigned HR rep and was seeking me out as a possible replacement. So, Mr. Jackson just what are you seeking in an HR Rep?"

"Well, I'm looking for someone I can build a working relationship with."

"You could have done that with the rep that was assigned to your desk."

"Yea, probably, but I'm looking for someone to share my vision, and I don't think the assigned rep would have shared or understood exactly where I'm coming from."

"And, you think I will share in your vision?"

"I'm not sure, but that's why we are here." I looked at her intently. I could tell my looking at her that way made her uneasy because she broke eye contact and took a sip of her latte. Then, she looked up at me and hit me with the burning question that begged to be answered.

"What is your vision, Mr. Jackson?"

"Well, before we get into my vision, let me ask you a question." She looked at me intently. "Why did you choose to go to Spellman to do your undergraduate work?"

"I wanted the experience of attending an African American college."

"And, how was your experience?"

"It was great! I wouldn't trade it in for anything."

"And, why did you choose to go Ivy League for your graduate work?"

"Well, to be totally honest with you, I felt the black college experience was nice, but in reality the business world perceives degrees from black colleges as a lower grade education, and I wanted to balance that perception to squash any questions about my qualifications."

"Do you think you received an inferior education at Spellman?"

"No, not at all!" She sat up, moved closer to the table, and replied with more conviction. "I don't share the same perception as the business world, especially since I've participated in the black college education system. I would have to say, my education at Spellman prepared me for the business world better than my Ivy

League school experience. One thing about the black college experience, it prepares you to compete and succeed against the odds. You can attest to that from your experience at Jordan. Am I right?"

"Yes, you are right. My education there was invaluable."

"Is that the reason for the out of the office meeting and targeting me as your HR Rep.?"

"Yes, I would like to add historical black colleges to the list of schools GPG recruits from for the Fixed Income Desk."

"When I first got here ten years ago, GPG developed this outreach program to historical black colleges that I headed, but every time I brought in candidates they wouldn't make it past the first round of interviews. And, I have to say the Fix Income Desk was the worst. They were even less civil to women. The program was eventually phased out and I was relegated to the convertible desk, working with that jackass bigot, Vince." She paused, realizing what she had just opened up and shared her real feelings and disgust.

Putting her mind at ease, I said, "Don't worry, what you say here is between me and you, and I promise I will not repeat it to anyone! I wanted both of us to be able to speak freely, which is why I wanted to get together outside your office."

"I appreciate that. Do you want me to head up the recruitment efforts of black colleges exclusively?"

"No, I want you to head up the entire recruitment effort, and I want you to add black colleges to our search for talent. You think you can handle that."

"Oh, yes!" She was interested, on board, and very perked up. "I appreciate the opportunity to work with you and help in your efforts to re-build the desk. I have a great admiration for what you are trying to do. Most people, when they make it, especially on Wall Street, never look back to give a helping hand to others."

"Well, I'm not one of them. My goal is not only to build a successful fixed income trading desk, but to give qualified African Americans opportunities that in other circumstances would not be offered."

"That is a commendable goal, but I must tell you, you have already raised many eyebrows with your recent hires."

"Really?" I said in a calm, but curious voice. I leaned in closer to get more color. Betty did the same speaking intimately and covertly.

"What I hear is that they have a watchful eye on you, and after your recent hires, the watchful eye has become a microscope. GPG has never had a black MD, let alone a desk with all key positions staffed by black men. There is concern by some of the top people in the firm. The word is, if you even stumble out of the blocks, you and your team will be eliminated immediately."

"Where did you get this information from?"

"Dorris, she is one of the Senior HR Reps."

"Why would she divulge this information to you?"

"She is my mentor and responsible for my working as an HR Rep with GPG. She knew we were meeting this morning and thought you could benefit from this information."

"Why would she want to help me?"

"She was in the conference room when you gave your presentation. She thinks you are a phenomenal young man with great charisma. After the presentation, she came back with nothing but praises for you. I also think she's been on Wall Street a long time and knows how," she raised her hands up to gesture quotes, "the good old boys' club works."

"I don't know Dorris. Is she black or white?"

"She's white."

"Knowing this information, are you comfortable with carrying out my plan for recruiting?"

"Yes, I'm comfortable, and to be totally honest, as a HR Rep, I just follow the directions of the MD, and act as your first line of screening. So in other words, my career will not be put in jeopardy." She paused, "If you are eliminated."

I smiled and chuckled at her. "I appreciate the information and your honesty."

We finished our conversation and ordered two more lattes to go. Betty's candor was refreshing and made me feel at ease with my decision to work with her as my HR Rep, which was a large piece of my plan. She could prove more valuable than imagined, especially with her relationship with Dorris. I already knew heads were going to turn when I brought everyone in, so raised eyebrows came as no surprise. It looked like they had me on a short rope, but no worries. All I needed was the rope, no matter how short it was, I would make it work.

Later that night I called our first war meeting at the house with Tim conferenced in by phone. I reiterated the conversation I had had with Betty, and let them know she would be a part of our team as our HR rep. Darrell and Charles voiced some concern, but I told them to be realistic about the situation. Given that we are practically an all black staff in a predominantly white owned company, and directing one of the most prestigious desks in the entire firm, we could expect to be held to a different and higher standard. Our situation was also unique in the way this opportunity had come about. Above all else, I told them, this was about the pride of Mr. Mackey. He wanted his track record unblemished before he transitioned to partner, and a rebounding of this desk would be a feather in his cap. And, if we could resurrect the desk from ruin, then we could write our own ticket. It was a hell of a challenge, but there was no doubt in my mind that we were up to the challenge. Bottom line, regardless of race, was making money, and we were primed to do just that!

After screening candidates for weeks, Betty had our first ten candidates lined up: three were traders with market experience from other firms; one African- American male, one Caucasian male, and one Italian American female, five sales people with experience from other firms; two African Americans, a male and female and three Caucasian males, two research analysts, both with limited experience but with MBA's from top schools; one African American female, and one Irish American male. Betty did an excellent job of finding quality talent to staff the desk. Three out of the ten candidates had MBA's from historically black colleges. I interviewed all candidates and they interviewed with the respective heads of their areas of expertise.

After Charles interviewed his candidates he was most impressed with the African American candidate for the trading position. I agreed with Charles that this candidate interviewed well, and had the background and experience that made him the best for what we were trying to do. For Tim, it was a tossup between two candidates; both were impressive during their interviews. He wanted to hire both of them, but we only had a need for one more analyst, with Big Mike's services at Tim's disposal as an analyst. Tim finally went with the African American female for his hire; I thought the decision was a good one. Darrell wanted to hire three out of the five candidates. He liked both of the African American candidates because they had good experience, and he liked one of the WASPs because he said his book was impressive. I agreed with him for the most part, but the WASP seemed to be self centered and self serving. We had him come in again for another interview and included Ted this time. Ted agreed with me that the candidate was 'small minded' as Ted put it. Darrell and I decided to go with the other two and leave him out. So, we had four new hires. They all happened to be African Americans. We all were satisfied with them, so I prepared the list for Betty to send out offer letters to each.

I emailed the list of candidates we wanted to hire to Betty. Not more than five minutes passed before I received an email from Betty asking me to come to her office. I made my way to her office and knocked on the door. She told me to come in. Once I entered, she asked me to close the door behind me. Betty had that same look of trepidation on her face.

"I received your list of hires." She looked at me in dismay. "You do know what you are doing and how much attention you will attract with these candidates?"

I was very calm, cool, and collected with my response to her question. "I can't concern myself with the attention I may get with these new employees. I am focused on putting the best professionals on my trading desk for the mission and goals of, not only the desk, but the company at large."

"And, all the black candidates met that criterion, but none of the others?"

"Yes, it just happened to turn out that way this time. The next round of hiring might be totally different. We'll just have to wait and see. By the way, when will you have some more candidates?"

"In about two weeks," she replied. Her look of dismay changed to cautious trust. "I sure hope you know what you are doing?"

'Don't worry, I have everything under control."

Betty's demeanor and body language told me she was more than concerned about my choices. As long as my choices added to the bottom line, there was nothing to fear. I was comfortable with the process and the candidates were high caliber and outstanding quality. Regardless of race, creed, or color the bottom line was producing, and I felt in my heart, in my mind, and because of my experience these new additions to the desk would be producers if given the chance.

Before our next round of interviews, we hired two more people; one person on the trading desk who was a referral from

Charles; the other, on the sales desk, which was referred by Darrell. Each of the candidates was a black male who used to work with Charles and Darrell at their previous company. Charles and Darrel both were concerned with their referrals being black. I assured them the only thing that mattered was their contribution to the earnings of the desk. If they did that, no one would or could question the decision to hire them. I told them we needed to get away from the subliminal quota for the number of black people we could hire. We were going to hire the best professionals that fit in with what we are trying to accomplish. If they all were black, then so be it.

After we made the official offer to Charles' and Darrel's referrals, I got a phone call on the desk from Junior's secretary, requesting my presence in his office immediately.

Once I arrived in his office, I saw that his face was beet red. He was breathing heavily, pacing the floor. He didn't have his suit coat on, so I could see the perspiration seeping through his white cotton dress shirt. Except for his hair, he didn't look like his usual self, not one hair was out of place. He looked at me with disdain as I stood in the doorway. He voiced his disgust by yelling at the top of his voice.

"What the fuck do you think you are doing? We are not building a basketball team or running a rib shack. I knew we made a mistake when we hired you as an MD. My father and I are the laughing stock of this firm. We gave you an opportunity and look what you give us in return, a desk that is better equipped to play in the NFL than to work on Wall Street."

His front office door was still open, so everyone could hear every single racist word that was coming from his mouth. Judging from his volume, he didn't care. I stood there, quiet and quite unfretted by his offensive statements.

"First, I resent the racial slurs that you are hurling at me on a consistent basis."

He responded quickly with the same reckless abandon. "Fuck You!"

I didn't let his profanity get to me. I continued with my explanation. "Second, I am following the plan I described in my presentation. I haven't deviated from that plan at all. As far as I'm concern we are on track to do great things."

"Great things? You just told a joke!"

"Where's your father? Maybe this conversation would be more productive if we included him."

"You don't worry about where my father is. He told me to deal with you because he is so disgusted, he can't stand to look at you."

Junior was starting to get to me. Now, if I were to walk up to him and punch him dead in the face, the police would charge me with assault and haul me out the building in cuffs. I knew that could have been part of Junior's plan. So, I continued to play it cool.

"If your father feels that way, given your display here in your office, the both of you are way off base in terms of my intentions for the desk."

"Oh please! Any blind man can see what you are up to."

"And, what might that be, Junior?"

Junior rushed towards me, stopped just a couple feet short of my face and let out another tirade.

"You don't ever call me Junior. It's Mr. Mackey to you. What gives you the audacity to call me Junior? Contrary to belief, you are expendable, and at this point I don't care if Ted walks out behind you. You had better think real long and hard about what you are doing and if it is worth your career. Now, get out of my face!"

Get out of his face? He was getting past the point of ignorance and bordering on insanity. I left his office without another word and went back to the desk as if the conversation had never happened.

The next day I got a call from Betty. In a concerned voice, she requested a meeting with me after work. She didn't want to have the meeting anywhere near the office. I suggested my home and even offered to cook a meal so that our stomachs wouldn't grumble during our meeting. She asked if it would be okay to bring her son over because she had to pick him up from her mother's after work. I told her, I would love to meet her son. We set our meeting time around 8:00 pm.

Betty wanted to meet outside of the office, which was somewhat of a surprise. She had something really heavy to reveal. Her concerned tone didn't really sound empathetic to my plight. I got the funny feeling that her concern was more for herself. The last thing I wanted to do was put her career in jeopardy. If she wanted out at this junction, I would have understood and allowed her to bow out graciously. I really had grown fond of Betty. She was very good at detecting and recruiting talent. I really thought she was one of the best in the firm, and no one recognized that but me.

Betty arrived at eight o'clock on the dot. I finished up the pasta dish and put the garlic bread in the oven. Darrell let Betty in, took her and her son's coats and led them to the dining area. Big Mike set the table and Charles picked a bottle of Merlot from the wine cabinet for dinner. We all sat down at the dinner table to eat, but we had to get a phone book for her son, Jerrod, to sit on because he was only six and could barely see over the table when he sat down without the phone book.

Betty looked nervous and her first words sounded as much.

"I thought we were going to have dinner alone?"

"Right now it's difficult to have dinner alone at my home while I have three roommates," I replied. "But, you can speak freely at the table … unless you think your son may divulge our conversation to GPG." Big Mike and Charles chuckled.

"If you are comfortable having this conversation, then I'm comfortable."

I gestured to Betty to move ahead with what she wanted to tell me.

"I've been requested by my boss, Larri, to turn over all files related to the latest recruitment of candidates for the Fixed Income Desk to Mr. Mackey and his son."

I didn't reply, and neither did anyone else. Betty's face was flushed with even more concern as she looked about the table.

"They have also requested to privately question me about the Fixed Income's recruitment and hiring policy.

Still no words were spoken by anyone; you could only hear silverware clanking against plates while everyone ate. Out of frustration, Betty shouted.

"Shane, you are not concerned with these recent developments?"

Everyone at the table was waiting for my response. I responded calmly.

"No, not at all. I should have informed you that this might be coming down the pipe, but I didn't expect it so soon. I thought they would at least wait until I had completed my first quarter as MD on the desk."

Betty stared at me with surprise and curiosity.

"Are you telling me you knew this was coming and you were not worried about such scutiny?"

"Yes." I nodded in the affirmative.

"You don't think there is a need for concern?"

"No, do you?"

"Yes."

"Why?"

"Your entire trading desk is black, and that's what's driving them up the walls."

Everyone at the table laughed. Big Mike and Charles especially let it all hang out. I thought they were going to choke on their food.

"This is not a laughing matter. You think they are going to believe that this is all a coincidence? Not likely," Betty responded to the laughter

Darrell gathered himself and responded to Betty.

"Betty, in this situation, all Shane did was to turn to people he knew and trusted to help him get this trading desk back on track. The people he turned to were professionals that have the knowledge and experience in his areas of need. No one in their right mind can claim some kind of conspiracy on our part."

"What about the new hires out of the pool of candidates I gave you all?"

I jumped back into the conversation.

"We hired the most qualified and best suited candidates that we felt would help us meet our objectives on the desk, and those objectives translate into profitability. Betty, listen to me, we have done nothing wrong. I would not put you in a compromising position where you would have to lie about our hiring practices or policy on the trading desk. Our hiring policy is consistent with the overall policy of the GPG. When they call you in for questioning, you answer each question honestly and truthfully and you will have nothing to worry about."

Charles put in his two cents.

"Yea, Betty there's nothing to worry about. You can tell them, hey I sent them clowns ten candidates, and the majority of those candidates were white. It's out of my control if they are trying to build a team to win the company's basketball tournament."

Charles let out a howl right after his statement, and we all laughed. We even got a chuckle and a smile out of Betty. I hadn't shared with anyone the conversation I'd had with Junior in his office, and they didn't know Charles' satire closely mimicked the sentiments of Junior. I didn't think at that time they needed to know. I wanted them to stay focused on our objectives and visions for the desk. I could handle everything else.

I cut through the laughter at the table. "Now Betty, please finish your dinner before it gets too cold. I didn't slave over the stove for the food to go to waste."

Betty began to eat her dinner. We changed the subject, and Betty got better acquainted with Darrel, Big Mike, and Earl. I could see that Betty was more comfortable now. She was engaging, laughing, and smiling more. I really wasn't going to lose any sleep over the request to review all the applications for employment; we had followed the hiring policy of GPG to the letter. The only change was that we expanded our recruiting to include black colleges, and in my opinion brought GPG closer to a true equal opportunity employer.

11

Year of Change

Our quarter numbers were in, and for that three month period, the fixed income desk wasn't in its usual spot at the top in profitability, compared to the other desk. But, given that we were less than fully staffed, we showed signs of potential. I was proud of that fact and our overall performance was solid. Charles was implementing some terrific trading strategies that were increasing our profit spreads on each sale and reducing the amount of interest rate exposure our inventory had to the market. Darrel was making miracles happen with his sales staff. As a group, they were bringing in solid new clients that were doing size and volume. Tim developed a market research report and analysis that really resonated with our clients and had been stirring up a buzz on Wall Street. The other staff, sales, trading, and research, all turned out to be solid performers.

The only concern I had was Big Mike. He hadn't brought in any new business and actually, some of our existing clients were complaining about his knowledge and service. I knew his strength was analytics, and I seriously considered making him a full time analyst, but Tim and Big Mike were not the best of friends and even more, their professional relationship was becoming combative and disruptive to the desk. Consequently, I had other plans for Big Mike, but I had to make him see the bigger picture of this move. I waited until we were in the privacy of our home, while Darrel and Charles were not around. We both were in the den watching Sports Center. I turned the volume down low and leaned in to the conversation.

"Big Mike, how are you feeling so far about your position on the desk?"

He looked up at me with a slight puzzled look on his face. "What do you mean how do I feel?"

"Are you happy with what you are doing?"

"I'm happy that I'm working with you, Darrel, and Charles?"

"That's not my question." I repeated my question once again. "Are you happy with what you are doing on the desk?"

"Shane, what's with the questions? I'm happy. Did you get another complaint about me from a client?"

"No, I didn't, but I'm concerned about my decision to put you into a position that may have not been the best for you."

Big Mike could see my seriousness, and he became a little tense. "Man, I'm doing my best. It's just that I'm not that pretentious, so when I'm disturbed by what someone might say to me, it shows."

"What are people saying to you that gives rise to a reaction that may be considered aggressive?"

"It's the little bullshit, like when clients greet me with "What's up brotha" I'm not their brotha, and I resent the fact that they're comfortable saying that to me." His voice got more intense. "Or when they meet me in person and try to give me a dap instead of a regular handshake. I'm not going to roll like that. I consider that bullshit. They have this image of the black man and they think all black men must cater to their narrow vision or image. And, I just want to let them know, I'm not the one."

I shook my head, letting him know I knew where he was coming from. "Big Mike, it's part of the game, and we have to play it in order to succeed."

"We don't have to do shit, but stay true to ourselves."

I shook my head in disagreement while I let out a chuckle. "That's true if we look at it from a human standpoint, but we want to take a business perspective. When we do that, then the playing field becomes clear and in focus. It's the white man's game, and the rules were set up and established long before we were allowed to play. For us to play Mike, we have to endure some inequities and slights that hopefully will change in time. Take for example, Jackie Robinson. He had to endure all kinds of racial slurs and racist treatment to play and succeed as the first black man in major league baseball. And, we have to take a page from his book and apply it to the world of finance."

Big Mike became more pensive. "I guess you're right, but man it's hard to take this bullshit with a smile. I feel like I'm an Uncle Tom."

"Man, everyone knows, you of all people are not an Uncle Tom. Remember this Big Mike, you have to win the game in order to change the way it's played."

"Yea man, I know what you mean," he said in a somber tone.

I took a good look at him and slid closer to him on the couch. "I want to remove you from sales and analysis all together." He sat up, intensity in his eyes.

"You firing me, man!" he said in a surprised and loud voice.

"Calm down, no I have something else in mind for you that will be essential to our survival in this game."

"What do you want me to do?"

"It involves sales and negotiations."

"Sales?"

"Not the kind of selling you are thinking about, but the kind of selling that is right down your alley, and with your legal background this will be a perfect match."

He looked at me with intrigue now. I explained that this assignment would involve some traveling, and as I laid out my vision and the details of the assignment, his eyes lit up with excitement. When I was finished, we both stood and gave each other a dap and a hug. Big Mike was overwhelmed and told me he wouldn't let me down. I knew he wouldn't and that's why I chose him for this position. There was one other thing I told Big Mike.

"This position and assignment has to stay just between me and you. I don't even want Darrel and Charles to know anything about this."

"Why don't you want Charles and Darrel to know? You know the four of us don't get down like that."

"Yes, I know, but I have my reasons, you just have to trust me on this one. Anyway I would like them to stay focused on the task at hand."

"Okay, Shane, I'm with you." He gave me another dap. "When do you want me to start?"

"Immediately, I notified HR of your change in position and your new title as VP of International Relations."

"I like that title, VP of International Relations."

I hadn't seen Big Mike this happy since he arrived in New York. It was good to see, and this was an assignment he could really sink his teeth into and show off his talents, which I know he possessed.

The following week I made the announcement on the desk about Big Mike's change in position and assignment. I was vague enough to totally convince everyone that I was putting him in a dead end job. Even Darrel and Charles pulled me to the side privately and voiced their concern about Big Mike's new position. I assured them, that I wasn't dumping Big Mike into never land. When the time was right I would reveal my plan to them. The move was a strategic one that I wasn't ready to reveal to anyone, but the person who was to be directly involved. Ted mentioned the decision to me also, but didn't object to the move because he felt Big Mike was struggling. Ted thought putting Big Mike in a position with less exposure to the critical profit components on the desk was wise, but he thought it would be even wiser just to let him go.

Ted and I had weekly meetings to go over the critical areas that were essential to the success of the desk. We usually grabbed an available conference room. These meetings were invaluable. I looked forward to them almost as much as I looked forward to my war room meetings with Darrel, Charles, Mike, and Tim at the House. These meetings also gave Ted and me a chance to connect and gave him a chance to check with me, making sure my head and direction were in the right place. .

"Shane, how are you holding up?"

"Good, a lot of hours and a little stress have impacted my relationship with Kendra, but nothing I can't handle."

"Kendra's a lovely young lady, but I think she understands what you are trying to accomplish and the challenges ahead."

"Yea, she does, but she's still affected by the lack of time I have to spend with her."

"Keep the lines of communication open and it will work itself out."

"You're right. That's the key, open lines of communication. Anyway, enough about my relationship. What are your thoughts about how the desk is progressing?"

"I think you are building a solid foundation and you have some smart people around you who are innovative in their thinking and highly motivated to make money. I don't think I have ever seen a more aggressive and hungry, and I mean that in the best of ways, group of professionals in my experience on Wall Street."

"I'm glad you approve."

"To be truthful with you, Shane, I had my doubts, so I took the liberty to review the file of every candidate you interviewed and hired, and one thing, maybe two things jumped out. One: They all were African Americans. Two: All came from meager backgrounds and all overcame substantial obstacles to get where they are at today." Ted adjusted his position and leaned in closer. "I do have to say, I'm a little apprehensive that out of the ten candidates none of the non African American candidates were hired, and some of their backgrounds were very similar to the ones hired. You only hired four out of that pool of ten, and there were at least eight that were qualified to work on the desk. What is going on?"

"There's nothing going on. The candidates I hired out of that pool were the people who basically had nothing and made something out of their lives. They were not strangers to struggling and making something out of nothing. The others definitely possessed qualities to be successful, but this desk is starting from the bottom, and I want people on the desk who know what it's like to start from the bottom and build. The other key consideration is, I want to keep the numbers small for now to build my foundation and nucleus, and let them grow and strengthen together before we bring anyone else on the desk. If the foundation is solid, we can build to the highest of heights."

Ted sat back in his chair and looked at me, as if studying me. We both were silent for at least a minute. Then, I asked,

"Are you still with me Ted?"

"Yes, I'm still with you, Shane, but I must warn you. If you are trying to make some type of political or social statement, don't do it! Steer clear of that type of stuff because it just muddies the waters."

I understood Ted's position, especially since he was the most non political person I've ever met. He had a genuine disdain for politics and games. Once he sat me down and told me a few stories about when he first started out on Wall Street; how he wanted to climb the corporate ladder, how his ambition and drive wrecked close friendships and cost him his first wife. He had been totally immersed in making it to executive management level and wanted to eat and rub elbows with political figures and world dignitaries. After eight years on Wall Street, he had reached his goal as Executive Management of Global Fixed Income Markets. At the same time, his first wife left him, and he said it was the most miserable time in his life.

He said, he went through a deep depression and didn't start to come out of it until he resigned and took a year off. During that respite, he reflected on himself as a person, and didn't like the type of man he had become. During his first eight years on Wall Street he did everything it took to advance. That included lying, backstabbing, and breaking SEC rules and regulations all in the name of being successful on Wall Street. So it was then he vowed to make a change, not only to be a better businessman, but also a better man. He met his second wife, had two kids and became one of the top salesmen on Wall Street.

Ted had been invaluable to my career, and he had put his reputation on the line for me to secure the MD position, but I had a higher vision and purpose, and if it cost me a high price I was willing to pay the price.

Another three months passed and our numbers were in. This gave us a full half year of the desk being together, and my plan was bearing fruit. The desk moved up to third place in terms of profitability. The nucleus of the desk was really coming together and running like a fine tuned engine. The camaraderie on the desk was exceptionally high. The new employees were productive and fit in well.

A culture of camaraderie developed because of the relationships between myself, Ted, Darrell, Charles, and Tim, and cultivated itself amongst the other professionals on the desk. Everyone was eager to come into work because they genuinely liked the people they worked with. But most of all, they all bought into the vision of returning the desk back to its top position as number one desk.

The only missing piece was Big Mike. I kept him on the road traveling, and his schedule was hectic, but much to my surprise he enjoyed the work more than working on Wall Street. He was making good headway towards the objectives we had set forth. His position and duties became more blurred as time passed, and I was constantly questioned about his traveling expenses by Management. I just told them he was opening up new markets and dividends from his work would be paid in due time.

Because the numbers were in I knew it was only a matter of time before Mr. Mackey and Junior would want a sit down with me. Especially since they had to realize the desk was moving forward. They had left me alone pretty much for the quarter; we had only brief interactions by phone and email.

When the call came, I was on the trading desk. Mr. Mackey's secretary said management wanted to meet with me after hours in Mr. Mackey's office. I agreed, and my mind raced quickly to Betty, so I called her up.

"Betty, what's up?"

"Hey, Shane, congratulations. I saw your quarter numbers, and they were impressive. Larri says you are creating quite a buzz as a new MD and a lot of people are starting to pay attention."

"Betty, congratulations to you also. If it hadn't been for you bringing in quality candidates, those numbers would not have been at the level they are at. I will make it a point to send out an email to Larri and Mr. Mackey commending you on your efforts to help me overcome the crisis on the fixed income desk, and how you have proven to be a valuable tool and an essential part of our success."

"Shane, that would be greatly appreciated."

"That's the least I could do for all your hard work. But, let me get to the reason for my call."

"Uh huh, go right ahead."

"Whatever came about with the review of the candidates that we brought in?"

"As far as I know, nothing. I gave the Mackeys all my files pertaining to all candidates brought in for interviews, and that was that. I never heard anything after that and it's almost been five months ago."

"Really?"

"Yes, I think it was like you said, we didn't break any hiring policies during the process and the bottom line is that you are making money now, so they might have thrown it by the way side."

"Okay, Betty. I appreciate the feedback. I'll get back with you later."

I thought it was strange that Betty hadn't heard anything about the review of our hiring procedures and policy. One would think the Mackeys would have some type of follow up with us either confirming that we were in compliance with GPG's hiring policies or we were in non-compliance. Either way, it would have given us valuable feedback and guidance, unless Betty was withholding information and feedback from the review from me. She had been pretty nervous when the files were requested. The Mackeys might have gotten her in a room and threatened her indirectly. Betty was a single parent with an eight year old son and a mortgage. Job security was number one on her golden list, but she'd had less job security before I gave her the opportunity to work on the Fixed Income desk. I hope her loyalties were in the right place.

I arrived in Mr. Mackey's office just before 6:00 p.m. He and Junior were looking at his computer screen and discussing something that was on it. . Senior was sitting down behind his desk and Junior was to the right of him, behind the desk, pointing at something on the monitor. I tapped on the door, which was already open. Mr. Mackey gestured for me to come in. I walked in and took a seat. They continued to chat between themselves in very low voices. I couldn't really make out what they were talking about, but there was no doubt in my mind that it was somehow related to me. About five minutes went by without their saying a word to me. When Mr. Mackey spoke, however, he congratulated me on my quarter numbers and said he wanted to talk in more detail about the numbers. As Mr. Mackey and I got into the numbers, Junior didn't say a word. He just watched in silence.

Given our last conversation, I'm surprised Junior didn't start on another one of his rants about me hiring a basketball team. I wasn't sure if he'd shared that conversation with his Dad, but Mr. Mackey had never brought up the topic to me. One thing I knew about Mr. Mackey, he was a bottom line person. If you were a producer, he wouldn't have any qualms with you, but if you didn't contribute to his bottom line, he'd just as well get rid of you. He was a stickler for the numbers, and as good as my numbers were, even with my limited staff, Mr. Mackey still had complaints about certain areas of the desk. Like He thought Tim could handle the research desk by himself and didn't need another analyst in that area. Besides, the company had a bigger research team that could give Tim ample support for any additional research or analysis he needed. I told Mr. Mackey that was true but the company wide research area was spread thin, and with clients relying on our research and advice we needed the added resources to support them without any delays. I reminded him of the limited resources.

He nodded in agreement, but his facial expression told me he wasn't completely convinced. Then, he hit me with Big Mike's expense report. He didn't understand why Big Mike was traveling to countries and markets where GPG didn't have clients. I explained that his activities were a part of my vision for the desk, and my plan was for growth. This included new markets and clients in non-traditional or unfamiliar areas. It would take some time to bear fruit, but in the long run it would pay off. I was vague on details, which Mr. Mackey didn't appreciate.

"I'll give you another year with this position, but if it doesn't start showing promise then it will be eliminated."

"Understood," I responded.

Then Junior finally spoke. "What are your plans about interns this summer?"

"I don't have any. I want to keep the staff numbers at status quo for another year. If I can keep this group together and focus on helping them reach their maximum potential then any new addition after the fact will not only benefit from my guidance, but the guidance of the desk as a whole."

Mr. Mackey chimed in. "I think that is a good plan."

"But, Dad," Junior quickly responded to his father's statement. "James is on summer break from NYU and wants to do a summer internship on the Fixed Income Desk. This would do wonders for his experience, let alone look good on his resume."

"Yes, you are right!" Mr. Mackey responded. "I didn't know he was interested in Fixed Income. He always talks about stocks."

"That's true, but some exposure to Fixed Income would only help his understanding of the markets."

"True," Mr. Mackey said.

Then, I interrupted their exchange. "Who is James?"

Junior quickly responded with authority. "He's my nephew and my father's grandson. And he will be your summer intern on the desk."

"These are critical times and there is a lot at stake, and I don't have time to baby sit."

"Baby sit!" His voice rose.

Mr. Mackey jumped in, "Alright, Alright, settle down you two. Shane, I think we should be able to accommodate my grandson this summer for an internship. I can appreciate your concern about time management, but my son can participate in the management of James's time and responsibilities."

I really had no choice and I had to choose my battles wisely, so I acquiesced and agreed to let James do a summer internship on the desk.

****

James had finished his second summer stint as an intern on the desk. We were really hopping on the desk and our production had improved significantly, which limited my interaction with James. Most of his time was spent on research assignments with Tim, and he reported directly to Junior. I didn't have anything against James, he just came at a pivotal time in the growth of the desk and my plan of keeping my staff lean had really paid off. Our numbers for the first half of the year were again solid. They showed signs that we could easily be one of the top two desks in GPG. Our hard work was paying off, encouraging and moving at a pace that kept all eyes on us, the Fixed Income desk.

We started getting more inquiries about transfers from other trading desks and visits from top executives dropping by to say congratulations. Most everyone in the firm assumed the Fixed Income desk had been dead, never to awaken again. For us to have revived the desk and return it to profitability within two years was considered a minor miracle. Mr. Mackey was ecstatic. He could see himself moving on to the Board of Directors and a Partnership, leaving the Fixed Income Desk strong and profitable -- in the same condition he had built it up to. And Junior was still Junior, never satisfied; he was still overly concerned about all the African Americans at the trading desk. Quietly around the firm and around Wall Street, they nicknamed the Fixed Income desk Black Street. A rumor began to spread that you couldn't get a job on the Fixed Income desk unless you were black. Because of Junior I think the rumors concerned Mr. Mackey and maybe some of the other top management executives. In the next meeting I had with Mr. Mackey and Junior they were pushing me to fully staff the desk. We were meeting, in one of the small conference rooms on the top floor.

Mr. Mackey started with praise. "Shane, you have done an outstanding job on the trading desk. You have accomplished so much in so little time, and have executed your plan to the tee, and it has paid off for you, us, and most of all, the firm. Everyone from top to bottom is singing your praise and deservedly so. I personally want to thank you for helping me go out on top, which makes my transition to Partner and the Board that much easier."

"We are not number one, yet," I responded.

"Given your current numbers, if you were to bulk up your staff, you would be number one by year's end."

"That's what we wanted to talk to you about," Junior interjected. "We feel it's time to open up the desk for new recruitment and get you fully staffed."

Before I could get a word in Junior tried to head off any objections that I might have had. "You were right to keep your staff lean and let them gel as a unit. It has served us well. Now they are seasoned and we are at that point where the only way you can push for the number one spot is to be fully staffed. We would like to have that number one spot by year's end. Then, by the beginning of next year my father can transition to partner and the board, and I can step into his shoes. Are you on board with us?"

There was no reason for me not to be on board. Junior was right this time. The desk had come together well and any additions to the desk at this point would be heavily influenced by their professionalism and work ethic. I knew they wanted to make the push for number one this year and the only way to do that was to be fully staffed. So, I had to agree with them.

"Yes, I'm on board and in agreement. If we want to make a push for the number one, we need to increase our staff of professionals. I can meet with heads of sales, trading, and analysis to see where the greater needs are to maximize profitability. Then, I will sit down with Betty and lay out a recruiting strategy."

Mr. Mackey and Junior responded in unison. "Sounds like a plan."

"Let's move on it immediately," Junior added.

Back down on the trading desk I was approached by Ted. He wanted to know how it went with the Mackeys.

"It went well!"

"With the numbers we're putting up I didn't think it could go any other way. We are finding our stride and the top position is ripe for the taking. Mission accomplished."

"Yea, that's the Mackeys' sentiment exactly. They want to push for number one, and they want to get fully staffed as soon as possible."

"Shane, along the lines of staffing, I wanted to update you on my plans. Can we grab an empty office or conference room?"

"Yea, let's check to see if a conference room is available." I knew Ted wanted to talk about his departure. At the end of this year I would have completed my second full year as Managing Director, and Ted only put off his retirement one year which will be at the end of this year. To lose Ted would be a blow to the desk, we would lose his experience, his wisdom, his leadership, and his example as the consummate professional.

I respected Ted and respected any decision he made about his pending retirement, but for some reason his body language had given rise to reservations on my part. I didn't think he would depart before his target retirement date. He had always been a man of his word, but the only time I had seen him act in this manner was over money. Was he thinking about delivering his book to someone else inside the firm or delivering the book outside the firm totally? I didn't want to think like a managing director, but my main concern was the protection and preservation of the profitability of the desk at all times. And if Ted decided to hand over his book outside the Fixed Income Desk, we would take a major hit and the run for number one by year's end would be a struggle.

"There's a conference room available on the 21st floor. I'll reserve it for an hour. Will that be enough time?"

"That's more than enough time!" Ted responded.

The 21st floor conference room was the smallest conference room I'd been in since I'd been at GPG. The room was only 12 X 12 and had six leather chairs surrounding a mahogany wood desk. No windows and only two water color paintings with wood frames hanging on opposite ends of the room. We both took a seat, I sat in the middle of the table on the right hand side and Ted took the seat opposite to me.

"It's coming to that time, Shane," Ted started off.

"Yes, I know the time is drawing near."

"I don't want any big party or parade." He became animated with his hand gestures. "Or recognition. I would just like to go off in the sunset quietly; sort of like a Humphrey Bogart movie," he said, kicking back and chuckling.

"I can't promise that we won't have a big party or parade. You are well liked around the company and my belief is, if we don't send you off in grand old fashion, than there may be hell to pay."

"Well liked, I thought I was loved." We both got a laugh out of that one.

Then a strange silence slipped into the room. We both were left looking at each other and I felt a need to change postures in my chair to make the moment not so sentimental. Then he came out with it.

"Once I leave, I would like to turn over my book to my nephew."

Who in the hell was his nephew? I had never met him, he had never mentioned him, and where did this nephew work? It was looking like this huge profitable book was leaving the desk. But, I wasn't going to panic until I found out more about his nephew, and saw the whole angle and picture of the situation.

"Where does your nephew work?"

"Well, Shane this is where you come in. I would like to hire my nephew on the Fixed Income Desk. Then have him train under me for about six months."

"What's his background?"

"Well, I don't really know. He's held down a few odd jobs and traveled a little through Europe and Africa, but now his life has changed … with a wife and baby on the way."

"I see, so you want to start him on a career in finance?"

"Yes!"

"Does he have a degree?"

"No." He said this hesitantly.

So, in essence he wanted me to hire his nephew, who doesn't have a degree, has no work experience and expected me to hand him a book that would generate a salary of over five million a year. That was nepotism at its best. Nevertheless, I really didn't have a problem with it because I'd been in the game long enough to know that's the way the game was played. I just needed some assurances that his nephew would stay with the desk after Ted trained him.

"Will your nephew stay on with the desk after you train him?"

"There's no guarantee that he will. He might take the book to another desk within GPG, or he might take it to another company altogether."

"Do you think he may be open to a signed agreement to keep the book on the Fixed Income desk for at least two years after your departure?"

"I'm not sure. You'd have to ask him that question."

Okay, I saw the way this was going. Ted was done, he was handing over his book and letting go completely. He didn't want to play company politics, but I'd thought for me he just might.

"Ted, your book is still a significant part of this desk's sales volume, and for it to walk out the door immediately behind you puts the desk in a precarious position."

"Shane, I understand your concern about the book, but the desk is solid and with a few more key people you are destined to be number one with or without my book. You have done an outstanding job in recruiting talented people. I don't think my book is going to make or break your desk."

"Come on, Ted, we both know it's not about making or breaking the desk. It will be a set back if your entire book leaves the desk. Matter of fact as Managing Director I have to try and protect the revenue sources of the desk. It's not as nonchalant as you are trying to make it out to be."

Ted's demeanor changed. His facial expression became harder and his face turned a slight cherry red. He sat erect in his chair. "No matter how nonchalantly I'm making this out to be … as you say, it's my decision and I've made it. And, as far as I'm concerned the discussion is over and I don't want to talk about it any longer." Then, he got up from his chair and walked to the door.

"Ted!" I shouted in a dismayed voice. But he didn't turn around. He walked right out the door.

Ted knew the game very well. He knew I had to react. The Managing Director can't just stand by and let a significant piece of the desk revenue source leave because someone is retiring and wants to set his nephew up in a cushy position by giving him his book. I had to protect this revenue source during this transition. My reaction to my mentor's nepotism, lack of judgment, and new found callousness would certainly put a strain on our professional, as well as our personal relations. However, I had to do it. I couldn't let my desk take such a hit.

Back on the desk, Darrell and Charles stared at me like something was wrong. I gestured to them like what's up? And then they both answered shrugging their shoulders like yea what's up. I realized my facial expression was one of deep and distant thought. I mouthed to them "War meeting tonight." They both shook their heads, yes.

I received a call on the trading desk from Betty. She informed me that she had finished a meeting with Mr. Mackey, Junior, and Larri. Her voice trembled a little. She said we needed to talk. I asked her what was the matter, but she didn't want to talk over the phone. So, I invited her to meet me at the house around 7:00 pm for dinner.

12
What's The Plan

It was seven o'clock on the dot and Charles, Darrel, and I had just sat down at the dining room table to have dinner and begin our War Room meeting. Just when we started to wonder where Betty was, we heard a knock at the door. It was Betty, with that same worried-to-death look that she'd had the last time she came over for dinner. This time though, she didn't have her son with her.

This meeting was going to be pivotal for all of us. Despite the desk's performance, there were some unfriendly waters ahead, filled with obstacles and pitfalls. The thing that weighed heavy on my mind was sharing my plan with them about building an all black professional Fixed Income desk and having them buy into my vision. My first thought was that Charles and Darrell would share my vision and buy into it one hundred percent. But Betty was another story, and from her perspective she had a lot to lose, and to a certain degree that was true, but she wouldn't have been in this situation if I hadn't picked her up from the land of corporate death.

So, I wanted to start off with her to ease her tension and concern.

"Betty, before we get started I just wanted to say you did an outstanding job in our recruitment effort, and your eye for talent is second to none."

Betty was eating some of her lobster pasta and couldn't respond quickly but managed to get out a thank you.

"I know you wanted to talk to me about your meeting with Mr. Mackey and Junior, so you have the floor." I raised my right hand and gestured towards her, then, I reached in front of me on the table and grabbed a piece of garlic bread. Betty seemed to be enjoying the tasty pasta because she was busy eating. We had to wait for her to finish before she could speak.

"Someone is enjoying the lobster pasta," Charles light heartily interjected.

"Oh, the pasta is good with a capital G. Who made it?" Betty finally spoke.

"Yours truly!' I responded.

"My compliments to the chef." She raised her glass of wine to toast me, took a quick sip and got right down to business. "Shane, I appreciate those kind words and I'm glad you are satisfied with the job I have done for you, but ….."

"There always has to be a but!" I replied

"No, not always but in this case, yes. My meeting with the Mackeys and Larri was unsettling, to say the least."

"What do you mean unsettling?" Darrell chimed in.

"Well, in no uncertain terms they made it clear that they wanted a more diverse professional staff on the desk."

"Racially diverse or gender diversity?" Charles asked.

"Racially! No one has a problem with gender, but the all black Fixed Income desk has raised some eyebrows."

At this time, I was listening intently. Charles and Darrel were engaging her, poking and prodding at her statements.

"What do you mean by raised eyebrows?" Darrell asked.

"People are talking about the all black Fixed Income desk."

"What are they saying, Betty?" Charles asked.

"Well, they're saying you can't get a job on the desk unless you are black, and they are calling the desk Black Street."

"Black Street! What is that suppose to mean?" Darrell quickly responded.

"Black Street is short for Black Wall Street."

I finally chimed in. "Did you hear someone say that yourself or did someone tell you that?"

"Larri pulled me into her office a few months ago and told me this was the type of talk that was coming from the top, and the Mackeys, even though they are happy about the desk performance, didn't like the connotation of Black Street and the notion that you have to be black to work on the desk."

All eyes were on me now. Betty asked the million dollar question.

"Shane, I know you wanted to create more opportunities for blacks on the desk, and you've done a great job in realizing your vision, but is it your intention to hire an entire black professional staff?"

I had the captive audience I wanted; now all three were looking at me intently. There was no more skirting around the issue, and we had a lot on the line. For me to ask them to possibly put their careers on the line, I had to share my entire vision and the reason behind my endeavors. I had to give them the choice of continuing on this journey with me or getting off and taking another train.

Darrel and Charles might have been a little surprised by my entire vision, but I knew they would have an appreciation for what I was attempting to do. They wouldn't leave me at this critical juncture. In the last year or so, however, Betty had made herself invaluable. Now, she was the key and I just didn't know where she would stand, but it was time to find out, so I answered her question in no unequivocal terms.

"Yes!"

"Ah, shit!" Charles exclaimed. "I knew it was too much of a coincidence for all the hires to be black."

"Man, what are you thinking?" Darrel questioned. "You have put all of our careers in jeopardy, and for what?"

"First, I must say that the only person whose career is in jeopardy is mine, and I've intentionally kept you all in the dark about my total vision for the desk just for that reason."

"Then, why tell us now?" Darrell responded.

"Because we've accomplished a lot and in the future we can do more. When it's all said and done the final decision and responsibility falls upon me, and everyone knows that, but I need your help and assistance to take it to the next level."

"So, you are willing to sacrifice your career to see an all black trading desk come to fruition?" Charles challenged.

"Absolutely!"

"Why?" Darrell Asked

"Because it's a vision I have to change the way we are perceived not individually, but collectively. We see all white trading desks on Wall Street all the time, but when an all black trading desk is being created, something is wrong. It doesn't look right for some reason. They think we are plotting an overthrow….. For Mr. White, who was the first Black Wall Street Broker and experienced discrimination every day, he worked on the street, for the young African Americans coming behind us wanting to participate and take the reins of the money capital of the world. For those who told me attending a historical black college for my MBA would land me in the unemployment line, and to make history on Wall Street by having the most profitable trading desk staffed by nothing but black professionals."

All this time Betty hadn't said a word. She was just sitting back listening. After my spiel about why I wanted to take on the big picture, she smiled and said in a soft voice, "I knew you had something up your sleeve when we had our first meeting at that coffee shop. You were sizing me up the whole time to see if I was trustworthy and if I could help you pull this off."

There was silence as she stared at me. Then, I broke the silence.

"You are right, Betty I was sizing you up, but it wasn't done maliciously. I knew you needed an opportunity to show your talents and I needed someone of your talents to reach my goal. It was a mutually beneficial partnership."

"The only thing is my job, is in jeopardy the same as yours. They are watching me in the same way they are watching you. They think we are in cahoots based on my last meeting with the Mackeys and Larri."

"Cahoots?" I replied upset. "It's just as I said. They think we are plotting. I guess were supposed to be conspiring to rob GPG, or create some kind of Ponzi scheme where we rob millions from them and customers, when all we've done is make money and restore the desk to profitability. They are paranoid!"

"Yes, and, to prove that I'm not in cahoots with you, they want me to give them daily reports on your recruiting and notes on all our meetings about potential hires, and they don't want you to know anything about it. "

"What?" Charles responded.

"Are you serious?" Darrell shouted.

"As a heart attack," Betty said.

"I'm not surprised! Junior has accused me face to face of using discriminating hiring practices."

"Why didn't you tell us about Junior's accusations?" Darrell asked.

"Because it was nothing to worry about, and I wanted you guys focused on revenue generating issues." I paused.

At that moment, I knew Betty was on board because she didn't have to tell us about the meeting with the Mackys. As for Darrell and Charles, they were worried about how I handled things and disappointed that I hadn't let them know from the start, but their body movement and facial expression told me that they understood.

"Look, all that is behind us now and ya'll my boys." I looked at both Darrell and Charles. "Are you down with me or what?"

"Come on, man!" Charles responded.

Darrell answered, "You know the answer to that question is, yes! But, let me ask you this. Does Big Mike know?"

"Yes, he knows. I gave him the plan a while back when I switched his position."

"So, what exactly do you have Big Mike doing?' Charles asked.

"It's better that you don't know at this time, so there's no culpability on your part."

"You don't have Mike doing anything illegal."

"No, not at all! I may bend some laws, but I would never break the law."

"So, what's the plan, Shane?" Betty asked.

"The plan is simple. We continue on the path we are on, and that is to build a qualified all black professional Fixed Income staff."

"They are on to your plan, so how do we protect ourselves?"

"There is no need for protection. It's a simple formula that is used all over Wall Street. Present ourselves as equal opportunity employers. Bring in a diversified candidate pool, then, we hire who we want. As long as we are interviewing a diversified ethnicity of candidates they cannot accuse us of discrimination."

"But, we all know the non-black candidates don't have a chance of being hired and that is discrimination," Darrell interjected tensely in voice at least an octave higher than usual.

"And, your point is?" I responded.

"It's wrong! It's reverse discrimination."

"Let's be real. Historically, and at the present, there is limited opportunity for black professionals on Wall Street. Yes, we have made some strides, but the good old boy network is still in effect."

"He's right about that, Darrell," Charles said.

I continued, "And, I just want to give the good old boy network a nice punch in the gut and wake them up to all the untapped talent in the black community. I want to dispel the rumors that we cannot be players in every aspect of Wall Street."

"Two wrongs don't make a right," Charles responded.

"But, it makes it even," I responded.

"Everything Shane is saying is true. It has gotten worse since they eliminated Affirmative Action. Initially they hired me to attract and recruit African Americans, and that lasted all of one year. When they killed Affirmative Action, they relegated me to menial tasks as if I were an administrative assistant. Who knows if it weren't for Shane I would be out of work."

"I know what Shane is saying is correct, but there has to be another way to make that point. Look, we have an all black staff now! You don't think we are making the point now?" Darrell vented.

"We are sending a small message, but I want the world to know. The top Fixed Income desk on Wall Street is now Black Street," I said. "Are you with me or do you want out?"

"Man, that's a stupid question to ask me," Darrell said raising his voice.

"I know, and I apologize, but I didn't want to put you in a position that you are not comfortable with. And, that goes for everyone. If you want out, now is the time. Betty, you are especially in a precarious position and if you were to opt out, I would completely understand."

"No Shane, I'm with you. But, how are we going to get this by the Mackeys?"

Everyone was intently watching me, waiting for me to lay out some kind of grand scheme. But like I'd told them earlier it's not as complicated as they want it to be. In the initial round of hiring I biased the process without anyone truly knowing; it raised some eyebrows, but everyone hired was qualified, and the proof was in their performance.

"It's simple. We let Betty do her job by bringing in qualified candidates." I looked towards Betty. "Betty, use the same process you used before, change nothing. We have about ten positions to fill. Let's get the best people in here, and then hire them all at once with the same starting date. Before they know what hit them."

Charles interjected, "Mission accomplished!"

"What about the notes and updates the Mackey's are asking for?" Betty responded.

"We will give them notes and updates, but it will not be of significance. As a matter of fact, bring in even more WASP to interview, but in the end the result will be the same."

Everyone shook their heads in agreement, then Betty asked,

"What's for dessert?"

"We have chocolate cake and ice cream," I told her.

"What flavor is the ice cream?"

"Chocolate," I responded.

"That's too much chocolate. You don't have any vanilla?"

"You can never have too much chocolate," Charles responded. "And why would a sista want a scoop of vanilla when she can have a scoop of chocolate?"

We all chuckled and laughed. I got up and got Betty a scoop of chocolate ice cream with a slice of chocolate cake. As I returned to the table with deserts in hand, I told them we have one more issue to address tonight.

Darrell asked, "What's the other issue?"

"It's Ted. He has decided to leave at the end of the year."

"We knew that, why is that an issue?" Charles rejoined.

"Is he trying to leave his book somewhere else besides the desk?" Darrell asked.

"Something like that, he wants to bring in his nephew who has never worked in the industry. I don't believe he's ever had a real job."

"So, what's the problem with that? Is it that he's white?" Charles chuckled.

"No, not at all, Ted is a part of our family on the desk and he has the freedom to do what he wishes and leave his book to whomever, but if that person's intention is take the book over and run out the door with it, as MD I must take measures to prevent that loss."

"What makes you think his nephew's intentions are to leave?" Darrell asked.

"Well, from my conversation with Ted, which wasn't the best, he wouldn't give any assurances that his nephew would not flee with the book."

"If we lose his book will it hurt us that much?" Charles asked.

"It would hurt us initially, but when we become fully staffed we should be able to recover," Darrell answered.

"Yes, we should be able to recover, but I don't want to let that book go without a fight," I said.

"What's the plan?" Darrel asked.

All this time Betty was silent but was listening intently. Her eyes moved excitedly from one person to the other, depending on who was talking at the time. A hint of a smile graced her face. I think she was truly enjoying this strategy session and appreciated being a part of this type of team since she started as a professional on Wall Street. I paused when Darrell asked the question, took a deep breath and laid out my plan.

"I want to have someone look into the background and character of Ted's nephew. Ted was pretty tight lipped about his background and experience."

"You mean like a P.I.?" Darrell asked.

"Exactly, I'm telling you, Ted is hiding something about his nephew and I'm determined to find out what it is. Use it against them to front run his book before he leaves."

Betty finally spoke up. "What is front running?"

Darrell answered her, "It's where you call the clients of a particular person, without their knowing and leak negative information about said person. Then you persuade the client to move his business to you."

"And, in this case the move is within the same company and same desk, so the sale should be a lot easier. And, depending on what we find out about his nephew, the negative information will be targeted towards him and not Ted because none of Ted's clients would believe anything negative about him. anyway." "Plus, if we build a negative campaign around Ted, we would lose those clients forever. This has to be done with tact and care, to guard against the wrong impression," Darrell stated.

"Darrel is absolutely correct and I think," I looked directly at Darrell, "you and I should handle this personally. I don't want anyone on the desk to know what we are attempting to do."

"Agreed," Darrell affirmed. "Who's going to get the P.I.?"

"I will take care of that," I responded.

****

Two weeks had gone by since our "War Room" meeting at the house. Betty put a list of potential candidates together, which had to be approved by the Mackeys before an invitation went out for an interview. I really had no problem with that as long as they approved enough Blacks to fill the positions that were needed on the desk. They also wanted to be involved with the interviewing process, which complicated things to a certain degree. It was really just Junior who wanted direct input. Being the only MD at GPG who had to acquiesce to such a request, I wasn't happy. So now, I had to push back on this point to ensure that my vision came to fruition.

My first stop would be to the man himself, Mr. Mackey. He was the only one who could put a halt to his son's request to interview each candidate. I had to make my stand firm and uncompromising. On my way into the office that morning, I stopped by to talk with Mr. Mackey before heading to the trading desk. He was an early riser, a habit he'd formed during his trading days, so I knew he would be in his office, catching up on the morning news. I knocked on the door to his office. He looked up at me and waved for me to come in.

"Mr. Mackey, how are you this morning?"

"Fine, what can I do for you, Shane?"

"I wanted to talk with you about my recruiting effort to hire an additional ten people on the desk."

"Is there a problem?"

He knew damn well there was a problem, and I was paying him a visit to complain about Junior. Mr. Mackey was a veteran, who played the game well, and I had never underestimated his savvy awareness. His tone was calm and welcoming, but he didn't offer me a seat. So, I stood in the middle of his office and stated my case.

"Yes, I have a problem with your son wanting to interview each candidate we bring in." I didn't give him a chance to respond or interrupt. "Since when did we adopt this policy? We had no such policy on our first round of hiring, and from all indications that was most successful."

"Shane, it has come to my attention….."

Just then, Junior walked into the office in a hurried fashion. "What's going on here?"

He must have overheard or eavesdropped on our conversation.

His father responded to his question. "Shane is concerned about you having input on the candidates for hire."

"Why?" Junior said in a high pitched tone.

"Well, I just wanted to know the reason for the change in policy," I stated.

"We don't need to give you a reason for the change," Junior said. "All you need to know is there has been a change, and I will be interviewing each candidate and having input as to who will be hired."

"That's not going to work," I retorted in a very level tone.

"What do you mean that's not going to work? You…….. " Junior, who had reached a boiling point, began to turn red when Mr. Mackey interrupted.

"Settle down, settle down," Mr. Mackey said looking at his son. "We are going to have a civilized conversation about this. "Now,

Shane," He looked towards me. I was still standing in the center of the office, and Junior was standing to the left of his father. "GPG prides itself on being an equal opportunity employer. It has come to my attention that we may have been practicing less than that in our first round of hiring."

"How could that be?" I responded

"Well, Shane, you hired nothing but African Americans."

"I don't see that as a problem."

"You don't think that is discriminatory?"

"No, not at all! I hired the most qualified of the candidates that were interviewed. If hiring the best is discriminatory, then yes I discriminated against the other candidates, but it was not based on race or gender. It was based on my opinion and judgment of how successful they could be in adding value to turning around the desk."

"You are so full of shit!" Junior retorted.

Mr. Mackey looked at his son with displeasure. Junior was a hot head. He telegraphed all his moves. To his credit or discredit, Junior was a straight shooter. Anytime people knew what you were thinking, they knew what to expect from you. From that standpoint, Junior didn't have a clue on how to play the game of politics on Wall Street.

In a monotone voice I told Mr. Mackey and Junior. "I will not tolerate being talked to in that way, it isn't warranted." There was a pause of silence. "It's surprising to me, with the success I've had in turning around the Fixed Income desk from the brink of disaster that I am treated in this manner."

"In what manner are you speaking, Shane?" Mr. Mackey rejoined.

"In this manner, of being spoken to in a condescending manner, having upper management interfere with hiring practices on the desk. Any other MD at GPG would surely find displeasure in these tactics. It's as if you want to sabotage my inevitable success on the desk," I said in an animated tone.

"Sabotage your success? Nothing could be further from the truth. You have done an excellent job and we have rewarded you for your efforts. Correct?" Mr. Mackey responded.

"Yes."

"We don't want any problems that could become potential lawsuits against the firm."

"Put your mind at ease. There's no need to worry about that," I told both of them.

"Okay, Shane. I will grant your request for complete autonomy over this hiring process," Mr. Mackey said.

"Don't make us regret it!" Junior added.

I bowed my head and said, "Thank you." As I was leaving the office Mr. Mackey asked,

"Have you talked to Ted?"

I turned back around to face him.

"Yes!"

"You know of his plans?"

"Yes."

"Is that going to cause you any problems?"

"No."

"So, everything is taken care of?"

"Yes."

"Good work! If you need my assistance, call me."

"Thanks." I walked out of his office.

With that small exchange, Mr. Mackey had given me the green light to do whatever was necessary to keep Ted's book on the Fixed Income desk. The bottom line for Mr. Mackey was profit and making money, as always. Junior had to learn a simple lesson about Wall Street, don't make things personal, keep it all business.

Ted and I spoke very little over the next two weeks. He brought in his nephew, Steve. I had Betty draw up an offer letter to hire Steve on the desk as a full time salesman. All Steve's training was Ted's responsibility, but I made it clear to Steve that he was under the Darrell's management.. He agreed, and appeared to be cordial and pleasant. Steve stood around 5'8", red hair, freckles on his face, thin build, and wore strictly Brooks Brothers suits, which I knew Ted had told him to wear. I had a P.I. do a background check to dig up any other pertinent information on Steve, but the P.I. hadn't gotten back to me yet. I did notice that Steve took a few more breaks from the desk than normal. Other than that, he seemed to be okay.

Meanwhile, Betty and I were getting into the full swing of bringing in candidates to fully staff the desk. Now we only needed nine not ten due to hiring Steve. Out of one hundred-fifty resumes submitted for the positions, Betty selected fifty that we would invite in for a formal interview. Thirty out of the fifty candidates were from

Ivy League schools. Five blacks, eight Asians, two Latinos, and fifteen Caucasians. We had another ten candidates from non Ivy League schools, all were Caucasians, and we had ten candidates from traditionally black colleges, all African Americans.

Out of fifty candidates, I had fifteen black candidates from which to pick the final nine positions needed on the desk. Five positions were in sales; three positions were in trading; and one position was in research and analysis. I wanted to have all the heads of each respective area heavily involved in the interviewing process. I also wanted to involve some of the other professionals from the desk with the responsibility of interviewing. This way we could get an indication of how the candidates might get along with each other. Everyone thought that was an excellent idea, but Tim raised concern over having everyone involved with all fifty candidates since the real candidate pool was only fifteen. I reminded him that the interviewing process had to be the same for all candidates, and any deviation would put us in direct violation of the recruiting policy of GPG.

I set a three week time period for us to interview all the candidates and make our final decisions. We were going to hire nine people. We made sure that we took no short-cuts and each step in the hiring process was reviewed and approved by the Mackeys. They were satisfied with the pool of candidates, especially the ones from top MBA programs. The ten candidates from historically black colleges raised an eyebrow, but we pushed it right past the Mackeys. My argument to the Mackeys was that I was a product of a historically black college, and if I wasn't able to reach back and present opportunities to graduates, who would? They had no choice but to respect my position, and Betty didn't have to worry about the notes she prepared for the Mackeys because everything was above and beyond reproach.

After Steve's first week on the desk, I heard from the P.I. It was as I thought. Steve had a checkered history. He did earn an undergraduate degree in social studies, but that was the highlight of his educational achievements. He'd had run-ins with the law for DUI's. He was thirty-two years-old and had not held a job for longer than one year. It seemed that Steve had acquired a reputation as a party boy while in college and never grew out of it. His father died a few years earlier of a heart attack, and Steve had a hard time coping. Eventually, he turned to drugs. He did a year at Molithan Hospital, a drug rehabilitation center and psychiatric hospital. So, not only was this guy a druggie, he was crazy too. It looked like Ted got involved when Steve fell under the influence of drugs by paying for his rehabilitation at Molithian Center at his sister's request. Steve had a newborn and a young bride who was twenty-one years of age.

I had enough to bury Steve alive with Ted's clients by front running them; but as I thought about my plan more and more, it became apparent that my plan was flawed. Ted's clients were loyal to him, not only because he was good at his job, but also because he was a good man. Any attempt to taint Steve would be an indirect shot at Ted, which wouldn't be looked upon kindly. Although most of his clients knew and liked me, they knew the history I shared with Ted. Ted had bragged about my accomplishments on the desk and made it well known that he was mentoring me. Any act of betrayal on my part toward Ted would jeopardize the whole book.

So, I decided not to make any moves until Ted retired and had left GPG for good. I needed to get a commitment from Steve to stay at least six months after Ted retired, and then I could make my run after Ted's book. With Ted out of the picture, traveling the world with his wife, the coup could take place smoothly without any immediate repercussions. Steve really didn't have a chance with Darrell and me handling the coup.

I immediately went to Darrell and informed him of my change in plans, and told him I would give him more details at the house. Then, I went to Ted and Steve and asked if they had time to sit with me for about thirty minutes. They agreed and we met in the conference room right off the trading room. I opened up the conversation with the most humble of tones and demeanor I could muster up.

"I called this meeting really to apologize to Ted." Then I looked directly at Ted. "You have been a friend, confidant, mentor, and father figure to me ever since I started working on Wall Street." Ted was silent and just looked at me to see if my words were sincere. I continued. "And, our last conversation wasn't the best. I was thinking like a Managing Director and lost sight of our relationship, and all you have done for me. If it wasn't for you, I wouldn't have gotten this opportunity. You stuck your neck out for me, stood by me, and gave me your support one hundred percent. For that I am eternally grateful. Ted, now I understand that you are just trying to give the same support to your nephew, Steve." I gestured toward Steve and acknowledged him. "My vision was a little blurry, but I see clearly now and ask for your forgiveness." Ted stood, I stood, and we embraced.

"Apology accepted! Shane, I understand the pressure you're under as MD, and the Mackeys are breathing down your back to get the desk to number one. There is no doubt in my mind that you will get there. If I believed my departure and bringing Steve aboard with no assurances would really hurt you, I would never take this course of action."

I said in a quiet voice almost just mouthing the words. "I know."

Steve then spoke up. "I'm sure glad to hear that I'm not obligated to stay on here after Uncle Ted retires. I have a buddy that's opening up his own institutional trading company and I will be joining his company as a partner."

Ted looked at him with disappointment, shaking his head in disbelief.

Steve is dumber than I thought. If I don't take the book from him, someone else will. How does one show his whole hand before the game even begins by revealing plans in front of his competition.

Ted spoke, "Always be careful of what you say and who you say it in front of, Steve. You not only have to be smart on Wall Street, but you must be savvy and strategic."

"Ted is right, be careful of your words and who you let into your circle of trust," I responded. "But being partner of a start-up sounds exciting."

"Yes, it is! I hope there will be no hard feelings about me leaving, once Uncle Ted leaves."

"No, not at all! It's business not personal, but I would like to ask one favor."

"Yea, anything!" Steve responded, and I saw Ted shaking his head again.

"Would you give me six months on the desk after the departure of Ted?"

Steve quickly turned his head and looked at Ted for an answer. Ted didn't say anything. I continued. "The only reason I have such a request is because six months gets me well into next year... after the year end numbers come in, which should solidify the Fixed Income desk back to its number one position in the firm. Now, having said that, I will probably reach that number one position without your book, Steve, but your book would make things a lot easier."

"I think that is a reasonable request, given the circumstances," Ted responded.

"So, what do you say, Steve?"

In a whining kind of voice, Steve said, "Ah, six months that's kind of long isn't it?"

"Six months will fly by before you can blink an eye. Look at me I've been MD for about two years now, and it just seems like yesterday when I got the promotion."

"Well alright if Uncle Ted thinks it's fair, I guess, I can do it."

"Great, thanks Steve! I appreciate that gesture of goodwill." We shook hands in agreement.

****

The interviewing process started with the fifty candidates. We figured that we needed to interview everyone in a two week period and reduce the number by week three to twenty candidates. Each candidate was interviewed by two people -- myself and the hiring manager. Weekends were utilized, which was out of the ordinary, but the time was needed to properly screen each candidate. We had no problem getting weekend interviews approved by the Mackeys.

Two weeks flew by in what seemed like a wink of an eye. We had our twenty candidates: Ten were African American, nine Caucasian, and one Asian. We did not disclose the identity of the final twenty candidates to the Mackeys which caused a little bit of an uproar from Junior, but Betty did disclose that four of the candidates where from black colleges in her weekly notes.

I did receive an irate phone call from Junior, but I brushed him off, telling him I had more important things on my mind than to discuss the ethnicity of the final twenty candidates. The bottom line for me and his father was the overall profitability of the desk and that was my single focus. "Have a good day." And, I hung the phone up. I fully expected him to give me a return call or come storming down to the trading desk, beet red, foaming at the mouth, but to my surprise neither occurred.

We changed the format of the second interview to a panel format for the first half of the interview and the second half would be the final interview with the hiring manager, then me. The panel consisted of other professional staff on the desk so we could get a peer point of view and get their input and opinions on the qualifications of the candidates.

Staff feedback was very positive for all the candidates, which was tribute to Betty's ability in bringing in top notch talent. In particular there was one candidate that caught everyone's attention. Her name was Emmy, an African American, and she was an Ivy League MBA from one of the top five business schools in the country. She was interviewed for the research analyst position in Tim's area. I wasn't able to interview her, the first go round, but Tim considered her to be the front runner for his open position. To say Tim was excited about bringing her aboard would be an understatement. He went on and on about her background and qualifications with vigor and enthusiasm, which led me to believe he was looking beyond her professional qualifications.

After her second round of interviews with the panel and Tim, I finally got the opportunity to meet and interview this young lady. As I suspected, Emmy was very attractive. Emmy stood about 5'8", brown skin, 125 lbs, with curves in all the right places. She was very afrocentric in her physical presentation: dread locks, cowry shell earrings, and a kente colored scarf that accentuated her beige business suit. She had these big brown eyes that could hold the average man mesmerized for quite some time, if he wasn't careful. I actually had to catch myself because I was staring at her. We were in a small conference room right off the trading floor where I interviewed her. I didn't have many questions, because based on the feedback from the people who had interviewed her, she would be a perfect fit for the desk. So, I really just wanted to get a feel for her personality and character, and I would have to say, I was surprised by her candor during the interview.

"So, I finally get to meet the one and only Shane, The Managing Director of Black Street," she said at the beginning of the interview.

"Black Street?" I responded.

"Yes, Black Street, you know that your desk is the talk of Wall Street?"

"No, not really."

She was silent for a moment as she glanced around the room, then looked back at me with curiosity.

"Come on brotha, it's just you and me. You mean to tell me, you don't know that the street is calling your desk Black Street? The word is, if you want to work on GPG's Fixed Income desk you better be black or get the hell back."

Now, I'm asking myself why she was being so forward. My first thought -- she was a plant by Junior to get me to admit my vision and goal for the desk, or was she just being sincere and wanted to be down. I still needed to play it safe because I didn't know her.

"I've heard rumors of the Black Street label, but I had no idea it was so prevalent. As far as a racial prerequisite there is none."

"Well, brothas and sistas are breaking their necks to get in here for an interview."

"I'm glad to hear brothas and sistas are looking for opportunities here because when I became MD I wanted to open the door for African Americans, but by no means does that mean every black that applies will be hired."

"No, I wasn't trying to imply that just because a candidate was black that he or she would be hired," Emmy replied in a hurried and nervous fashion. "The word on the street is that you only take the best of the best, and you have an eye for true talent." She paused and there was silence as she tried to assess the results of her candor. Then she continued by trying to explain her position in a slow and deliberate fashion. "We are just proud of you, brotha, for what you have accomplished at GPG and the doors that you continue to open for other African Americans. The success you've had only indicates that there are talented African Americans that can produce and add value on Wall Street. Sometimes it takes extreme measures to set examples."

"You think it's extreme to have an all black desk on Wall Street?"

"Very, unless the company is black owned, and sometimes you will not see 100% black at these companies. As you know the major players in this game are still old white men, but now they are taking notice to what's happening here, and I want to be a part of this history."

"You do?"

"More than anything I've wanted to do this for a long time. I like the team you have assembled already, and Tim is a sharp and intelligent economist from whom I can learn a great deal."

"Oh, you don't think you could learn anything from me?" She had left the door open on that one. I just had to walk through it.

"Okay, I walked into that one, but when I say, I want to be here and be a part of history being made, that is a direct reflection on you. And anyone I learn from on the desk, I'm indirectly learning from you!"

"I appreciate those kind words, but I was just having some fun with you."

"I know you were." She flashed a big smile and batted her eyes.

"Maybe you might be a better fit in sales with Darrell?" I said.

"Why would you say that?"

"You seem to have the gift."

"But, I'm not a salesperson."

"What do you mean you are not a salesperson? You're sitting here selling me now."

"Well, I'm trying to get the job."

"And, that's what sales is all about, getting the deal. I know your background and your interest is in research, but a lot of times salespeople ask their research analyst to go on a sales call with them to help secure business."

"I understand," she replied.

There was a knock at the conference room door. I looked at my watch and saw that it was 3 o'clock, and our time was up. Then the door opened slightly, and I requested just another minute before the room would be theirs. Then I turned my attention back to Emmy. "Looks like our time is up, but I've enjoyed our conversation." We ended the interview professionally with a hand shake.

"When can I expect to hear if I have the job or not?" she asked

"Well, we'll take a day or so to discuss the final candidates, and then send out the offer letters by the end of the week."

We ended the interview and I escorted her back to Tim. Emmy was a very sharp and aggressive young lady. She had all the necessary qualities to make it on Wall Street, and the way Tim was carrying on she was a shoe in for his open position.

13
Black Street

After talking with everyone about the candidates, it didn't take long for us to choose the final nine. Understanding the vision I had for the desk and buying into my plan, each of the managers, Charles and Darrell, made their choices with my blessing. Regarding Tim, I knew his choice before he uttered a word, so we were set to go.

I gave the names of the final nine to Betty on a Thursday night with instructions to send offer letters out first thing in the morning. I was meeting Kendra for drinks and dinner in Uptown Manhattan and running a little late. Hence, I was brief with Betty, and told her not to give the list of the final nine to the Mackeys, and not to let anyone know we had chosen our final nine.

"Betty, we need to give the impression that we haven't finished the interviewing process."

"That's going to be a little difficult once the letters are sent out by my admin," she responded.

"I know. That's why I want you to send them out personally, and when you send them out, use an outside source."

"What do you mean?"

"Don't send them out from this office or use any corporate accounts with any of the couriers."

"You want me to go to the post office and send the letters out?"

"Exactly!"

"Do you want to send the letters out on blank paper in a blank white envelope, so we can keep the image of a covert operation?" she asked sarcastically.

"Very funny."

"So, is it your plan not to let anyone outside your desk know you have hired your final nine employees until they're sitting on the Fixed Income desk, working?"

"Exactly!"

"You're crazier than I thought," Betty exclaimed.

"I have to get going. I'm running late to meet Kendra. You'll make sure those letters go out in the morning, huh?"

"Yes, I will personally see to it."

I walked out of the office and headed for the subway to meet Kendra Uptown. We were meeting at a little Greek restaurant and bar called "Akili's." I hadn't seen or talked to Kendra in about seven days. We had been playing phone tag and I think she was a little frustrated, so she left a message to meet her at Akili's after work.

Akili's was crowded as usual, but the wait for dinner was worth it because Akili's had some of the best Greek food in the city. I made my way through the crowded lounge toward the bar, and about ten feet away I saw Kendra sitting at the bar dressed to impress. She had on a black strapless halter dress with some diamond earrings, along with the diamond necklace I had bought her a few months back when I was feeling bad about not spending enough quality time with her. Her hair was pulled back in a bun and she looked fantastic. I slowly walked behind her sitting at the bar singing Toni Braxton's *Seven Days*.

"Seven long days and not a word from you, seven long nights and I'm just about through. I can't take it no more, I can't take it no more, had about enough of you, you better be on your way."

Kendra turned towards me and without a word, stood up and gave me a passionate kiss. To say we drew attention to ourselves would be an understatement. When she finished kissing me, I took both of her hands, took a step back and looked her up and down.

"You look beautiful," I told her.

"Thank you, babe," She responded.

I was looking at Kendra as if she were the meal for tonight. "You want to get out of here and go to my place?"

"No, I want to have a nice dinner with my man, first, and be treated like a queen."

"You are a queen!" I pulled her back in close to me and gave her my version of a passionate kiss.

Just then, my name was called for a dinner table. "You put my name on the list?"

"Yes, let's go eat?" She led me toward the hostess to be seated.

Kendra and I were sitting down, catching up. She told me her business was growing, especially in the men's suit department. She told me not only have my boys Darrel and Charles been ordering suits, but my street hustler friend Ice came in yesterday to have a suit made."

"Did you tell him, I made your suits?"

"Yes, one day on my way home from work he stopped me and asked where I got my suits and I told him from you. He thought I was kidding, but I told him besides women clothing you do custom tailored suits for men. I gave him your address."

"Well, he came in and I sized him up for two suits. He gave me a cash deposit, so I'm not complaining."

Just then, a shadow fell over our table from behind me. I saw Kendra's attention shift from me to someone approaching from behind me. By the time I turned around to see who it was, the person had reached the table. It was Emmy, to my surprise.

"Hey, Emmy, what are you doing here?" I stood up to greet her.

"I'm having dinner with my husband on the other side of the room. I told my husband, I thought that was you, but we were so far away I couldn't tell. I was trying to be discreet coming over here just in case it wasn't."

"Well, I'm glad you came over." Then I turned and gestured to Kendra. "Emmy I would like you to meet my queen, Kendra." I always introduced Kendra that way because she truly was my queen.

Kendra stood and shook Emmy's hand. "It's a pleasure to meet you," she said.

"Likewise, my sista!" Emmy responded.

"Emmy interviewed for the research/analyst position in Tim's group earlier this week," I interjected.

"Oh, okay!" Kendra rejoined, and shook her head as if everything had just became clear to her.

Given Kendra's reaction to Emmy, I wondered if she thought Emmy might have been some competition. She must have known by that time there was no competition.

"I better get back to my husband. Have a great dinner, and by the way, the Cajun shrimp pasta is the bomb." She said goodbye to us with a half wave and a smile, then she walked off.

Kendra and I sat back down. "Shane, did you hire her?"

"Betty's sending her an offer letter tonight."

"She's kind of cute," Kendra exclaimed

"Yea but, she's a little on the chubby side," I returned, without looking up at Kendra. Once our eyes met we both chuckled.

"So, you do think she's attractive?"

"Why are you asking me that question?"

"Because I want to know if you think she is attractive. She was looking you up and down, I know you saw that."

"Yes I did, but her intention was not what you are thinking. She was trying to detect through my mannerisms if she had been hired or not."

"Why didn't she just ask?"

"It's too bold of a move."

"Yea, you're right."

The waitress arrived with our food. I was hungry, but I was really ready to head to my place or hers because Kendra was looking good and her little episode of jealousy kind of turned me on. After about ten minutes into our meal and talking about taking a vacation together, Kendra happened to look up and whispered to me.

"Your new employee is headed this way with her husband."

I didn't look back, but when they reached our table and stood in front of us, I was totally surprised by her husband. I'm not one who is easily surprised. Given Emmy's demeanor, her speech pattern, her style of dress, and the content of her conversation, I would have never imagined her with a white man, but there he was standing in front of our table looking down at me, and me looking up at him. He was the typical prototype of a handsome man in American culture. He stood about 5'10", medium build, blonde hair and blue eyes, clean cut, wearing a navy blue suit with a red tie. I couldn't hide the surprise on my face; I was stunned and the expression on my face showed it. Kendra had to nudge me with her foot to bring me back. I tried to play it off, as much as I could, but my initial reaction was obvious. My vision shifted from Emmy's husband to her, and I could tell my reaction to her husband caused her some discomfort. I quickly tried to make up for it. I popped up to my feet and introduced myself to her husband with a handshake. I was all smiles but the moment was awkward and I couldn't start it over.

After about five minutes of small talk Emmy and her husband left. I took out my phone to text Betty. Kendra asked what I was doing, and I didn't answer her. The text I sent to Betty was as follows:

Did U send out OL yet?

Reply: *No, not yet.*

Do not send out Emmy Whites – Changed mind, will talk tomorrow.

Okay.

Kendra was growing a little impatient because I never answered her question. "So, what's the text messaging all about?" she asked

"I just sent Betty a text, telling her to not send out Emmy's offering letter."

"Why did you do that?"

"Trust."

"What do you mean Trust?" she said in a concerned voice.

I had shared my vision for the desk with Kendra on several occasions, but I didn't give her blow by blow details on my run-ins with the Mackeys, especially with Junior. I thought she had enough on her mind with operating her own business, and I didn't want to weigh her down with my problems.

"She might be a plant by Junior," I said in a subtle voice.

"Plant! What are you talking about, Shane?"

"There is a strong possibility that Junior is trying to put a spy on the desk to set me up so he can take me down.'

"What?"

"Yes, we've had it out on a few occasions concerning the desk being all black. He's told me, he knows what I'm up to and vowed to put a stop to it."

"Shane, it is admirable what you are trying to do, but you might have to abandon your vision....I"

"Never!" I interrupted. "I'm not afraid of him or his father, and if it costs me my job so be it."

Kendra looked at me with frustration and concern. "Is it worth it?"

"Yes," I said in a calm voice.

"So, you really think that young lady is a plant by the Mackeys?"

"Yes, when I interviewed her, she was saying she was very proud of me and what I had accomplished with an all black trading desk. She mentioned that the word on Wall Street was there was no need to apply for a job on Black Street unless you were black."

"Black Street?"

"Yes, that's the nickname for the desk around Wall Street."

"I'm still confused as to why you think she is a plant."

"She's talking all this I'm black and I'm proud stuff at the interview and brotha this and brotha that. She even referred to you as sista when she met you, and she's married to a white man."

"Because she is pro black and married to a white man you think she is a plant by the Mackeys."

"Exactly!"

"You think her pro blackness is not sincere?"

"I don't know if it's sincere or not, but she is a walking contradiction."

"So, you're saying you can't be pro black and married to a white person."

"Yes, that's what you would call a sell out."

"Sell out?" Kendra's voice rose to a high pitch.

Our conversation started to go south quickly. Kendra obviously became more and more disturbed with my comments about Emmy. We had never really discussed race, but we had discussed the history of our people in America, and Africa. I thought we were on the same page about racism in America and the black tax, but given her reaction to my statements, I wasn't sure of that anymore.

"Yes, I believe she is pretending to be pro black. Her choice in a spouse shows her true feelings about black people, especially about the black man."

Kendra was completely silent. The look on her face was one of disbelief. "If anyone would have asked me if you were prejudiced I would have said, no way."

"I'm sorry to disappoint you, but I am prejudiced. In my line of business I prejudge people and situations all the time. If I didn't, my success in this business would have been short lived."

"I can't believe you are justifying being prejudiced."

"I am not justifying anything. I'm just telling you what's, what." I started to get irritated with the conversation and my voice rose. "I don't know one person who is not prejudiced or biased about something. All people show favor to something based on their experience and environment."

We really began to have an argument at the table. It's not like Kendra and I had never had an argument, but this one was the worst and in the worst possible places, in a public place. I had never seen Kendra like this, arguing a point so vehemently. Tears swelled up in her eyes and her voice got shaky, with a nervous tone. Then, she finally hit me with it.

"Do you think I'm a sell out?"

"What kind of question is that?"

"Just answer the question?" she screamed.

"No, I do not think you are a sellout. What is going on with you?"

"Well, maybe you should." Her voice was calm and cool. "About two years before I met you, I dated a white guy for three years and was very much in love with him. We planned to get married, but he was killed in a car accident. Those were the best three years of my life. I was looking forward to spending the rest of my life with him."

I was stunned and shocked, to say the least. Kendra and I had been together going on three years, and she had never even mentioned this guy. She'd told me she had been in some serious relationships in the past, but never serious enough for marriage, and she never mentioned a white guy. I was silent. I didn't have a response. Kendra's eyes were steady on me, and my silence really said a thousand words, and ninety percent of those words Kendra did not like or appreciate.

We hadn't eaten the rest of our food because we were too engulfed in our heated conversation. A perfect start to a wonderful date ended in a quick descent into the dark abyss. I had no words for what Kendra had just revealed to me. I felt betrayed. I requested the check and paid without a word.

"You have nothing to say, huh?" Kendra asked in somewhat of a sarcastic tone.

I was silent. I couldn't even bring myself to look at her.

"I think in all the time we spent together this is the first time you haven't had anything to say to me," Kendra said

We got up and left the restaurant. Kendra gave her keys to the valet, and I waited alongside her in silence. The valet pulled up in her car, Kendra walked towards it, then she stopped and turned towards me because she realized I was not following her.

"Are you coming home with me?" she asked

I just shook my head, no.

"Do you want me to take you home?"

I shook my head, no again. She just stood there without a word for about a minute, and then she turned towards her car, walked to the valet, gave him a tip, got in her car and drove off.

****

Two weeks later, on a Friday afternoon, there was turmoil on the desk between Tim and me because he was upset that I'd changed my mind about hiring Emmy. I really didn't give him a good reason. I just told him I changed my mind, but it didn't sit well with him. So, I focused and vocalized my concern on his physical attraction to her, and that she might be more of a distraction for him than an asset. He really flipped his lid when I said that. Our communication broke down after that conversation.

Ted and I were on better terms, but I could see it was a struggle with his nephew Steve, who was not focused enough and lacked the necessary drive to be a successful salesman. We had some short discussions about him, but Ted was very hesitant to bad mouth his nephew, it wasn't his style. I reassured him that as long as Steve was here, on my desk, that I would help him in any way that I could. I knew damn well when Ted walked out that door I would try to take seventy five percent of that book during the six months Steve promised to stay. One part of me was torn about misleading Ted this way. Another part was convinced that it was just business, nothing personal, however I wasn't sleeping well at night.

Some of my sleepless nights were due to my crumbling relationship with Kendra. I hadn't talked to her since our date at the Akili's. She tried to contact me by email and phone, but I didn't respond to her emails. I screened her calls by caller ID, and any calls from numbers that didn't look familiar, I didn't pick up. Although I missed her deeply, I still had no words to express what she told me. I didn't know if I was more upset at the idea that she had loved someone else enough to marry them or that I never knew about the relationship. Plus, it didn't help the situation, knowing the guy was white. Kendra was my first and only love. I guess, I wanted to be her one and only, so in a way my ego took a big hit. She used to say my ego was too big, but sometimes what people see as ego is just a black man's confidence.

I really had little time to worry about my relationship woes because Monday morning was the start date for the new hires. Betty had done a tremendous job in holding off the Mackeys, but come Monday the gig was up. Our hand would be shown for all to see, as far as I was concerned. Well, I wasn't concerned. Betty was, so I had a meeting with her after work at the same coffee shop where we'd had our first meeting. When I walked in, Betty was sitting at the same table where we met the first time. She had a cup of coffee in hand and a worried look on her face. I knew I would have to put her at ease and give her some assurances that we would make it through this okay. I ordered a cup of coffee and joined her at the back table.

"Betty, Betty, Betty, Be-e-tee!" I said in very slow, sensual and soft voice. Betty smiled and let out some chuckles. "Betty, I bet you were something else back in the day. Driving brothas crazy?"

"I'm still something else and I'm still driving them crazy!"

"I bet you are," I responded. We exchanged looks. Betty batted her eyes and looked down at her cup, regrouped and then spoke.

"Okay, Mr. Shane, Monday what's the plan?"

"There is no plan. We have reached the mountaintop. So, the only plan is to make our push in the next six months to the number one spot."

"You think they are going to let you get away with this. Once they see that every last new hire is black, things are going to hit the roof."

"Betty, the bottom line on Wall Street is profitability, and as long as we deliver the number one spot to Mr. Mackey before he makes his ascension to partner, we will be untouchable."

"Shane, I don't know," Betty said with concern creeping into her tone.

"It's too late for them to react. Their hands will be tied."

"What happens after you deliver the number one spot? What then?"

"Like I said, we're untouchable."

"I sure hope you are right."

"No worries, Betty, I got you. No way will I let you take a fall. Trust me, you my sista and I will keep you out of harms way."

"I do trust you or I wouldn't have gone along with you, but sometimes I think you are too confidant for your own good."

People had been telling me all my life what Betty was telling me, but look where it's gotten me. My mother always told me that people would mistake my confidence for arrogance, which is just a reflection of their own insecurities. My mother always said to be independent of the good opinions of others, be your own man, and follow your own mind.

I truly believed that I would be able to see my plan through to its completion without any repercussions on me, my staff or Betty. I believed that to the core of my heart, if I didn't, I would have never involved her.

Finally, Monday arrived, all the new hires reported to Betty in the Human Resource department at 7:00 a.m. sharp. Betty had them fill out the necessary paper work for new hires and upon completion guided them down to the trading floor. Once they arrived I welcomed everyone, then I let each of the managers take their respective new employees and get them situated on the desk. At that time, Betty pulled me to the side and told me there was a tremendous buzz going around upstairs when the new hires arrived, and about fifteen minutes into completing their paper work Junior showed up.

"What did he say?"

"Not much, he walked into the HR conference room took a look around turned red and walked out the door before I could introduce him."

"I'm not surprised. He's probably complaining to his dad, as we speak."

"What should I do?"

"Nothing, carry on with the rest of your day as usual, but if they contact you or try to isolate you, call me."

Betty nodded, yes, and then left the trading floor. Junior was probably steaming hot, but his father would let cooler heads prevail. Mr. Mackey could see the finish line. He didn't particularly care how he crossed the finish line as long as he crossed first. So, my focus was to bring the new hires up to speed and get them producing to contribute to the bottom line of the desk.

About halfway through the day, Ted approached and asked if he could have a word in private. Now, Ted and I had been speaking regularly and we even discussed the progress of Steve occasionally, but we hadn't had any lunches together or had any strategic sessions about the desk. It was almost as if Ted had gone from being my mentor to just an acquaintance.

Ted was sharp and politically astute. I wouldn't have been surprised if he knew about my plans to take over his book once he walked out the door for good. There have been plenty of times when Ted told me that by reading a person's body language, you can tell if he was withholding information, straight out lying, uncomfortable, comfortable, and you could determine a man's character if you study him long enough. He repeatedly told me never go by a man's word, but always go by his actions. His actions would always speak louder than his words or his lack of action would. At this time, I'm not sure what he was reading from my behavior, but I didn't really care. I had too much on my mind and too much at stake to let his book walk out the door with no attempt to retain some of those clients for the good of the desk.

We grabbed the small conference room right off the trading room; the same one where we had the confrontation about him turning his book over to his nephew. So, if we were going to have another confrontation then this would be the appropriate place, but much to my surprise the conversation took on a different tone.

"Congratulations, Shane," he said in a very calm and subdued voice.

"On what?" I answered

"On seeing your vision for the desk to fruition. I always knew your ambition went beyond just making money, and I admire you for that. I guess that's why I was so willing to mentor and help you, but I have to say I'm not in agreement with what you have socially accomplished on the desk. The civil rights era was about unifying people of all colors not separating them."

I wanted to blast Ted and tell him that the civil rights era did not bring about economic equality for blacks and that the social equality we attained came at too high of a price. I wanted to explain to him how the mental scars of slavery had manifested themselves into an inferior vs. superior relationship between blacks and whites. How we never felt that we were on the home team, but always on the visitors side, but I held my tongue out of respect for Ted.

He continued. "What you are doing is clearly separation. The civil rights leaders of your community would be disappointed with your strategy and your efforts. You are actually going against what the civil rights movement stood for."

"And, what's that Ted?" I interjected.

"Unity. Shane, your social agenda will not stand. The Mackeys and all the top brass will stand against you, bring you down along with everyone on the desk, and I cannot and will not help you out in this situation. You are on your own."

Right then, I understood clearly where Ted was coming from. He was with me as long as my vision agreed with his vision for me. Once my vision for my life wasn't in accordance with his vision for my life, the support could no longer be there. It was just like what Ralph Ellison articulated in the "Invisible man". The white man has visions and dreams for the black man, but he never sees what dreams and visions the black man has for himself, or he doesn't think the black man is capable of his own visions and dreams.

I respected Ted's opinion even though I didn't agree with it, but he had done so much for me. This wasn't the appropriate time to disagree and debate with him about my vision and the tactics implemented to achieve my vision.

He continued. "Given all I just said, I think the time is appropriate to give you my two week notice. I haven't told anyone but Steve about giving you my notice. I will follow up our conversation with an email to the Mackeys."

"Okay," I said in slow, methodical way.

"I have to tell you, Shane that Steve is not at all comfortable on the desk. He wanted to renege on his six month agreement with you, but I talked him out of it."

Comfortable! Now I'm thinking, black people sat on the trading desk, buses, trains, airplanes, and academic classes all the time without seeing another black person, and felt no discomfort or threatened by that situation, but when the shoe was on the other foot, there's a problem. I had to ask Ted how he felt about that.

"I appreciate you getting him to honor his word, but I have to ask. What do you think about that?'

"I don't really want to go into it. I was just letting you know his current state of mind. If you really are curious about why he feels that way, then I would advise you to ask him."

"Okay, I just might do that," I responded

Ted stood up and exited the small conference room, leaving the door slightly cracked behind him. I stayed in the conference room thinking about the conversation that just took place with Ted. I felt a little sorrow about Ted leaving. He helped me so much, his friendship, mentorship had been invaluable in my growth and my accomplishments at GPG. Now, for it all to end, not on the best of circumstances wasn't sitting well with me.

About ten minutes later, there was a knock on the conference door. Charles stuck his head inside.

"You ain't in here crying are you?"

"You just told a joke," I said in my most sarcastic voice. "Who's that behind you?"

Charles walked in the conference room followed by Tim and Darrell. They all took a seat around the small conference table.

"So, what's up?" Darrell began

"Ted just gave his notice," I responded

"Is his nephew going to stay on?" Tim asked

"He's committed to six months, but that may be in jeopardy."

"Why?" Darrell shouted.

"Evidently he is not comfortable in the current environment," I said

"Damn, so he might jet on us?" Charles asked

"Well, I think Ted has bought us some time with Steve, but I don't think he is going to live up to his six month commitment to us."

"Should we put our plan into effect?" Darrell asked.

"Well, I think it's still prudent to wait until Ted walks out the door."

"What plan, and why does it have to wait for Ted to leave? What kind of underhanded stuff are you guys up to?" Tim asked.

Tim hadn't been privy to all the conversations that had taken place at the house, and seemed a little disturbed about being in the dark. I tried to let him know, it wasn't done intentionally. Since he didn't live with us, it was hard keeping him in the loop about every detail pertaining to the trading desk.

"Just like the decision to not bring on Emmy that directly affects my area?"

"Are you still harping on that?"

"Yes, she was a qualified candidate on the verge of getting hired and at the last minute you rejected her," Tim said as he leaned on the conference table to engage me.

I had to diffuse this quickly, so I focused on his attraction to her.

"Man, you must really have the hots for that girl."

"I did not have the hots for her!" Tim shouted.

"Oh, ya'll talking about the young afrocentric sista with the nice little frame?" Charles rejoined. "Yea, Tim, you were salivating over her, you had that wolf look every time you got around her."

"I did not!" Tim shouted again.

Charles had a way of getting under people's skin, and he really enjoyed getting under Tim's. Charles lost a little respect for Tim when we had to take him home after his drunken stupor.

Charles needling Tim some more with Darrell and me taking little jabs at him, became a too much. Tim stormed out of the conference room.

"What is up with your boy?" Darrell asked. "He has no sense of humor. He must have been really diggin that young lady."

"Yea, I think so, but he'll be alright," I said, paused then looked at Charles and Darrell. "We have six months to take this desk to the top."

"No sweat, we are practically there," Charles said

"Being fully staffed will give us the added push we need to get the number one spot," Darrell added.

My mind wandered in thought for a minute, and then a smile came across my face. "Black Street, we did it," I said to both Charles and Darrell. Smiles appeared on their faces.

14
Number One Spot

The first month of our six month push to become the number one trading desk at GPG was probably the most intense month I had had on the desk since joining GPG as a salesman. Ted had left on a world tour with his wife. Even though we'd parted ways on not the best of terms for some reason, I expected a call before he left.

As for his nephew, Steve, we started on project takeover full force once we got word Ted was travelling the world with his wife. Steve threw little hints that he didn't want to be held to the contract that stated he would stay six months after Ted's retirement.

"Hey, Shane, can I talk to you?" Steve said as he approached me while I was sitting on the trading desk.

"Yea, what's up?"

"Can we go to a conference room and talk in private?"

"I don't have time right now, but if you have something you need to get off your chest then the floor is yours." I knew this would make him uncomfortable. By this time, I didn't care how he felt. For some reason, I wanted to make him feel uncomfortable and force him out. Of course, without Ted's book in tow.

"Well, what I wish to discuss is kind of private," he responded.

"Can it wait until tomorrow?"

"No, I need to talk to you now," he shouted.

Since he shouted, I was going to be accommodating. I looked up at him from my sitting position and in a calm, conservative voice told him. "If you need to talk to me now, then you better begin talking." By this time, we had everyone's attention on the trading desk and a few others nearby.

"I don't want to stay here for six months," he said in an authoritative voice.

"You don't have a choice, Steve. You signed a contract stating you would stay at least six months after Ted's retirement."

"Well, I've changed my mind."

"I'm sorry that you've had a change of heart, but there's nothing I can do to accommodate your request to leave before your obligation is up." My calm tone really irritated Steve. Then, he showed just how bad of a salesman he really was.

"I'll just take my clients and leave. I was just staying here as a favor to my uncle, and I'm not comfortable working here on Black

Street." You could hear some chuckles around the desk and from some other colleagues.

"First of all, your so called clients are really the clients of GPG. Any attempt to take those clients without the permission of GPG would be in direct violation of Securities and Exchange Commission client tampering act. We would not only prosecute you, but we would go after any company that welcomed you into their firm." Then, I just stared at him. "Your uncle is no longer here to hold your hand, and you are like a fish out of water. Instead of making enemies you need to be making friends. You understand what I'm telling you?"

In a subdued mood, shoulders slumped, he said, "Yes." "Now carry your ass back to your desk and make some money" I said in a stern voice. Then I brought my attention back to what I was working on, which was taking Steve's so called clients away from him right under his nose. The desk was pretty quiet after my exchange with Steve. I looked up at Darrell, who smiled and chuckled. I did the same.

Darrell and I focused in on that book like snipers aiming at their target. We personally contacted each of Ted's clients, and voiced our concerns about Steve's abilities. Our tone was tactful with a hint of concern. We knew Ted's clients were old school and didn't want too many ruffles? ripples in the water, especially the ripples that could be avoided. So, we were careful not to put them in a state of panic.

I knew most of Ted's clients personally, so I made the initial contact by phone. I then followed up with a personal visit to their headquarters. Darrell joined me so I could give him a proper introduction and let him shine as he always did on sales calls. Just like any other successful book of salesmen there are about two to three clients that make up for 50% of their book. In Ted's case there were three. The Big three were all pension fund managers that had combined assets under management of over 21 billion. All three were huge in the Fixed Income markets and Ted was the major player in filling up their appetite. In order to pull this coup off we needed to convince them their business was much better off in the hands of Darrell and me instead of Steve and his fly by night start- up company.

The first was Mr. Jacobs, just across the water in New Jersey. He was about sixty years of age and managed several pensions, ranging from teachers' unions, to united construction workers' unions. The total amount of assets he had under management was approximately 5 billion. Mr. Jacobs was very conservative and didn't like to touch any exotic derivatives or any other synthetic fixed income securities. He was a straight shooter, no nonsense. He wanted everything in his portfolio to be easily understood each bond representing a simple business model. His fund never had above average returns, but when the market took great losses, he was always able to turn a profit. Mr. Jacobs had been the manager of the fund for over twenty years. Ted used to say his understanding and timing of the market was second to none.

On Monday, Darrel and I arrived at Mr. Jacobs's office after market hours. Mr. Jacobs was very accommodating, and the three of us had a private meeting.

"So, Shane, what exactly is your concern about Steve's ability to handle my account?" Mr. Jacobs got right to the purpose of our meeting.

"I just want to say before I express my concerns that this is probably the most difficult conversation I've had to have, since becoming an MD."

"Well, Shane, I have to say, I was disturbed and concerned from the phone call I received from you and Darrell. Knowing Ted for over twenty years, I don't think he would put my business in the hands of someone who was not capable."

"Yes sir, but I would have to say in this case Ted's judgment was motivated by his nepotism. I know that's hard to believe, if you know the man like you and I do, but just take a look at Steve's resume." Darrell handed Mr. Jacobs Steve's resume. Mr. Jacobs put on his reading glasses and started to review Steve's history. As he continued with his review I continued with my subtle assault. "As you can see, Steve lacks market experience and knowledge. His undergrad degree is in history, and he has never worked in the financial industry. Plus, there are about ten years of his life unaccounted for."

The ten years of unaccountability really got his attention. "What else do you know about Steve?"

"I know he has plans to leave GPG and take Ted's book to a start-up company that doesn't have one third of the experience or resources of GPG. So, you can see the predicament that I find myself in as a MD."

"Yes, Shane." He said in slow thoughtful voice. "Are you sure his plans are to partner up with a start-up?"

"Yes, he hasn't left at this point because he is under contract for six months with GPG."

"Have you talked to Ted about this?"

"I tried on several occasions before he retired, but to no avail."

Mr. Jacobs went into deep thought, and then another man joined us. Mr. Jacobs introduced him as one of the portfolio managers of his fund. Julius Jones was his name. He stood about five foot eight, Brooks Brothers suite, well groomed with slightly graying brown hair. His demeanor was very conservative with a privileged air. Mr. Jacobs filled him in and brought him up to speed on our discussion.

"I hear you guys are running a regular chocolate factory at GPG Fixed Income."

"What, who did you hear that from?" Darrell responded.

"From Steve. He says you guys only hire Blacks and the nickname for the desk is Black Street."

"That is not true!" Darrell exploded.

I put my hand on Darrell's shoulder to calm him down.

"Shane, is this true?" Mr. Jacob rejoined.

In a very calm and confident tone I answered. "Yes, it is true that we have an all African- American trading desk, except for Steve. It is also true that we have the second most profitable trading desk at GPG and that's without being fully staffed. It is true that our research on the fixed income desk is rated in the top ten on Wall Street, but what is not true is that you have to be black to work on the desk. It just so happens that the most qualified candidates in the hiring process happened to be black and it proved itself in the numbers. We are well on our way to being the number one desk, since we are fully staffed now. Anyone, who would suggest that being black is a prerequisite to working on the Fixed Income desk at GPG, should know we are an equal opportunity employer and that interviewing qualified black professionals is part of that process. No one on my desk is a token hire." I gave a glance over at Mr. Jones.

"Number one desk? Ted was right about you. You are bright, driven, and a visionary," Mr. Jacobs said.

"Thank you," I responded

The room went silent. Then, Mr. Jacobs stood up, walked from behind his desk and approached me with his hand extended. Both Darrell and I stood and shook Mr. Jacobs's hand. Mr. Jones and Darrel walked out of the office toward the elevators in front of Mr.

Jacobs and me. Mr. Jacobs put his arm around me and began talking in a low private voice.

"Shane, I like you, and I watched your professional growth from salesman to managing director. I would have to say you have tremendous drive and ambition to accomplish what you have in the four years you've been at GPG. But I must tell you, Ted anticipated your move. He knew you would try to take over his book from his nephew, Steve, upon his departure. He came to me and requested that I keep my book with Steve even if he left GPG to go to this new start-up company. He also guaranteed me that there would be no drop in performance or service when he left. He pledged to keep current on capital markets and advise Steve for the next two years. I gave him my word to stick with Steve. If it's any consolation, I don't think Ted did this to hurt you, but just to help his nephew out. We all need a helping hand from time to time. Don't you think so, Shane?"

I was stunned by the words that came out of Mr. Jacobs' mouth. My mind raced, thinking if Ted had this conversation with Mr. Jacobs, then he'd had it with his entire client list. I responded to Mr. Jacobs's question as if I were just coming back into consciousness. "Yea," I shook my head up and down. "We all need a helping hand from time to time." When we got to the elevator, Darrell and I both thanked Mr. Jacobs and Mr. Jones for their time once again. Then Darrell and I walked on to an empty elevator. The elevator doors closed behind us.

"How do you think it went?" Darrell asked.

I didn't respond immediately because I still was recovering from what Mr. Jacobs had just told me, and then I noticed how Darrell stare at me, waiting for a response. I looked at him in somewhat of a daze.

"You think he will keep the book with us?" Darrell asked.

"No, I don't think he will keep his business with us. I think this will be our last visit to Ted's clients."

"What? Why?" Darrell responded in puzzlement.

"Yea, and we'll turn Steve loose immediately, so he can take and do whatever he wants with Ted's book."

"Huh!"

Then as we stepped off the elevator, I shared what Mr. Jacobs told me as we walked through the lobby. Darrell was surprised, too. We both agreed that our future efforts to take over Ted's book would be futile, and our energy would be better spent making the last push to become the number one trading desk at GPG.

I thought for a short time the student would be able to outwit the teacher, but that was premature. Ted had been my mentor for over four years and had taught me many lessons in that time, and just like Ted, he taught me another lesson on his way out; staying true to his words that some of the lessons would be subtle and some not so subtle.

****

I hadn't talked to Kendra in over a month, my focus and concentration was bringing my trading desk to the finish line in first place. Every time I thought about Kendra my whole body went numb. What was even more surprising, I really hadn't heard from her in a while. Maybe she didn't love me as much as I thought she did. If she did, how could she walk away from me that easily and not fight for what we were building together. When those thoughts went through my mind, I got angry. It was best for me at the time to push my feelings and thoughts about Kendra to the darkest and deepest part of my subconscious mind. I didn't want those thoughts to creep into my consciousness unless I took the effort to recall them.

I hadn't told my mother about Kendra and our little dispute, but I did wonder if Kendra had contacted my mom. They were pretty close, and as far as I know, my mother was still ordering dresses from Kendra and having them shipped to California. My mother and I kept in contact, and I relied on her more and more as my confidant and mentor since Ted's departure. She was my biggest supporter, and in her eyes I could do no wrong. I missed my mother, even though we talked on the phone at least two or three times a week; we hadn't seen each other in about two years. Her business was flourishing in L.A., and my responsibilities as a managing director and the push to become the number one desk at GPG kept me busy on the East Coast. My mother was understanding and never made me feel guilty for not making it home in two years.

The desk was in full swing, each of us was concentrating on bringing the new staff members up to speed and helping them to add to the bottom line of the desk. We were a relatively young group. At thirty-four, Charles was the oldest on the desk. Darrell was attacking each day like a posse after a bank robber in a western. I think, he felt he had let me down by not being able to convert some of Ted's clients. I assured him the blame didn't fall with him, but with me. We all were pulling fifteen hour days and extended our work week to six days when needed.

I figured it was time to have something like a pep rally to encourage and share the goal of being the number one desk at GPG with everyone. I scheduled a meeting for the entire desk; research & analysis, trading, and sales to meet in the largest conference room at GPG after market hours.

As they arrived for the meeting, I stood at the front of the conference room with a black marker in hand and a 25 X 15 white board as my back drop. There was enough space in this conference room to seat all twenty professionals from the fixed income desk. Once everyone was seated and comfortable all eyes were on me. I quietly turned around and wrote in big bold black capital letters BLACK STREET. Then, I turned back around and faced the room.

"Everyone take a look around at each person in this conference room." Everyone looked around the room at each other. "The one thing we all have in common is that we are all black. Some would have you believe this was done purposely. The only purposeful act was to choose you talented people for the skills and talents you possess, and how you fit into the vision and strategy to get this desk back to its number one position." I started to walk around the room. "Now, because of the composition of people on the fixed income desk the name Black Street has been branded to the desk." I pointed to the big black bold letters on the white board spelling out Black Street. "Now, ask yourself… is that a racist label?" I paused to let the question sink in. "Yes, it absolutely is a racist label. Do they call any of the other desks on Wall Street that are at least 90% Caucasian, White Street? No, because it's inferred that Wall Street represents the majority population that works on it. But we are not going to take the label Black Street that way. We will wear it with a badge of honor." My voice began to rise like a preacher at Sunday's sermon. "We will be proud to work on Black Street and brag about being the first all black trading desk on Wall Street." There were shouts of yeah and we'll show them. "We will be a force in the fixed income market that no one on Wall Street has ever seen since Drexel Burnham controlled the Junk Bond Market. Any company with major fixed income issuances will look to GPG underwriting because of the prowess and dominance of Black Street. Our research and analysis is in the top five on Wall Street and continuing to break new ground with our weekly publication. Our trading is in the top three on Wall Street, thanks to the excellent mind and strategy of Charles, our head trader. Our sales is also in the top three on Wall Street for fixed income instruments due to the drive and determination of Darrell, our sales manager. With the addition of all our new people, we are fully staffed. Our push to be number one inside GPG is inevitable. However the real goal is to be number one on Wall Street." There was a resounding roar throughout the conference room. You would have thought we were at a NY Jets football game and the Jets had just scored a touchdown. I moved back to the front of the room. "All this is within our grasp. Tomorrow when you come in for work, I want everyone to start saying we are the number one desk at GPG and the number one fixed income desk on Wall Street."

"Who do we say it to?" One of the traders asked.

"Anyone and everyone. Let it be known that we are number one."

"But, we are not, at least not yet!" One of the sales persons stated.

"But, we will be. We will speak it into reality. First you think it, then you say it, and then you achieve it. If you say it enough, people will believe it. All of you are a part of Wall Street history. You'll be able to tell your kids and grandkids that you were a part of Black Street! There will be books and articles written about all of our accomplishments on this desk, and how we were better than any other fixed income trading desk in the world" You would have thought, we were having a revival with all the shouts of affirmation and clapping after I finished my pep talk. Everyone was on their feet clapping and shouting. As I exited the conference room, everyone in the room wanted to touch or shake my hand. I never felt so much power and influence in my life. I felt as if I could conquer the world.

The next three months, the desk gelled and became the closest thing to a family on the trading desk. We became a community within the Wall Street community. We gathered for a lot of happy hours together, and dinners as a group. From the attention we drew when we were together, you would have thought we were some kind of popular rock band. With all the number one talk in and around Wall Street about us, Black Street became a self fulfilling prophecy. There was no official word, but the rumor was the numbers we were putting up far exceeded any other trading desk at GPG, and we were at the number two spot compared to all of Wall Street fixed income trading desks.

I would have to say that the trade room as a whole became a little closer with the success of our trading desk. Initially, there was some resentment. When the final numbers came out they were so impressive, no one in their right mind could resent that type of success and commitment to excellence. We had non-stop visitors coming by just to congratulate us on our accomplishments. There was a sense of pride throughout GPG from the top brass to the mailroom. We had accomplished our goal; we were the number one trading desk at GPG, and the number two desk on Wall Street.

Darrel, Charles, Betty and I had a small celebratory dinner at the house. Big Mike was missing. He was still away on business. The dinner was lively with good conversation and just basking in the success that we all worked hard for. The long hours, sacrifices, and risks were well worth it. Everyone was in agreement. Betty was the most enamored by our accomplishment.

"We did it! We beat them at their own game. I thought that we could do it, but I must admit I didn't believe it a hundred percent," she said in the most joyous voice.

"You didn't believe it?" I asked.

"Truthfully, nah. I thought it was a beautiful dream worth chasing, but I didn't think we would accomplish the dream."

Just then the door bell rang. Darrell got up from the dinner table to get it. Betty, Charles and I were still engrossed in our conversation. A few minutes later Darrell returned to the dining room alone. Betty, Charles, and I stopped our conversation and looked up at Darrell.

"Who was at the door?" I asked.

"You have company in the front room." Darrell said.

"Well, tell them to come back here and join the celebration."

"Shane, you have someone who would like to talk to you in private in the front room."

Immediately, Kendra came to mind. My body went numb. We hadn't talked or seen each other since we parted ways at the restaurant. All my emotions and feelings about what took place at the restaurant were buried deep into my subconscious to avoid dealing with them while accomplishing my vision. Now, she was in the front room of my home, it was time for me to salvage my personal life. I was in total confusion. I hadn't taken the time to think about our relationship, so I wasn't prepared or ready to talk to her now, but I did want to see her.

I walked to the front room and there she stood in front of the fireplace, wearing an overcoat and warming her hands. As I entered the room, she turned toward me and didn't look the same. Her vibrant smile and demeanor were subdued. Her usual energy that had exuded confidence and beauty was not evident. Her eyes penetrated my body to search my soul and heart, but I tried my best to give them cover.

"Cold out, huh?" I started off.

"Yes."

There was silence as she tried to make eye contact and as I tried to avoid it as much as possible.

"I hear congratulations are in order," she said.

"Yea, yea, we pulled it off," I said, pep in my voice. "I have a great group, they all believed, well most of them believed in what we were trying to do." My thoughts went back to what Betty had said.

"I always believed in you," Kendra e interrupted.

"I know."

There was that silence again that seemed to creep in at the most inopportune moment. Her eyes were penetrating my soul again, as I tried to avoid their focus like a player in a dodge ball game.

"So, how did you find out about the good news?" This probably was a question I shouldn't have asked.

"Darrell, I still make and tailor his suits, even though I don't do the suits for the person who referred him to me."

I had no response to that statement. I had left myself wide open and she knew it. Once again, silence.

"Shane, what is going on?" I was silent, so she continued. "I haven't heard from you in six months. The only way I know that you are alive is because of Darrell. I called several times and left messages, but you never returned my calls." Her voice started to crack. "I love you more than anything I ever loved in my life, and I thought we had something special." She paused. "You are breaking my heart, and I don't deserve it." Tears started to roll down her face.

I still had no words. My body and mind were numb.

She continued. "You mean to tell me that because I dated a white person years ago you don't want to have anything to do with me?" Her tone changed to anger, but she didn't yell.

"Did you love him?" I asked

"Yes, I loved him, Shane. He was a good man, but the love I had for him pales in comparison with the love I have for you!"

I couldn't hear what she was saying. My temperature rose when she said she loved him. I didn't want her to ever have loved anyone else. I wanted to be her first and only. The fact that I wasn't, did not set well with me. I didn't respond, because I knew something inappropriate would come out of my mouth.

"Shane, did you think I had never been with anyone else?"

"No, I didn't think that."

"Then, is it because the person happened to be white and somehow you perceive me as tainted? You are not racist. I've been with you long enough to know you are not a racist, but your pro blackness clouds your judgment at times. You denying that young lady the opportunity to work for you because her husband happened to be white was absolutely wrong, and I hope God forgives you."

This conversation was over. She had finally pushed a real sensitive button with me. That decision was another thing I didn't want to deal with. I stored it in my subconscious until a more convenient time presented itself so I could deal with it.

"If you are going to attack me, then this conversation is over."

Tears streamed down her face. She stepped closer to me, looking me dead in the face. "Look at me," she said in a calm voice.

My eyes met hers, but revealed no emotion. This was the sales job of my life. The woman I truly adored and loved stood before me, and I looked her dead in the face like a dingy grey stone, emotionless.

"I'm not going to wait another day for you to come around," she said in tearful voice. "Because I don't have to."

"Yes, I know you of all people don't have to wait for anyone. You might just try something new. Oh, but for you, it's something old."

She looked at me as if she didn't recognize me, then turned around, walked to the front door, paused, opened it, walked out and closed the door behind her. When she closed the door behind her, I felt loneliness, emptiness, despair, and loss all at once.

I didn't go back and join them in the dining room, I went straight to my room and fell on my bed and went to sleep fully dressed.

By the start of the New Year the desk was fully staffed and we were beginning the New Year in the number one position at GPG. Our goal, for the coming year was to move from the number two position on Wall Street to the number one and that was no small order. This goal would be a larger challenge than taking over the number one position at GPG, but we had the talent in place to get it done.

Mr. Mackey would be making his transition to the board in another month and Junior would be stepping into his shoes. I was a little concerned about Junior because he took things more personally instead of looking at them from a business perspective. I felt I could handle him and accomplish my goal of being number one on Wall Street.

Something was going on with me. It was as if I were walking through life in a fog or a daze. I couldn't snap out of it. Every day seemed to be moving in slow motion. I didn't smile very much, and socializing with others on the desk wasn't my top priority. Most times I opted to go home and rest. Darrell, Charles, and Tim were constantly asking me if I was all right. My response always was a quick nod of my head.

About three weeks into the New Year, I saw Emmy, the young lady I didn't hire, in the trade room. She had been hired to work on the convertible desk. The convertible desk was still hanging on by a thread, and the managing director was still that miserable bastard Peter. Emmy was a talented young lady, and I thought she would land another job on Wall Street after we refused her. Her presence at GPG on the convertible desk made me suspicious. Emmy came by the desk to say hello to Tim. He was ecstatic. You would have thought they were childhood friends who hadn't seen each other in over twenty years. When they finished their conversation, she chatted with a few others on the desk, including Charles and Darrell. She then came over to say hello to me.

"Hello, Shane."

"Hey, Emmy." I stood to greet her.

"How are things my brotha?"

"Things are good."

There was a moment of silence.

"Congratulations, I knew this desk was headed for great things. I'm just sorry I could not be a part of it," Emmy said in a factual tone.

"Yes, we're sorry too."

"I've landed on my feet, though. I'm working on the convertible desk in sales."

"Yea, I saw you over there. How's it going so far?"

"So far, so good, but I'd rather be in research."

"Well, you do have the personality for sales, as I told you when we first met."

"Yes, but my heart is in research."

"Sales can lead to research, look at Tim."

"Yes, I guess you're right. It was good to see you again, my brotha and keep up the good work. Eyes are upon you." She shook my hand and walked off toward the convertible desk.

Not even five minutes after Emmy left, Tim rushed over to me with a look of excitement on his face.

"Let's pull her over to our desk. I still need to fill the research analyst position."

I tried to keep my head down without acknowledging him when I answered.

"No."

"Why not?" he said in an animated voice.

I still didn't look up to acknowledge him.

"She's not a good fit," I said in a calm voice.

"That's bullshit!" Tim slammed his fist down on the trading desk next to me. He had my attention then. I looked up at him with dismay. Tim continued. "What is going on with you? You are not god. I am supposed to have a say in who is hired into my group."

"You do," I responded

"Then I want her," he demanded

"But, I have the final say."

"Bullshit!" he shouted. Then he walked back to his office and off the trading floor.

I guess he was so disgusted with me he didn't want to sit at his place on the trading desk and look in my face. I understood where Tim was coming from, but there were two things working against his wishes: One, my mind was somewhere else and I really didn't want to revisit the subject of hiring Emmy. Second, I didn't want to lose face on the trading desk, giving the appearance that I'd made a mistake by not hiring Emmy. Mistake or no mistake I was willing to live with my decision.

Tim's little outbreak drew attention to the desk while Junior happened to be on the trading floor. He casually strolled over and asked me, in a very low voice, if everything was okay.

"Yea, everything is everything," I mumbled back, without looking up from my screen.

"You're not losing control of your desk are you?" he continued in a low voice.

"No, everything is copasetic," I responded with my attention directed to my computer screen.

"I see you guys know Emmy."

"Yea, uh she interviewed with us for a research position."

"You didn't hire her?"

I looked up then. "She's working on the convertible desk so obviously I didn't hire her," I said sarcastically.

"Yea, I got her the job on the convertible desk. I know her husband."

"Good for her. Is there a point to this little conversation? Because if there isn't, I have a lot of work to do," I said in an irritated tone.

"No, no point to the conversation. Just know it's a new year and there's a new sheriff in town."

I shook my head and kind of shrugged his last comment off, considering him to be an arrogant prick. My mind was on Kendra. The fact that she was out of my life finally caught up to me. The separation was affecting me in the worse way. After all the drama that morning, I just wanted to go home and get my head together. I called it a half day and headed home, to the dismay of Charles and Darrell. I told them to handle the desk for the rest of the day, and I could be reached at home if anything came up that needed my immediate attention.

About an hour into my nap on the couch in my dimly lit den, fully clothed in my suit and tie, the phone rang and woke me. I sat up and looked at the caller ID. It was an international number. My mind was so foggy. It didn't register to me that this phone call could be from Big Mike, so I laid back down. However, my cell phone rang and it was the same international number, so I answered it.

"Hello this is Shane," I said in a groggy voice and half awake.

"Hey Shane, its Big Mike, where you at?"

"At home."

"Yea, Charles said you went home because you weren't feeling well but I just called there and you didn't pick up."

"Yea, I was kind of out of it but you have my full attention now. What's up?"

"You all right?"

"Yea, Yea… What's up?"

"I just got a telegram from Junior requesting I come back to New York."

"Really!" I was completely awake and attentive now. "What did the telegram say exactly?"

"Just that my assignment has been terminated and GPG requests that I catch the 8:00 a.m. flight back to New York tomorrow morning."

"Okay…" I said in a concerned voice.

"Shane, is it beginning?"

"Don't know, but it just could be that Junior thinks your assignment is not paying enough dividends for the desk. That's probably what that asshole meant when he said there's a new sheriff's in town," I mumbled aloud.

"What?" Big Mike responded.

"Nothing, take that 8:00 a.m. flight but don't come into the office. I will meet you here at the house after work."

"Okay, see you tomorrow."

After Big Mike hung up the phone, my mind wandered back into the abyss of misery that I found myself in. The loss of Kendra finally caught up with me. I slept the rest of the night on the couch in my suit and tie.

The next day my mind was still in disarray when I arrived at work and I didn't really have the energy to face what I knew was going to be a difficult day. Junior was taking over and asserting his power over the desk. This was evident from his request to have Big Mike take the next flight back to New York. I was sure, he would be calling me in for a face to face that day. I didn't have the energy or the desire to deal with him, but I knew I didn't have a choice. As much as I tried, I couldn't snap out of the withdrawal I was going through over not having Kendra in my life anymore.

My face to face with Junior came sooner than I expected. I was only on the desk for a couple of hours when I received his call requesting my company in his father's office. I took the elevator up immediately. When I walked up to Mr. Mackey's open office door, I could see that he was in his usual position, sitting behind his desk, facing the door, and Junior was flanked to his left, standing and chatting with his father. I lightly knocked on the open door. Mr. Mackey gestured for me to enter.

"Shane, have a seat," Mr. Mackey said.

I walked directly to the seat opposite him and to his left. Once I sat down, Mr. Mackey didn't waste time, he got right to his point.

"What happened to Ted's book?"

"Well, Ted got to his client list before I could get to them." I looked over at Junior who had this irritating smirk on his face.

"I thought you told me everything had been handled with his client list," Mr. Mackey said.

"Yes, I did tell you that because at the time I thought I had everything under control."

"Well, how did it get out of control?"

"Ted made a move that I didn't anticipate."

"As a managing director isn't your job to anticipate moves of others that might adversely affect the business?" Mr. Mackey said in a stern voice.

"I would say that is a part of my job."

"Then, what happened in this circumstance?"

"Basically, I anticipated that Ted would not intercede on a personal level to keep his book with his nephew. It's never been his M.O. to take business personally, but in this case he made an exception." The drilling from Mr. Mackey, with his son standing right by his side, angered me, but I realized what was going on. Mr. Mackey was letting me know, I no longer had his support. The loss of Ted's book was the reason. It was a substantial loss, but I still delivered the number one spot and I had to let him know, so I continued. "I played the odds. They didn't fall in my favor, so I took my bumps and moved on. I concentrated on the real prize of delivering to you, on schedule the number one trading desk in GPG and not to mention the number two spot on all of Wall Street."

"That, you did Shane, but you're missing the bigger picture. You lost a significant portion of our profitability when you lost Ted's book, which by my calculations would have put us at the number one position on Wall Street."

I had no response. What he'd said was true, but there was no reason to think that with our personnel we couldn't achieve that goal by next year. He knew this, but for me to argue that point would be futile, so I let it go. The next thing I heard was out of Junior's mouth.

"Shane, you have been accused of discriminatory hiring practices."

"By whom?" I said, as if I didn't know.

"Emmy White."

I didn't respond to the name. I just gave Junior a blank stare. So he continued.

"She accuses you of discriminating against her because of her interracial marriage."

"That's ridiculous!" I said in an authoritative voice.

"No matter how ridiculous it sounds, the charges will be heard by a mediator in two weeks," Junior said with a smirk.

"Mediator!" I shouted. "What is going on here?" Mr. Mackey didn't say a word. He sat silent, watching me and his son go back and forth about a mediation hearing.

"Shane, we take these charges seriously, and we here at GPG pride ourselves in being an equal opportunity employer. Anything to the contrary, to that practice is in direct opposition to company policy."

"So, based on one person's word, you are going to subject me to a hiring discrimination mediation hearing?"

"It's not just one person's word," Junior said with a smile.

Stunned and confused, I didn't have a response. The stunned look must have shown on my face because Junior looked as if he were thoroughly enjoying this moment. I didn't want him to have too much enjoyment at my expense. I abruptly rose from my seat, put on my best poker face, and told them I would see them in two weeks at the mediation hearing. Then, I asked. "Am I on mandatory leave?"

"Until the charges are heard there's no reason for disciplinary action," Junior responded.

They had something up their sleeves and I needed to figure it out quickly. I left the both of them chatting in Mr. Mackey's office.

Someone had sold me out. The more I thought about it the more it angered me. There were only five people privy to my dream and vision of an all black trading desk. Anyone else besides them would just be repeating hearsay and conjecture and Junior wouldn't go to mediation with that. I went back to the trading desk to contemplate my next move. As I looked around the desk, I caught the attention of Charles and Darrell. They both gestured to me, asking what's up. I mouthed to them War Room Meeting tonight.

In my mind I knew three of the five in no way had any hand in betraying me and that was Big Mike, Charles, and Darrel. That left Betty and Tim. Betty had been nervous and afraid from the start, but Tim's behavior had been peculiar every since I overruled his decision to hire Emmy. Both may have had an incentive to expose me, but which one? I couldn't see clear enough to determine. My judgment was still clouded because my focus was not 100%. Kendra was still heavily on my mind, I couldn't push those thoughts aside long enough to give this situation the concentration it warranted. I decided to use Big Mike, Charles, and Darrel to help me sort out this situation.

Charles, Darrel, and I caught the subway home that night. Once we hit the door to the house, there was Big Mike sitting on the couch in the front room with a big plate of food. Darrel and Charles erupted with shouts on sight of Big Mike. He looked good, in good health and spirit.

"What's up?" Charles shouted.

"Big Mike!" Darrell followed with a bellow.

I stood back and watched the three of them give greetings and handshakes. It was a good sight. These three men were good people and good friends. Most of all I considered them family, a sense of comfort came over me when I'm around family.

"What up, Shane?" Big Mike greeted me.

I walked over to him gave him a hug then stepped back.

"Good to see you big man. I see you been eating well."

"Yeah, a brotha been eating good. Speaking of food, I picked up some Chinese on my way in from the airport. There's plenty in the kitchen, y'all go help yourselves and join a brotha."

Charles, Darrel and I made our way into the kitchen fixed our plates of Chinese food and rejoined Big Mike in the front room.

"So, am I out of a job?" Big Mike asked as he looked at me.

"I'm not sure. The Mackeys called me into their office today and said there were charges against me for hiring discrimination."

"By whom?" Darrell asked

"Emmy."

"Isn't that the young lady Tim wanted to hire?" Charles asked

"Yes," I responded.

"Then how can she charge you with discrimination? She's black."

"Yea, what's the deal with that?" Big Mike rejoined.

I was silent. With all that had taken place with Kendra, I started to re-think my decision not to hire Emmy. When I first made the decision to rescind the offer I thought I was standing on solid ground. I didn't know how much of that decision had been based on my notion that she may have been a plant by Junior or my questioning of her character based solely on her choice for a husband. Either way, I had to come clean with my friends. My silence indicated that something was wrong.

"What in the hell did you do to that girl?" Charles asked.

I took a deep breath. "Long story short, Kendra and I were at dinner right before the offer letters went out. Emmy saw us, came over and introduced her husband who happened to be white."

"What? Isn't she Ms. Afrocentric? Always talking brotha this and sista that," Charles asked in a surprised tone.

"Yea," I responded, finding comfort in Charles's surprise at Emmy being married to a white man.

"Tell me, you didn't hold her husband against her, Shane. Please tell me you are more conscious than that?" Darrell questioned.

"I would like to think I am but at this point I don't know. At the time, I saw her as a threat to everything we were building on the desk. Her demeanor and conversation were so pro black, but when I saw her husband, I colored her sell out."

"I can't believe you did that," Darrell said.

"Shit, I don't have a problem with that at all. I've never met her but from what I hear she's playing the role of Angela Davis, but her actions read Aunt Jemima- sell out!"

"How can you say that with a straight face?" Darrell asked Big Mike.

"Darrell, coming from a law background and spending time in prison I put less on what a person says than what that person does. Action always speaks louder than words."

"I have to agree with that," Charles agreed.

"I can't believe you guys. Anyway let's move forward. What happened after you met her husband?" Darrell continued

"After they left the restaurant, I texted Betty and told her not to send out the offer letter to Emmy."

"Did you give her a reason?" Charles asked.

"I don't think so, but I'm not sure."

"No wonder Tim was so irate when you rejected her at the last minute. He knew something was wrong," Darrell rejoined.

"Okay, where are we now?" Big Mike asked.

"There will be a mediator who will hear the evidence and help GPG and myself come to some kind of resolution. I know Junior will be pushing for my dismissal."

"The way I see it, Shane, it's just your word against hers. Any impartial mediator worth their salt will lean in your favor," Big Mike said

"Junior said they have someone else to support her charges."

"Who?" Darrell asked.

"He wouldn't say, but it has to be Betty or Tim," I said

"My money is on Tim," Big Mike said.

"I'm long on him, too," Charles responded

"Betty has a lot more to lose than Tim. She put her career on the line for you, Shane. Junior might have gotten to her, when she was making her regular reports to the Mackeys," Darrell explained.

"Yea, but my gut tells me it's Tim. Even though he didn't agree with my decision not to hire Emmy, he took it too personal."

"I've seen Tim and Emmy in his office with the door closed, and taking lunches together on the regular since she's been hired at GPG," Charles said.

"No matter which one it is, you are going to need a legal advisor to negotiate for you on procedural controls and presenting evidence during the mediation," Big Mike said.

"I'm going to need your help on that one Big Mike."

"I got you, don't worry."

"Aye man, you know I got your back," Charles added.

"Even though I don't agree with what you did, I'm behind you 100 percent," Darrell assured me.

We had two weeks to prepare for my hearing in front of a mediator. From my perspective, it wasn't looking good. One or two of the people from my inner circle would testify against me. I couldn't fully wrap my mind around the seriousness of the situation because I feared I was in a far worse situation with my personal life. I had lost my woman and there was no turning back the hands of time to repair what I had damaged.

Big Mike handled my legal advisement and negotiated on my behalf for cross-examination of any testimony against me and my right to testify on my own behalf. Big Mike also had a say in who would sit as the mediator. The mediator was a retired Wall Street attorney named Jefferson Pete. According to Big Mike, he had sat as mediator on several disputes with other Wall Street firms and came highly recommended because of his ability to keep an objective point of view and confidentiality.

Two weeks sped by quickly. The fog that had clouded my mind for the last several weeks had gotten thicker. My mind was constantly on Kendra, which left little energy to focus on my mediation at GPG. My lack of focus and attention to the discrimination matter left Big

Mike, Charles, and Darrell puzzled and frustrated. I have to admit it left me frustrated. Despite how I was feeling about my personal life, my day of judgment was upon me.

The mediation took place in the executive conference room on the top floor. Big Mike, Darrell, Charles, and I all entered the conference room at 7:00 a.m. sharp. There was Mr. Jefferson Pete sitting at the head of the conference room table. To his right, and seated next to him facing the conference room door in sequence were Mr. Mackey, Junior, Larri- Head of Human Resources, Betty, Tim, Emmy, and the intern that Junior had forced me to hire last summer. As we entered, Mr. Pete offered us the other side of the conference table across from the others. Big Mike sat next to the mediator followed by myself, Darrel, and then Charles. As it happened, the seating order put me right across the table from Junior. He had this unassuming smirk that I think he had perfected over the years.

I surveyed the room; Tim avoided direct eye contact with me. As a matter of fact he never made eye contact with any of us; Big Mike, Darrell, or Charles. Betty was a different story. She looked frightened and lost. Emmy also avoided direct eye contact. Their behavior led me to believe none of them were completely comfortable with what they were about to do. I especially felt sorry for Betty because it was my responsibility to protect her and I failed to do so. Junior looked like he had the deck stacked against me and had two people from my inner circle ready to testify against me.

Mr. Pete started the mediation. "Hello, my name is Jefferson Pete. I will be your mediator today in the discrimination claim against Mr. Shane Jackson by Garvin, Pratt, and Gooden. We will hear the evidence against Mr. Jackson. Then Mr. Jackson or his legal advisor, Mr. Michael Strands, who is seated to my left, will have the opportunity to dispute the evidence presented.." He then gestured toward Big Mike, and Big Mike nodded his head in agreement. ""When all pros and cons are complete on the discrimination claim, I will then render my opinion on the evidence presented. I will simply state whether there is enough evidence to substantiate the claim or if there is insufficient evidence to support the claim. At that time, if need be, we will enter the resolution phase, and I will give possible options to resolve the dispute. Are there any questions?"

Big Mike looked at me. I shook my head, no. The Mackeys shook their heads, no, also. Mr. Pete then announced the beginning of the hearing.

Junior had a small folder and note pad in front him on the conference table. He was taking the lead on this one, which reminded me of the time when Ted and I were campaigning on my behalf for the MD position in the very same conference room. I shut Junior down with my stance for a permanent hiring to the MD position. I knew he was going to enjoy this. This was his opportunity, no one was going to steal his thunder, not even his dad.

Junior began to state his case. The charges against Shane Jackson......." But he was interrupted by Mr. Pete.

"These are not charges," Mr. Pete said. "We are not in a court of law. These are claims of discrimination."

"Okay, well these claims of discrimination have been a long time coming." Junior's voice sounded as if he were giving a lecture to a class of 100 college students in a small auditorium. "Ever since Shane Jackson was hired on as Managing Director of the Fixed Income desk he has been on a mission to hire nothing but African Americans on the trading desk. We were never able to substantiate these claims until now. He made the mistake of discriminating against one of his own because of who she is married to. We will hear evidence from Brad Downey, an intern who worked two summers on the desk; Emmy Duncan, a candidate who went through the interviewing process for the Fixed Income desk; Tim Doogan; head of Research, and Betty Johnson, HR Rep. Their collective testimony will unveil a plot and a scheme to populate the Fixed Income desk with nothing but African-American professionals to the detriment of other professionals of different ethnicities. Not only will the testimony you are about to hear give evidence of discrimination against white candidates but against other ethnicities including Asian, Latino, and Middle Eastern candidates, as well.

Junior laid it on pretty thick. You would have thought I was Adolf Hitler. He described efforts? on a playing field that has been uneven since its creation. The actual words stock market and Wall Street came from buyers and sellers coming to market with African slaves as stock. Wall Street represented the Wall they kept the slave stock behind so buyers could not get advanced looks at the slaves. When a person becomes an agent of change in a discriminatory environment using the tactics that have been used historically against him and his people, I don't call that racism or reverse racism. I called it intelligence.

Junior called on his first witness, Brad. Brad's testimony wasn't that damaging. He actually said he enjoyed the two summers he spent on the desk and that everyone on the desk made him feel like he was part of the fixed income family. His testimony made Junior irate, and he turned beet red.

"What the hell do you mean you enjoyed your summers on the desk? Didn't you tell me one of the traders told you the fixed income desk was the black hole and any race other than black would get lost forever trying to be a part of it?" He yelled at his nephew.

"Yes," Brad responded. "But when he said it, it was kind of jokingly."

"Jokingly! What the fuck are you talking about?" Junior's yelling continued,

Mr. Pete had to interject and calm the situation. "He gave his testimony, Mr. Mackey. Let's just move on."

Junior moved on to Betty. She wasn't that much help in proving his claims against me. The only part of her testimony that gave Junior a boost was her collaborating the time of my call, requesting her not to send out the offer letter to Emmy.

Mr. Pete interjected once again. "Did Mr. Jackson give you a reason for changing his mind?"

"No, he just said he had second thoughts about her and told me to hold off."

"Around what time did this call take place?"

"8:00 p.m."

"Thank you."

Betty looked at me with trepidation after her testimony. I gave her a look back of acceptance to let her know it was okay.

Emmy was next. For some reason she started to look a scared. I really thought she would be out to get me, along with Junior, for the way I had rescinded her offer at the last minute, but something deep down inside was disturbing her. I could see it with every word she spoke. It was as if she had to force each word through her lips and the pressure was causing her much pain.

Mr. Pete had questions of his own. "At anytime did Mr. Jackson offer you the job or indicate there was an offer being sent out to you?"

"No," Emmy responded.

"Did he at anytime say he disapproved of your choice in a spouse?"

"No, but his reaction to my spouse when I brought him over to his dinner table and introduced him said it all," she said with authority.

"Mrs. White, was Mr. Jackson's reaction one of surprise or disapproval?" Big Mike asked.

Emmy paused. She looked surprised that Big Mike asked the question. She looked as if she were struggling with telling the truth or giving an answer that would support her claim. After a few moments, she answered. "Surprised."

"One last question, Mrs. White, what time did all this take place?" Mr. Pete asked.

"I would have to say between 7:45 pm and 8:00 pm."

"Thank you, Mrs. White."

Up to that point, there had been nothing real damaging except the timing of my call to Betty to rescind the offer to Emmy. Junior knew he hadn't hammered the nail in my coffin yet, but he was banking on his ace in the hole, Tim.

Before Tim could speak one word, Big Mike asked one question of Tim. "Were you offered anything in exchange for your testimony here today?"

Tim looked like a deer in the headlights of an oncoming Mac truck. His next move wasn't the smartest. He quickly looked in the direction of Junior. Junior looked away. Then his focus came back to Big Mike.

"I don't quite understand the question," he stuttered.

"It's a simple straight forward question. I think we all would like to hear an honest straightforward answer," Big Mike returned.

One thing I knew about Tim from way back in our undergrad days, he was an honest man and lying was not something that came easy to him. Hence I expected he would tell the truth.

"Yes, I was offered the MD position."

"What the fuck?" Charles muttered.

"Damn!" Darrell exclaimed.

"What a dumb fuck," Junior mumbled.

The room went into a quiet rumble, but Mr. Pete kept us on track. He asked Tim to go ahead and tell all he knew of the claims against me. Tim spilled the whole bag of beans. He told about the war meeting at my home, and how I had devised a plan to hire an all African-American Fixed Income trading desk. He named himself, Darrell, Charles, Betty, and me as insiders to my grand scheme. He left no detail out. He even included my strategy on handling the Mackeys with Betty, keeping the desk profitable, and how we leveraged Mr. Mackey's aspirations to become partner and board member at GPG.

Mr. Pete questioned Tim. "What about the claims of Mrs. White? Did Mr. Jackson ever tell you he didn't offer her the open position because of who she is married to?"

"No, he never said that to me. He just said he changed his mind, which I thought was absolutely crazy. She was perfect for the position."

"Did he ever say that?" Mr. Pete asked Tim.

"No, not exactly...."

"Okay." Mr. Pete interrupted and silenced Tim. He turned to me. "Do you have a response or defense to these accusations and claims?"

I sat up in my seat, and in a calm and cool voice responded with, "Yes." Unlike Tim, I really didn't have a problem with bending the truth especially for the greater good. If that meant saving my own skin and protecting those who believed in my vision, the truth didn't have a chance. In my mind there was a thin line between the truth and a lie.

I first called on Charles and asked a very simple question. "Do you know of any conspiracy on my part to populate the Fixed Income desk with only African American employees?" His response was short and to the point.

"No."

I posed the same question to Darrell and Big Mike. They gave the same answer as Charles.

"No."

I then turned to Betty and she responded firmly.

"No."

So, my attempt to neutralize the explosive testimony of Tim had worked effectively. It was his word against the word of four others. In order to knock him flat on his back I had a question for him.

"Tim, do you have any other evidence to support your testimony here today?" I always filled Tim in later about the developments that took place at the war room meetings. We always talked in private and to my knowledge, he never took notes or recorded our conversations.

"No, I do not."

An eerie silence came over the room. Heads were turning toward each other and facial expressions exchanged, but no one spoke. Mr. Mackey kept his eyes on me but never said a word. He just observed. Junior on the other hand was breathing heavy and at a steady pace. His coloring was getting paler by the minute.

Next, was Emmy's claim. I simply made a statement to explain changing my mind about hiring her on the research desk.

"As for me changing my mind about hiring Emmy, it had nothing to do with our encounter at dinner that night or who she is married to. Her choice in a husband had no bearing on my judgment of her ability to be an effective part of the research team. There were only two issues that concerned me about Emmy. First, in the interview with Emmy, we discussed getting some experience in sales on the desk. She was hesitant and almost refused."

Junior interrupted. "Why the hell did she need to work in sales when the opening was a research position?"

"Well, she didn't have that much experience. I thought a rotation in sales would give her more product knowledge along with client interaction. This is something that Tim himself had to go through on the convertible desk, and in my opinion made him one of the best research analysts at GPG... May I continue?"

Mr. Pete gestured for me to continue.

"Secondly, this is something I would not ordinarily confess because it is a violation to the hiring practices of GPG, but ..... I detected a strong attraction to Emmy on the part of Tim. I thought she might be more of a distraction for him than an asset. I let those two issues factor into my decision in changing my mind about hiring Emmy. Right or wrong, my first priority is to the bottom line of my desk. It is my duty to protect the desk from any situation or person that adversely affects production. After my statement in my defense, there was really nothing else for anyone to say. I could see Mr. Mackey slightly shaking his head in agreement; almost like he was proud of me and the action I took to protect my bottom line. This was the first time he made direct eye contact with me since the beginning of the mediation. The mediation hearing drew to a conclusion. Mr. Pete asked for twenty four hours to consider all the testimonies and said that he would render an opinion tomorrow. We all thought that was reasonable, except Junior who went off on a short tirade until his father stepped in and gave his blessing for a twenty-four hour period.

****

Twenty-four hours passed quickly. Before I knew it, Big Mike and I were on the subway headed to Wall Street to meet up with Charles and Darrell. On the ride, my mind was reflecting on all the decisions I had made and I questioned the morality and validity of some of them. What about my vision for an all black trading desk? Had it been self-destructive or even a valid effort to try something like that in this day of age? Was I a reverse racist? I thought about my efforts to try and steal Ted's book from his nephew. Was it betrayal on my part, after all Ted had done for me? This question was one that made my stomach weak. I tried to justify it in my mind as just business, but was it really? Did it say volumes about my character? I didn't have the answers, which was frustrating in itself.

What about Darrell, Charles, Big Mike, and Betty, did I let them down? Was it right for me to involve them in my plan when it was already in motion? They had little or no say about their involvement. I really felt bad about Betty because if this mediation didn't go in my favor she would be left on the chopping block. There wouldn't be anything I could do about it. I told her, I would protect her. Yea right, in this game I realized I was powerless.

The stupidest decision of all, which was downright ignorant, was my decision to sabotage the great relationship with my lady, Kendra. This decision kept me up at night and clouded my mind, leaving me with little energy to think or strategize, when I needed it the most. Visions of her lovely face haunted me. Her sweet scent, once so vivid had become faint, I missed her companionship, but most of all her spirit, which resonated into my personal being and inspired me to be the best that I could was no longer there. My lady was gone and there was no one to blame but myself. How could I have let such a gentle and loving creature leave my life? It was beyond my comprehension. I had fucked up!

Big Mike and I finally made it to the headquarters of GPG. There, we met Charles and Darrell at the trading desk. Once we arrived, there was chatter among all the traders, salespeople, and analyst. – They were all standing, as if they were in a football huddle, the trading desk was the quarterback kneeled down in the center. They all had a look of concern and dread on their faces. Right away, I knew what they were thinking. If Shane goes down, we all go down. They all were right. I had no words to console them and to tell them everything was going to be alright, or that I had everything under control, would have been the furthest thing from the truth. I avoided eye contact as best I could, moved quickly toward Charles and Darrell, and then walked to the elevators toward the conference room.

Big Mike, Charles, Darrell, and I were the first to arrive at the conference room this time. Mr. Pete hadn't made it in yet, neither had the Mackeys or any of their so called witnesses, including Tim. We chatted it up. Surprisingly, we reminisced about the time Darrell got me to paint Cheryl's apartment and pulled Charles and Big Mike along for good measure. We were having a ball just the four us laughing and joking about the good old days, when Tim stepped into the conference room all by himself. Once he saw it was just us four, he tried to back out of the room, but I didn't let him.

"No, my brotha," I gestured for him to come into the room. "Come on in!"

He then walked into the room and sat in the same seat he had occupied yesterday.

"Benedict Arnold arrives!" Big Mike said.

"No, not Benedict Arnold,, but Uncle Tom," Charles added.

"Not Uncle Tom.... maybe Step and Fetch It," Darrell joined in.

Charles couldn't resist, so he went into his best southern drawl to mock Tim. "Yes sir, Mista Charlie, we sick boss?"

Tim erupted, "Fuck all of you. I'm no sell out!"

"Then what would you call it Tim?" I asked.

"You fucked up, Shane and you know it."

"Even if I did fuck up why would you sell me out after all that I've done for you?" The anger had built up in me about Tim's betrayal. "I taught you the art of selling, picked you up, dusted you off and helped you reach your potential. I fucking saved your career. If it wasn't for me you wouldn't even be working on Wall Street any longer. Don't you remember, just a short time ago, you were the butt of jokes and nobody respected you?" Then I stood up, lost my cool, and my next words came deep down from my diaphragm. "FUCK YOU, YOU FUCKING SELL OUT!" Just then, Mr. Pete, the Mackeys, Emmy, and Betty entered the conference room. I sat back down in my seat.

Tension was in the air when they walked in and it was evident to everyone entering the room. Mr. Pete asked, with a puzzled look was everything okay. We all nodded in the affirmative, including Tim. Everyone took a seat around the conference table with Mr. Pete taking his same seat at the head of the conference table. Once seated, he wasted no time in giving his opinion:

"I thought long about this mediation case and to be quite frank, this is a peculiar case. On the one hand, we have a Managing Director that has been highly successful, taking a desk that was on the brink of going under to the number one trading desk at Garner. Pratt & Green. We have one of the top investment banking firms on Wall Street benefiting from accomplishment, but the way in which this accomplishment was brought about broke the hiring rules of GPG. I have to say that this type of case is a first for me. I have never in my thirty plus years as a professional and as a mediator on Wall Street ever heard or been a part of anything of this nature. Upon hearing the background of this dispute during my interview process to mediate, I was intrigued, but at a loss because I had not heard of anything so bizarre especially on Wall Street. I couldn't understand why GPG would want to dispose of a managing director that has been so successful, because of one person's claim of discrimination. There haven't been other complaints from any of the other applicants that were from diverse backgrounds."

At this time, my confidence was starting to build. I was thinking I might just make it out of this with little or no damage to me or my friends.

"But, when you look at the makeup of the Fixed Income desk, all African- American professionals ... this raises some warning signs. I asked myself. How can you have a Fixed Income trading desk of all African American professionals when they only make up less than 12% of the population and less than 1% of the financial professional population? This goes to the physical evidence in this matter, which doesn't hold well for Mr. Jackson, but I wanted to give him the benefit of the doubt, so with the help of Ms. Betty Johnson, I reviewed each of the candidate pools from which Mr. Jackson put together his desk. I would have to say if you were just to look on paper, without the benefit of physical appearance, you couldn't knock any of his hiring. But, when you take in the physical appearance, there is a trend which lends itself to a prototype that Mr. Jackson has found an affinity. The common trait in this prototype is ethnicity."

"Ah huh!" Junior stood up and pointed directly at me. "It's just like I've been telling you, Dad."

Mr. Pete interrupted him. "Please, Mr. Mackey, let me finish. The testimony of Emmy White seems to contradict this trend of hiring only African Americans and goes a little deeper to the choice of one's spouse. I would have to say in this case that I believe Mr. Jackson. He had second thoughts about hiring Mrs. White based on his observations and her interview. There is no evidence that he changed his mind because of her husband being white. Although the timing of the phone call to Ms. Johnson throws up a red flag, that still doesn't support the premise of denying her the position because of her spouse. In regards to the last testimony of Tim Wayne, I believe the testimony of Mr. Wayne."

All of us erupted. Charles, Darrell, Big Mike, and myself. We made scoffing sounds, mumbled small profanities, and then adjusted our bodies in our seats. Mr. Pete paused and gestured for us to come back to order. For the first time, I really saw my career at GPG slipping away and the slope was becoming more slippery.

"In my opinion, Mr. Wayne is a credible witness and an insider. Evidently, he was privy to all the intimate details of Mr. Jackson's vision to create an all black trading desk at GPG. There are problems with his testimony, given he was offered the managing director position in return for his testimony, however that is typical in getting an inside guy to turn on friends. Having said that, it is my opinion that Mr. Jackson was and is in direct violation of the hiring practices of GPG and did knowingly and willingly discriminate against employee candidates based on race." then Mr. Pete paused, then went on.......... "IT IS MY RECCOMENDATION THAT MR. JACKSON RESIGN FROM THE POSTION OF MANAGING DIRECTOR IMMEDIATELY AND THAT THE FIRM GARNER, PRATT & GREEN PAY HIM OUT HIS FULL SALARY FOR THE REMAINDER OF THE YEAR!"

I couldn't believe it. Just like that, they wanted me to resign on the spot. Junior had never looked more satisfied and content. Tim's head was down, tears rolled down Betty's face, Emmy looked regretful, and Mr. Mackey was expressionless. On my side of the table, we looked the same, stunned.

"What if I refused to resign?" I said.

"Then you'll be fired!" shouted Junior.

Mr. Mackey tapped Junior on the hand for him to settle down.

"No, Mr. Jackson, you wouldn't be fired," Mr. Pete responded. "But this hearing would probably go to arbitration and to be totally honest with you, there is no arbitrator in the world that's going to see this in your favor. I will admit to you the testimony against you is weak, except for Tim's, but all one has to do is look at the makeup of your desk to know that in order to accomplish such a feat, some hiring policies were broken... to put it mildly."

There it was, I looked to my left at Charles and Darrell, then to my right at Big Mike. "What will happen to my staff?"

"That decision will be up to the Mackeys," Mr. Pete said.

I knew eventually the staff would be disbanded and reassigned to other desks and other areas inside GPG. They really couldn't afford to let them go all at once, and initiate another mass exodus of the number one desk at GPG again. So, I conceded to resign. As part of my agreement to resign, Big Mike made sure that none of the accusations or charges nor the mediation hearing would be a part of my permanent employee record. The official word would be that I was leaving the firm for another job opportunity.

I felt really down after the hearing, losing my job was bad enough, but there was something else. I had believed the risk would be small to my employment at GPG as long as I delivered the number one desk, but I knew the risk was there. In my mind it was somehow worth it. I didn't like to lose, and losing to Junior left a thorn in my side, but I would get over it. So, why was I feeling like such a loser? It was Kendra. The loss of my lady hit me hard once Big Mike and I left the head quarters of GPG. We were on the train headed back home. I told Big Mike I needed a little time alone. I got off the train few stops before our station.

Redemption

When I got off the subway, I had no particular place in mind to go. I just wanted to walk along the streets of Harlem, clear my head or bury what I was feeling deep inside me,. Kendra had been a precious jewel in my life and in the end, I'd treated her like she was just a piece of coal. My mother used to tell me, when I was younger, you never really appreciate the good things in your life until they are gone. I didn't appreciate all I had in Kendra, when she was a part of my life. If I had, I wouldn't have let her go that stupidly.

It was a sunny, cool day with clear and blue skies in New York. As I wandered around the streets of Harlem, my alone time wasn't the remedy I was seeking, for my free fall into the abyss of self pity continued. But each time I raised my face to the sky the sunshine was the light I was looking for to lead me out of this darkness. It seemed too far away. After an hour and half of walking through the streets, I came upon a bar and lounge called "Just Us".

I walked in. The place was small, about six hundred square feet in a rectangular shape. The bar took up about half the room, extending from the front door to a few feet short of the stage, which was at the back of the bar. The rest of the room had small wooden round tables with wood chairs that didn't look that sturdy. There was a base player, drummer, piano player, and singer on stage laying down some serious blues music. They didn't sound that bad. The lead singer was a heavy set black woman in a tight sequin dress that looked like it had come from a second hand store. She sounded a little like Etta James; her voice was soulful and had a maturity to it that hinted of a life of struggle and pain. It was dark inside and the place had about seven patrons, including myself.

I didn't venture too deep inside "Just Us". I took a seat at the bar, the closest seat to the front door facing the stage. I asked the bartender for a shot of whiskey and decided right then that I was going to drown my sorrows and take in the blues music to sooth my soul. I had arrived at the right place, a dimly lit bar with some second hand blues music, few patrons minding their own business, and a bartender that was good at following directions without questions.

"Another shot, bartender," I said. He filled my glass quickly. I sat in that bar for over two hours, and seven shots later the whiskey had taken its effect over my mind, body, and soul. The band was into a serious rendition of Funny Valentine and the sista was putting her all into this one like it had special meaning for her. I appreciated the way she was singing the song, so I shouted out to show my appreciation. "Sang that song you bitch." The bartender quickly walked over to me.

"Keep it down brotha," he said in a low voice.

I couldn't regulate the volume of my voice because of my drunken state. My response to him was just as loud as my shout out to the sista who was singing. "Man, that bitch is sanging her ass off."

"Man, be cool!" The bartender said in a low voice, trying to warn me. But little did I know that the four brothas sitting up front were the husband and brothers of the lead singer. They let me know my words weren't appreciated.

"What the fuck did you say, nigga?" one of them shouted back at me.

"I said that bitch can sing her ass off." Before I knew it those four brothas were out of their seats and surrounding me at the bar.

"Who you calling a bitch?" one of them asked me.

The bartender tried to intercede on my behalf. "He's had too much to drink fellas. He's not aware that he's being rude."

"Fuck that, that nigga knows what the fuck he sayin. Don't you nigga?" another one of them said.

"Yea, I said that bitch up there can sang, and I'm going to toast to that bitch as soon as the bartender gives me another shot."

Before I knew it, one of the brothas grabbed me by the shoulders of my suit coat and lifted me off of my barstool. I still didn't understand the gravity of the situation I had gotten myself into.

"Hey brotha, you messin up my suit. I'll have you know this is a three thousand dollar suit you have your hands on," I slurred.

"The least of your worries is us messin up yo three thousand dollar suit," one of them responded.

"We gonna take you out back and stomp yo black ass like the piece of shit you are," another one of them declared.

The bartender tried to intercede on my behalf once again, but to no avail. They dragged me through the club, with little or no resistance from me. It was as if I didn't mind them taking me out back and whipping my ass. I wanted to be completely numb to all that I was feeling about the loss of my woman, my job. I figured the whiskey had numbed about fifty percent of what I was feeling, and maybe this ass whipping could numb the other fifty percent.

As they dragged me by the last table, before taking me outside to the back of the club, I looked at a couple sitting there. I recognized the man as Ice and he recognized me and stood up.

"Shane!" He looked at the brothas who were dragging me. "You brothas gonna have to get your hands off my partna," he said in a demanding voice.

"Man, fuck you! You better stand yo little ass back before you join him," one of them shouted.

"No, you mutha fuckas better stand back and get yo hands off my nigga!" Ice repeated. Then he pulled back his coat to reveal a silver plated .38 special automatic on his hip.

All of them quickly took a step back and let me go. I fell to the ground, and Ice helped me back up.

"Man, you alright?" he asked.

I couldn't seem to get my balance, so Ice sat me down at his table. He instructed the bartender to bring over some coffee. I chatted for a while with Ice and his lady friend and filled him in on why I had come into the bar.

"Yea, I was surprised the last time I was in Kendra's place and asked about you, she said you guys were no longer together. Man, truthfully I thought ya'll was two steps from the alta," Ice said.

Even Ice knew Kendra was my soul mate and that I'd pushed her away like an unwanted puppy. It was time for me to get out of there. Ice had just saved my butt but the conversation brought back emotions the whiskey had numbed. I stood up with the help of Ice. He asked, was I going to be alright and did he need to hail a cab for me. I told him no. I was going to walk off some of the whiskey, and I wasn't that far from the house.

I slowly made my way through the front door of "Just Us". When the sunlight hit my face, I became a little dizzy and needed to lean up against the outside wall of the bar. I was in the typical pose of a wino who didn't have all his faculties about him. My lean against that wall lasted at least fifteen minutes and still, I felt as if all my internal organs were going to rush to my mouth and spew out on the sidewalk. Somehow, I was able to keep it together and head toward home at a very slow pace.

My walk home was a sight to see. I attracted so much attention with my wobbly two steps forward, stop, lean or swerve, catch my balance, and then proceed again. Little kids were passing by me pointing and asking "Mommy what's wrong with that man?", but I was making it down the street. About four blocks into my drunken journey back home, I saw a couple walking toward me. I really wasn't paying too much attention to them because my concentration was on preventing myself from falling over. The couple got closer and closer and I felt something was very recognizable about the young lady. However, my vision was blurred and I really couldn't make her out. It wasn't until we crossed paths that I recognized the young lady. To say the least I was shocked; it was Kendra.

It had only been a few months since our break-up. She was already out on a date. All carefree looking, like she was enjoying herself, while I was waddling in self doubt and pity. She looked good, as usual, which really pissed me off. When we crossed paths, she didn't see me, but her date noticed when I stopped in my tracks, turned and gave them a look like I had caught my wife cheating on me. He turned back and asked me, "What's your problem?" Kendra turned, looked, and the shocked expression on her face was almost as if I caught her cheating on me. Still in my inebriated state with my slurred speech and wrinkled suit that had gotten roughed up from my bar altercation, I told him he was my problem. More like, "yuus my problemmm." Then I stumbled two steps slightly to the right . He didn't like my response so he attempted to shorten the distance between the two of us. Kendra stepped between us.

"Shane, what is going on with you?" she asked in a concerned voice.

I didn't respond. I just stared at her with betrayal in my eyes.

"You are drunk, and you look a mess. What happened to your suit? It's all wrinkled and your shirt collar is ripped, along with the strap to your brief case. Have you been in a fight?"

I didn't answer any of her questions. I responded in the most disrespectful and distasteful way imaginable. "You better not be fucking him because I won't take you back, if you are."

I've seen Kendra sad, disappointed, and even angry, but never have I seen so much rage on such a beautiful woman.

She stepped closer to me, faced me directly and looked into my eyes. "Don't you ever talk to me that way again! First, it's disrespectful and I will not tolerate that from you or anyone else. Second, this is the third time you've hurt me with your words and actions, and I don't deserve that from you. Third, what gives you the audacity to think that I even want you back? I always knew you had an ego, but I had no idea just how big it was until now. Let me tell you one other thing, the next time we cross paths and you make me feel the way I'm feeling now, I'm going to have someone kick yo ass!"

Before I could say anything or react, her date said, "I'll kick his ass for you." He pushed Kendra to the side and hit me with an over hand right to the left side of my face. It landed just below my eye on my cheek bone. I fell to the ground, on my back in a daze. I tried to get to my feet, but the alcohol was still working within my system and getting hit with a Mike Tyson power shot didn't help. The guy quickly was on top of me, pulling me up by my suit coat. At that moment, I think Kendra wanted to see me get a little payback for the way I had treated her. Her date then grabbed both sides of my suit coat in his left hand and delivered a Joe Frazier upper cut to my stomach with his right hand. Needless to say, in my condition the upper cut served as a release for all that was dying to come out of my stomach; I puked all over this guy.

This liquid chunky brown and yellow substance covered his clothes and hands. He reacted violently, pushing me away, spinning my body around, leaving my back side exposed. I was bent over, feeling another spewing attack coming on when he took his foot and shoved me in my butt, hurling me forward, face first into the side walk, where my face slid to the edge of the curb. He cursed me, but I paid him no mind because there were other things that had my attention. Like the burning sensation on the right side of my face and another spewing episode which began face down along the curbside. He couldn't have cared less about my helplessness at that moment. He was too enraged about me throwing up on him, so he charged toward me to deliver more punishment, but Kendra threw her body on top of mine to protect me. Facing him, she yelled.

"Leave him alone! He's had enough." A hint of sorrow in her voice.

"What?" He reacted surprisingly. "I thought you wanted someone to put this asshole in his place."

"Just leave him alone. Just leave us be."

"Are you kidding? After the way he talked to you? You have compassion for this piece of shit."

"Please, just leave us alone," she said in a pleading voice.

After all I had put this woman through, she still had my back in the end. Right then, I realized I wasn't worthy of her love or to have her in my life. My behavior towards her during the past months wasn't the behavior of a real man, but of an asshole. Her date finally walked off in disgust. She wrapped her arms around me, set me up straight, took a handkerchief out of her purse and wiped my mouth.

"Let me help you get home," she said in a soft voice.

When I looked at her, her eyes were tearing up, but she wouldn't look at me. She helped me to my feet, put my left arm around her shoulders, and wrapped her arm around my waist. She helped me walk home without a word. I was moved by her protecting me, like a lioness protecting her cubs, but I was afraid to say anything to her because I knew I would break down. So, I kept quiet.

We arrived at the front door of my home. I tried to dig in my front pocket with my free hand, but my keys were in my left pocket which made it difficult to get my keys. Kendra went into my pocket and got my keys and opened my front door. She helped me inside the house. Big Mike was coming down the stairs, when he saw us standing in the doorway.

"What the hell happen to you?!" he shouted.

"I got my ass kicked by Kendra's 6'3", 240 pound Bob Marley look alike Rastafarian boyfriend," I said jokingly.

She chuckled. "He wasn't my boyfriend."

That was music to my ears. "Well friend, whatever, he whipped me like I stole something from him." Then I chuckled.

"Well, he is a boxer."

"Are you serious? So, in other words, when you jumped in, you saved my butt from a much greater beat down."

We both laughed.

"I don't know what all the laughter's about, but look at your face," Big Mike said.

With Kendra's assistance, I turned and walked toward the mirror in the front room. The face that was looking back at me was swollen under the left eye and on the right side, there were long scrapes and dry blood from my forehead down to the jaw line. I ran my hand over my wounds, but it looked much worse than I felt. The shots of whiskey had numbed some of the pain. I knew tomorrow would be a different story. Kendra kept her head down the whole time that I was looking at myself.

I reached for Big Mike's help to take the burden off of Kendra and to face her. I wanted to apologize and thank her for helping me, but the words were difficult to find. Tears were falling from her eyes. This time she didn't look away. Our eyes locked. The time was now for me to let her know how foolish, stupid, disrespectful, hurtful, and egotistical I had been toward her and that I would give anything to turn back the hands of time to erase all of it. It was time for me to get down on my knees and beg for her forgiveness, promise to honor and love her the rest of her days and treat her like the beautiful queen she was.

"Kendra ...I'm sorry........." I was too emotional. The words stopped and the tears flowed, and I started to drop to my knees when Big Mike quickly grabbed me and lifted me over his shoulder, then faced Kendra with my backside to her.

"Kendra, I'll have him give you a call, okay?." he said. Then he quickly took me up the stairs .

I shouted, "What are you doing, man?"

Big Mike took me into the bathroom, turned on the shower and held me up with both hands under the shower fully dressed with my brief case. The water felt ice cold. I squirmed and yelled. "What the hell, man!"

"You need to sober up, and you are not in any condition to have that kind of conversation with Kendra right now."

"But, I love her," I whimpered.

"I know, but you need to take some time. Too much has happened today, you need a clear head when you talk to her. Your words should be for her ears only."

Big Mike was right. I was in the wrong state of mind. Surprisingly, the cold shower became soothing. After about five minutes Big Mike pulled me out, handed me a towel, and left me. I managed to get out of my wet clothes, dry myself off, stumble to my bedroom, and fall face first into my bed.

I slept a complete day. No one bothered to wake me, and I didn't rise from my comatose state until 8:00 p.m. the next day. I woke feeling like someone had a sledge hammer on the inside of my head, trying to hammer their way out. I threw on my housecoat and made my way downstairs. There, I found Big Mike, Charles, and Darrel sitting in the front room watching Sanford and Son on television and having their way with some snacks. No one said anything when I entered the room. I took a seat in the empty love seat, and they just passed the snacks my way along with a bottle of old fashion root beer. We sat around for the next two hours watching the Sanford and Son marathon laughing, joking, and eating junk. It was quite a release from yesterday's activities, but I knew sooner or later what had happened yesterday after the mediation would come up.

"So, Big Mike said Kendra's new boyfriend got in that ass yesterday," Charles declared.

"That brotha didn't have a weapon, did he?" Darrell asked.

"Weapon?" I responded.

"Yea weapon, judging from your face it damn sure looks like he slap the shit out you with a brick or something," Charles said.

We all laughed. I put my hand to my face because I hadn't looked in the mirror since my incident yesterday. I did feel a huge knot on my forehead along with some scrapes on the top and side of my face, and my right eye was swollen.

"I've been sitting here with you guys for over two hours and no one offered me any ice."

"We kind of wondered to ourselves why you didn't go and get yourself some ice," Darrel mentioned.

They were right, but I was still physically and mentally numb from all that had taken place and watching Sanford and Son had allowed me to escape for a couple of hours. After joking about my appearance, Big Mike got me an ice bag and the conversation turned serious.

"What's our next step?' Charles asked.

"We should start our own firm," Darrell responded.

"We're two steps ahead of you," Big Mike Declared.

"Is that what that overseas assignment was all about?" Darrell asked.

"I will reveal all in due time, but first there are more important matters," I said.

"What could be more important than our employment situation?"

"Kendra!" I said in a subdued voice.

We all looked at each other. They didn't know what to say to me about her, but they knew I wouldn't be able to move forward without having an opportunity to set things right with her.

"How can we help you with that situation?" Darrell asked.

"What can I do to get her back?"

"Beg!" Charles responded. "I mean like Keith Sweat begging."

"He doesn't need to beg," Big Mike rejoined.

"Oh yea, he needs to beg," Darrell said.

"Big Mike this man fucked up the best thing in his life and for what, nothing. I'm not trying to come down on Shane, but I'm just calling it like I see it," Charles said.

I didn't respond. I just agreed with him non-verbally.

"So, how do you want us to help you beg?" Darrell asked.

I had been thinking of a way but I needed their help to put everything in motion. I shared with them my idea, which included each one of them helping in some capacity. There was some hesitancy on Big Mike's part, but for me he said, he would go to hell and back. Darrell and Charles thought the plan was brilliant and just might help me get Kendra back. So, the plan was in play. We gave ourselves a week before the big date, to make sure we all knew our parts, and all the little details were covered.

****

One week went by like a tornado through a small country town. The big day was upon us and everyone executed according to the plan. Big Mike made sure the block where Kendra's shop was located, was blocked off between the hours of seven and eight p.m. Charles made sure all the band members were on time, set up and ready to go. Darrell made an appointment with Kendra for a suit fitting at six thirty p.m. that day and made sure he kept her occupied in the back until the appropriate time for her to come out front. With everything set up in front of Kendra's shop, we drew a small crowd, but it wasn't enough to draw Kendra outside prematurely.

I had a four piece band with two background singers. We had rehearsed all week. Let me tell you this band was dynamite. Kendra and I had heard them play around Harlem and became friends with a couple of the members. I informed them about the situation between Kendra and me, and how I wanted to go about trying to get her back. They all climbed aboard without hesitation. The keyboard player was the vocalist of the group. He rehearsed with me overtime just to get me to sound decent on the song I wanted to sing to Kendra. He was patient because he saw in my face the dedication and commitment to pull this off. We had some late nights. I'd never worked so hard at anything in my life, including building my book when I worked on Wall Street.

Everyone was in place, the band members were dressed in black linen. I was dressed in all white linen. The summer months in Harlem could be extremely hot, so the attire was appropriate, along with the time of day. As the band began to play, I saw Darrel usher Kendra outside, along with some of her friends, who must have been inside the shop. The shocked expression on Kendra's face told me this was a good beginning. Her friends huddled around her, whispering back and forth. I had sung for Kendra before, and she always said that I had a good voice, but she was my lady and singing to her in private was a little different than singing to her in the middle of a city block with about twenty five on-lookers.

Looking at Kendra, I missed the lead in by the band for me to start my song. All the people, who had gathered around, made me a little more nervous, so I closed my eyes and listened for the band to bring my lead in back. When they did, I just let it go!

How did I ever let you slip away
Never knowing I'd be singing this song some day
And now I'm sinking, sinking to rise no more
Ever since you closed the door

My eyes were still closed; I was focused on the words, giving each one emphasis, meaning, and harmony. To my ears, the sound coming from my mouth was sweet and above all sincere. It was time for the hook. I opened my eyes so Kendra could not only hear the sincerity in my heart, but also see it in my eyes.

If I could turn, turn back the hands of time
Then my darlin' you'd still be mine
If I could turn, turn back the hands of time
Then darlin' you, you'd still be mine

Funny, funny how time goes by
And blessings are missed in the wink of an eye
Why oh, why oh, why should one have to go on suffering
When every day I pray please come back to me

I grabbed the mic off the stand and moved in closer towards Kendra.

If I could turn, turn back the hands of time
Then my darlin' you'd still be mine
If I could turn, turn back the hands of time
Then darlin' you, you'd still be mine

And you had enough love for the both of us
But I, I, I did you wrong, I admit I did
But now, I'm facing the rest of my life alone, whoa

Never have any words come from my mouth that had more truth to them than the words that I was singing to Kendra. I was being as soulful with this song as my voice would allow.

If I could turn, turn back the hands of time
Then my darlin' you'd still be mine
If I could turn, turn back the hands of time
Then darlin', you, you'd still be mine

The background singers kicked in and pulled me through to the end of the song.

I'd never hurt you
(If I could turn back)
Never do you wrong
(If I could turn back)
And never leave your side
(If I could turn back)
If I could turn back the hands
There'd be nothing I wouldn't do for you
(If I could turn back)

Forever honest and true to you
(If I could turn back)
If you accept me back in your heart, I love you
(If I could turn back the hands)

(If I could turn back)
That would be my will
(If I could turn back)
Darlin' I'm begging you to take me by the hands
(If I could turn back the hands)

I went down to my knees at this time right in front of Kendra. I heard a couple of brothas in the background shout "Don't do it", but getting on my knees and begging this sista to forgive me was the plan.

I'm going down, yes I am
(If I could turn back)
Down on my bended knee, yeah
(If I could turn back)
And I'm gonna be right there until you return to me
(If I could turn back the hands)

(If I could turn back)
If I could just turn back that little clock on the wall
(If I could turn back)
Then I'd come to realize how much I love you
Love you love you love you
(If I could turn back the hands)

Kendra joined me down on my knees, tears in her eyes. She gave me the warmest and tightest hug. Then she whispered, "I thought, I had lost you forever."

"The loss would not have been yours, it would have been mine," I whispered back in her ear.

She then gave me the most gentle and loving kiss any man could desire from a woman he was in love with. All the onlookers cheered and clapped. When I looked around at some of them, they had teary eyes.

I was a lucky man. Although my career on Wall Street had come to a screeching halt, and the woman of my life had been lost because of my ego and pride, I somehow managed to resuscitate my life for a new beginning and a new career with Charles, Big Mike, and Darrell. Most importantly, Kendra, my greatest inspiration, was back in my life!

Made in the USA
Columbia, SC
02 June 2019